A Dark Place

Neive Denis

Book 10 in the Sonoma Whittington series

Copyright

Cataloguing-in-publication data
Creator: Denis, Neive, author

Cataloguing-in-Publication details are available from the National Library of Australia
www.trove.nla.gov.au

ISBN: 978-0-6454907-0-1 (paperback)
ISBN: 978-0-6454907-1-8 (digital)

Cover design: T A Marshall, Mackay, Australia

Contents

Three Days Earlier

Why is there a wall here? ...And why would anyone want to put a wall here right across one end of the front room? Is there a door somewhere? How do you get into it? After asking herself a barrage of questions without answers, Kirsty took a couple of paces back and cast her eyes over every inch of the offending wall.

"If it is a room, why build it here, and where is its door?" Kirsty asked aloud. "If it's not a room, what is it for, and why is this wall here at all?"

Her questions went out to the universe, but no replies were forthcoming. She found herself wishing Bill Branigan would hurry up and arrive. He said he'd be there at eight o'clock, and was now almost nine. "I suppose it would be a bit rude to call and ask him where the hell he is," Kirsty muttered.

As she pondered the mysterious wall – and the equally mysterious whereabouts of Bill Branigan – Kirsty wandered back out onto the front verandah, with no other purpose in mind other than to breathe in fresh air. The only place to sit and wait was on the top step or the on the floor of the verandah.

While she was wearing her newly purchased work clothes and wasn't too fussed about getting them filthy, the verandah floor looked like she might catch something unmentionable if she planted her backside on it. On the other hand, she deserved a bravery award for having negotiated those front stairs in the first place... And, they were no cleaner than the verandah floor. At least the decking was solid and posed less risk of her falling through it. Yep, her best option was to sit on the verandah and dangle her legs over the edge.

1

Decision made, she moved to the front edge of the verandah and was about to lower herself to the floor when she spotted a cloud of dust coming up the track. "Please God, if you let it be Bill Branigan creating the dust, I promise to be good for a month," she whispered. Then the truck arrived and she read the signage along its side. "Damn," she exclaimed. "I should be more cautious about promises I make." Her next thought gave her a fit of the giggles. What were her chances of being anything but good for the next month? Her behaviour couldn't be any better if she lived in a convent.

Bill Branigan was a large bloke, probably measuring six and a half feet tall in the old scale, and with a tanned, leathery looking hide. As he jammed his battered old felt hat on his head, she couldn't help but think he looked a lot more at home out here than he did in his office the other day. Although he owned the business, this was a man used to hard work. While he was a big bloke, he looked lean and solid; didn't appear to carry any excess weight.

"Sorry about being a bit late," he called as he slammed the truck's door, "was held up by a call from a supplier just as I was about to head out. If I hadn't wanted to give him a mouthful about late deliveries, I probably would have let the call go through to messages. Never mind, I'm here now. Let's get started. What exactly do you want me to do today?"

"Thanks for coming, Bill. I want to start on making the house a bit liveable, and I thought I should have you check it out before I did anything too serious to the place. Maybe the first thing to do is to identify any load-bearing walls, so I don't do anything silly and have the whole place come down on me."

"Good move. Let's have a walk through the place to see what can be done without too much drama happening."

At the bottom of the front stairs, he paused midstride. "Is this the only way up onto the verandah?" Kirsty nodded. "You're game. I think I might weigh a bit more than you do, but I suppose, if there is no other way up there, I will have to brave them too."

2

Their 'walk through the place' took 'walk through the place' took long than expected, and left Kirsty in no doubt Bill was a professional. He went to great pains to examine every wall before delivering his verdict on whether it was a load-bearing part of the structure, or something she could remove without causing anything to collapse. Starting at the top of the house, they worked their way down, with Kirsty making copious notes as they went. Once they were on the lower level, it didn't take them long to confront the mysterious wall in the front room.

After tapping along it in several places, Bill asked, "Right; what's this wall doing here then?"

"Er, that's my question, Bill. You are supposed to tell me why it's there. So, what do you reckon?"

"Buggered if I know, Miss McGregor. There is no rhyme or reason for it as far as I can see. It's a lot newer than the rest of the place; a more recent construction. What's behind it?"

"Well, if I could find a way in – a door of some sort – I'd be able to tell you. As I haven't found an entrance, I haven't a clue. All I know is, I don't think I want it there. Does it have to stay, or is it one I can remove?"

"No, knock it down if you want to. It's not supporting anything. And, as you say, as there is no way in, knocking it down is the only way you're going to find out what's behind it."

A few minutes later, Bill finished his tour of inspection and was dealing with a phone call from his tradesmen. As he climbed into his truck, he shouted, "Gotta go to sort out a problem on another job. Let me know when you've worked out what you want to do and you're ready for me to install a builder's pole."

She stood watching him create another cloud of dust as he headed down the track and off the property. Then her eyes strayed to the notes she made during their inspection of the house. It would take her a while to make sense of some of the stuff she'd written. But, before she considered doing anything, she had to give some thought – more than *some* thought – to the ultimate layout of the house she wanted to live in. There was no point in knocking down walls only to find out later she wanted them there.

There was one wall she knew would not be replaced at some later date: the newish wall across the end of the front room. Attacking it would give her something to do while she thought about the future interior of the place. And, the physical effort involved would help ease the frustration created by not being able to enter the place, let alone do anything to it, for so long.

"Right; then why am I still standing here?" Kirsty asked the universe. "Tools… I need some tools." And they were what she didn't have.

A pinch bar would be handy but, never having felt the need to carry one around in her car, she didn't have one. "I don't suppose I'm likely to find one anywhere around here. I might not find a pinch bar, but those outbuildings must contain something I could use to begin the demolition," she announced.

While never entertaining any inclination to enter any of those buildings before, her current situation required she overcome her distrust of them. 'They probably won't come down around my ears if I enter them', she told herself. Anyway, it was either search the buildings, or drive all the way into town for a quick visit to a hardware store.

Chapter 1

"Is this where I might find Ms Sonoma Whittington?" a vaguely familiar voice asked.

I looked up to see who owned it and saw no one. So, pushing my chair back from my desk, I was about to stand up, when a head slid around into view in my open doorway. The body it belonged to remained hidden in the corridor outside my office. I didn't need to see the rest of my caller to recognise who owned the shock of ginger curls and the dimples.

"Kirsty Williams! What are you doing back in Millhaven… and when did you arrive? Come in. Come in and explain yourself." The rest of Kirsty emerged and, giggling, came towards my desk. I hurried to meet her halfway and wrapped her in a hug. After a moment, she wriggled free.

"Is that a coffee machine I spy on yonder bench? Perhaps my explanation should be accompanied by coffee," she suggested

After as long as it takes for the machine to do its thing, and for me to open a new packet of TimTams and tip a few onto a plate, we were seated in the two ancient lounge chairs in the front corner of my office. "Okay, now we are settled, tell me what brings you back to Millhaven after all these years. God, I haven't seen you since about twelve months after we left university. Sarah's wedding was the last time we saw each other, wasn't it? Come on, we've more than a decade of catching up to do. Let's start with why Millhaven, and why now? When did you arrive and where are you staying?"

"It's good to see you haven't changed. As soon as you stop talking for long enough, I'll make a start on my story – and it might even provide you with some answers."

"Apologies; please continue," I said, accompanied by a contrite gesture. "You have the floor. So, please get on with it."

"Where to start…? Well, I arrived in Millhaven about a week ago. Crikey the place has changed since I left here at the end of primary school. I suppose it was a few years ago now, so change is only to be expected. To answer a couple of your questions, my return to Millhaven is all part of a long story, and my stay here looks like being a lengthy one. For the time being, I've rented a unit in the new tower block in the city heart, and probably will be there for about another week – or two."

"You could have stayed with me. About how long is this 'lengthy stay' you're planning to spend here?"

"The simplest answer, and best guess for the moment, might be *for the rest of my life*."

"What… here in Millhaven? You must be mad. What prompted this … this prodigal-son-like return after all these years? There has to be something quite traumatic behind it."

"More like a series of events rather than one major episode. And it brings me to the reason I'm here… here in your office I mean. Sonny, sometime after I arrived, I discovered you were a private investigator."

I nodded, but didn't see the need to do, or say, more. She seemed troubled and I wanted her to continue. After appearing to have gathered her thoughts again, she continued.

"Sonny, I think I need your help... probably both as a private investigator and as a friend. While I don't know exactly what you do, or how you operate, I need help and you are the only person who might be able to provide it."

Although I was stunned and couldn't think how to respond, I was saved the embarrassment of stumbling through an unprofessional reply when my phone opted to play its tune at the appropriate moment. She motioned for me to answer it.

"Ben… what has you calling me at this hour of the day? … Tonight…? I don't know yet. I have enough to wrap up the case I've been working on, but I might give it one more night for good measure. Will it cause a problem if I do work tonight? … Oh, I see. Well, it might be better if you plan on eating alone. Okay, I'll see you in about a week, or whenever you return, whichever comes first."

As the call ended, I looked up to see Kirsty standing, and preparing to leave. "Kirsty, what's wrong. I'm sorry I interrupted our conversation to take the call. Please sit down and tell me what is going on."

"You don't need to apologise. I just realised this is your office, and not your lounge room. I came blundering in here totally oblivious of the fact you probably were working and had appointments and other commitments lined-up. I'm sorry; I just didn't…"

"Oh, do shut up, and come and sit down again… please. You asked for my help. I need to know why and what has happened. Now, do you think we might be able to get on with this long story of yours?"

She hesitated for a moment before resuming her seat. "I don't know how or where to start my story. It all seems so… so surreal … even to me and I'm living it. So, I don't know how you're ever going to understand what has happened."

"Right; trust me. I've had plenty of episodes like this. I'm not nearly as dumb as I look, and I usually manage to follow a story along okay. So, pick an event which might have been the one to precipitate everything you've encountered since then. Or, if you find it easier, just tell me what it is you need my help with now."

"I'll choose the latter option if I may."

I nodded and gestured for her to continue. "You have the floor." Another brief pause followed before her story began tumbling out.

"Sonny, I've found some bones – *human bones*."

Then it was my turn to hesitate for a couple of heartbeats while I tried to persuade my mouth and my brain to sync properly. I felt a shot of excitement. This had the promise of a 'real' investigation, one involving something other than surveillance on often cold and wet nights, and following targets around town all day. While such run of the mill stuff is profitable and readily available in and around Millhaven, it does make for a humdrum, dull life. Kirsty's discovery could be just the thing to revive my bloodhound instinct – depending on where she found those bones.

"Did you find these bones here in Millhaven, or wherever you were before you came here?" As I asked the question, I struggled to rein-in my anticipation – and tried to prepare for disappointment.

"…Here in Millhaven, and I think they might have something to do with the strange sequence of events responsible for my being here at all."

"Okay, but I think we need to go back to the first event in the sequence, which seems to be the underlying cause of your concern. Think back to the first event which precipitated everything else."

"More like a series of events than one trauma. I suppose, to start at the beginning, I'd have to go back a few months. Anyway, the upshot of everything was, I needed to get away from Sydney … to lose myself … to find the proverbial rock and climb under it."

"And Millhaven is your chosen 'proverbial rock'?"

"Only because things transpired in such a way as to bring me here. But, here I am, and here I am planning to stay. So, now it's your turn. Whittington Investigations: what's that all about?"

"Well, I suppose it is another long story, but it is what I do for a living these days – and have done for some time now. I'm a Private Investigator, and crimes and other matters requiring investigation in Millhaven and its surrounds manage to keep me well occupied. You said you thought you might be in the rented unit only for another couple of weeks. What are your plans beyond then? Have you lined up somewhere more permanent to stay? If you would prefer, you still could come to stay with me, even if it's only until you sort out yourself and your future accommodation."

"Thanks, Sonny. But, no, I do have other plans in place. Nevertheless, you are likely to be seeing a lot of me from after this."

"Okay, but I still think we need to go back to whatever the first event was which sent you scurrying back to Millhaven. Think back to the event which was the trigger."

"Can I ask you something first?" I nodded. "Have you ever had to prove you are who you claim to be? Argh, I don't mean like when you have to show some form of identification. I mean having to prove you are really you."

Her question wrong-footed me. All I could do was to shake my head and murmur, "No, I can't say I've experienced such a situation." In spite of my rubbish answer, my brain already had worked out how difficult it would be.

"No, I don't imagine most people have experienced anything like it, but I've been living such a situation for more than a month. And now I've found bones … and I daren't go to the police about them. It just would be too hard to explain."

"So, how is this relevant to your story? Please go back and start at the beginning."

"I'd have to go back a few months ago to when Mum died. Her death and the events which followed turned my world on its ear for a while – and continue to do so. Add in a broken heart in more recent times… No, in the interest of honesty and full disclosure – and telling it like it was – it was a brutal break-up of a long-term relationship. Safe to say I was an absolute mess – and probably still am."

"Right… I agree. It sounds like a long story, and definitely one I want to hear. It has gone five o'clock. I suggest we go somewhere more comfortable than my office to indulge in a drink and dinner. While we are about it, you can tell me your story. Where would you like to go?"

"My story can wait until tomorrow if you are supposed to be working tonight."

"I was of two minds about it, but I can tell you now, without any doubt, I will not be working tonight. So, do we go to a quiet restaurant somewhere, or do we collect some takeaway and head to my place?"

"There is a restaurant on the ground floor of my building. It's always been quiet so far, and there is a nice little alcove tucked away in the back corner. I could go now and reserve the alcove for us."

"Sounds great; I'll meet you there at about seven o'clock."

I walked her down to street level and let her out of the building before hurrying back to my office to prepare for what could be shaping up to a long night of hard work. A bit over an hour later, I had finished dealing with emails and messages, freshened up as best I could, and stuffed all I thought I might need into my oversized tote bag. Then I was on my way, on foot, to dinner with Kirsty. I knew parking close to the restaurant would be just about impossible. No point wasting time trying to find a parking place when I could be listening to Kirsty's story.

The restaurant was ideal for the session I planned for this evening. Kirsty was already seated in the alcove when I arrived. She stood and waved to me as I came through the door. A few minutes later, with our drinks in front of us, I eased her into the story I was dying to hear.

"Did you manage to give any further thought to what might have been the precipitating incident which triggered your concern?"

"As I said earlier, I suppose, to start at the beginning, I'd have to go back a few months to when Mum died. Her death and the events which followed spelled the end of my world as I knew it. To add to the trauma of it all, her death came in the midst of a difficult period when a long-term relationship was souring. So, throw into the mix a broken heart, followed in more recent times by the brutal break-up of that relationship ... and the stage is set. So, those were the triggers for everything which followed."

"I'm sorry to hear of your mother's death. I didn't know about it until you mentioned it. What about your father, where is he now?"

"Oh, he died nearly ten years ago. It was hard for Mum at first but, in reality, life was a whole lot better for her without him."

"Yours always seemed a happy, solid family. Your comment is a surprise, and I'm beginning to suspect a whole lot more of your story will be surprising as well."

"Yep, probably... Right... back to my story... As I said before, it starts with Mum's death. Dad had been gone for about nine years by the time Mum died. She was a fair bit younger than Dad, so she was a young widow. Then, when her death happened while she was still quite young, it came as a shock. But, the real shock came later, when I was sorting out her affairs."

"I can understand how her death hit you hard. I'm struggling to accept it now."

"Well, it was hard, but the next incident rocked me... I discovered Fred and Dulcie Williams were not my parents. Well, not my real parents – not my birth parents, is what I mean. I discovered my birth mother died when I was about two years old. Of course, I have no memory of her. When the authorities discovered I appeared to have no living relatives who could take me in, I was placed in an institution – an orphanage. I have no memory of being there.

After a brief stay, I was fostered out to Fred and Dulcie Williams. A couple of years later, when no one had come forward to claim me, the Williamses embarked on the long process to adopt me. They had no family of their own and were both getting on a bit by then. In fact, Fred was well outside the allowed age limit for adoptive parents, but Dulcie was okay age-wise. As the authorities appeared to consider the Williamses did a good job as foster parents, and still no family member had come forward to claim me, they allowed the adoption to go ahead."

"In this day and age, it is difficult to imagine someone going through life without ever knowing they were adopted. I don't think I condone parents' withholding such information from their adult adopted children. I can't know how the Williamses felt about you. But, from what I saw of them when we were young, they didn't seem to treat you in any way different from how other parents treated their natural children. Although you knew nothing of your adoption, is it fair to say the life you had with Fred and Dulcie was happy enough?"

"Yes, and as a child, I knew nothing different. So, I suppose it is safe to say I was happy. In hindsight, it was after I came home from university when I started noticing things I hadn't seen before. I don't mean they weren't there before. I suppose the younger me just hadn't noticed them.

In reality, underneath his pleasant veneer, Fred was not a nice person. He was a control freak, and treated Dulcie as some dim-witted lower form of life, in much the same way as he saw every other female on this earth. Throughout his life, he always maintained a misogynistic, dinosaur-age, male superiority outlook. Although she never complained, I realised Dulcie had suffered in silence for their entire marriage. I didn't go home much after I finished university. I knew if I did, I wouldn't be able to hold my tongue, and I would end up making things worse for her."

"But, you were unaware of any of this while you were growing up. So, while Dulcie's life might not have been the greatest for all those years, the Williamses were gracious enough not to allow it to impact on your life and your upbringing. Perhaps it's something to be thankful for."

"I suppose… But, regardless, discovering Kirsty Williams was adopted, and was in fact not Kirsty Williams, created a whole wagon load of emotional response – not much of it good."

"It would come as a shock, and the situation would have been compounded by the fact both Fred and Dulcie were gone. You had no one to ask about anything to do with your origins."

"My real name never appeared on any documents after the adoption. Once the adoption papers were signed, I became known as Kirsty Williams, and that was it. So, of course, I wanted to know who my real parents were. I hired a professional researcher."

"I can understand your curiosity, but you must have felt some apprehension about what digging into your background might turn-up."

"It's true. I did experience a whole world of hesitation and trepidation about whether to embark on the journey or not, but I had to know. The professional I engaged knew what she was about. She realised even just the bit we already had discovered was affecting me. She sent me away to think things over for a few weeks, and wouldn't talk to me again until I had done so and was sure I wanted to proceed. By the time I was ready, and she was prepared to see me again, I was quite certain about what I wanted to do, and couldn't wait to start on it."

"You must have been bursting with curiosity by the time you were ready to continue digging into your origins. How did it go once you got into it again?"

"Well, then the next major incident occurred. In fact two incidents happened at almost the same time. Given the state I was in, neither of them was easy to understand or to manage. As you would expect, my first move was to contact my researcher to confirm I was ready to proceed with the research we had discussed. The outcome almost knocked me off my perch."

"Argh, don't tell me she had changed her mind about helping you, or had taken on another major investigation in the interim period."

"No, it was nothing so simple. I tried every way I knew, but I couldn't contact her. It didn't take me long to realise the situation suggested something serious was amiss. The bottom line was, I thought I'd been scammed. I paid her several hundred dollars as a retainer and to cover an initial program of research. After a couple of weeks of stewing about how I thought I'd been the victim of fraud, I decided to contact the Australian Society of Genealogists to see if they knew anything about the woman."

"Somehow, I'm guessing their response was not something you wanted to hear. What did they tell you about your researcher? Were you the victim of a scam?"

"I suppose I should have been relieved. No, my researcher was the genuine article. The reason I couldn't contact her was because she was a victim of a vicious mugging gone wrong in the Sydney CBD. It left her in a coma and on life support. It appears the attack occurred around the time I first tried contacting her again. The woman at the Society of Genealogists told me the previous day's update indicated no improvement in the woman's condition. They offered to keep me posted on her progress."

"Okay, in some way, it must've been a relief to discover you weren't being scammed but the news was disappointing. Was discovering what happened to your researcher the second major incident you mentioned?" Kirsty shook her head but didn't answer, so I continued. "With your researcher possibly now out of action for months, if not forever, how were you going to proceed with finding information about your parents?"

"For a few days after I learnt of what happened to my researcher, I didn't know what to do. In cold hard mercenary terms, I had paid her a considerable sum of money without having anything to show for it. If I were to engage a replacement researcher, I again would have to part with another large lump of cash for the same research as I had negotiated with the original woman. Oh, I don't think it was just about the money. It was more about my not coping with yet another setback; another disappointment."

"So, is this when the second major incident occurred, or is there more to the researcher saga before we come to the next incident?"

"It was while I was sitting stewing over what to do about a researcher, when the next incident occurred. A solicitor from Millhaven contacted me. His name is Nathan Jones, and he is a member of the firm of Truman & Parsons. Again, my first reaction to his contact was to assume he might be a scammer. He had a hard job convincing me he was a real solicitor and his contact was genuine. I told him I'd call him back if I wanted to talk further. As soon as the call ended, I looked up the Truman & Parsons phone number and called them. They confirmed Nathan Jones was one of their solicitors. In keeping with the way things were going, they told he had gone to appear in court, and would be there for the rest of the day and probably all of the next day as well."

"As you say, things were not going well. Nevertheless, as you are now here in Millhaven, I guess you did make contact with your solicitor and have been working with him. How did this Nathan Jones come to know about you, and what prompted his call?"

"While I thought my researcher hadn't done anything for me during all those weeks I was sent away to consider whether to proceed or not, it appears she had been busy on my behalf. Although she didn't know what my decision might be, she continued digging into my origins. Her research put her in touch with the legal firm of Truman & Parsons."

"Why did she choose that legal firm I wonder? There are several more well-known legal firms in Millhaven. While Truman & Parsons has been established here for a long time, they are not a high-profile operation. Did they give you any indication of how it came about?"

"No. I think it was a bit of a surprise to them too. Anyway, they appointed Nathan Jones to work with my researcher to follow-up on the claims she made."

Kirsty was forced to pause her story when staff came to deliver our platter of bruschetta. Although I hoped it would be a short pause, I should have realised I would hear no more until after we made inroads into our starter.

Chapter 2

At last, having dispatched half the bruschetta, I was able to encourage Kirsty to return to her story. "Before food so rudely interrupted us, you said how Nathan Jones had worked with your researcher, and everything fell in a heap when she was attacked. How much had Nathan done with her before she ended up comatose in hospital?"

"He spoke to her on two or three occasions before the incident. It appears my researcher believed she had established a sound case to claim a deceased estate here in Millhaven. She asked Nathan what evidence he required to prove I was the rightful heir. He wasn't sure my researcher wasn't just another crackpot trying to make a killing. Without too many details of the possible claim, Nathan gave her only basic guidelines on the types of evidence required."

"It's not hard to understand Nathan, and Truman & Parsons, treating your researcher's approach with some degree of caution, but they must have learnt enough for them to contact you. Did Nathan say how it came about?"

"In the last conversation Nathan had with her, she outlined information already discovered. My researcher asked for clarification of what else she needed to provide. From their conversation, Nathan couldn't ascertain what evidence she already had gathered. To enable him to provide her with accurate guidance, he asked to see copies of it. She agreed to post certified copies of everything to him by the end of the week."

"Progress seemed okay up until then. What prompted him to start dealing directly with you?"

"The last time Nathan spoke to my researcher was two days before she ended up in hospital. When the promised copies hadn't materialised, he started making enquiries amongst his colleagues in Sydney and discovered what had happened. He discussed the situation with his firm's senior partners who, labouring under the misconception I knew everything my researcher had discovered, instructed Nathan to approach me directly."

"But you didn't have any of the information your researcher dug up, did you?"

"No; none of it. I faced beginning the research again from scratch… and I did do a bit. But, in reality, I just gave Nathan the authority to obtain the relevant information. Anyway, he found enough to feel confident I had a genuine claim against the deceased estate, but still needed more to prove it to the court.

I had to prove beyond doubt I was who I claimed to be. It doesn't sound like an almost impossible task until you have to do it. And, you have to remember I was still in Sydney at the time, and Nathan was doing everything from here in Millhaven. So, in those early stages, I saw nothing and knew nothing – other than anything Nathan told me over the phone."

"Couldn't he at least email scanned copies of the information to you? After all, this is your life he was digging into. I would have thought you had the right to know everything he discovered about you."

"You would expect so, wouldn't you? And, yes, I did ask to see whatever he discovered, but he said it was illegal to copy some of it. So, after about three weeks of such nonsense, I came to Millhaven to become more involved, and to see what he had discovered."

"No doubt, with more than a little trepidation involved in finding out. So, how did it go? Had he done much work by the time you arrived?"

"He had done an enormous amount. Well, I doubt he did it. I suspect one of the office people or his articled clerk undertook all the research. By the time I arrived, he had enough to feel sufficiently confident about who I was and the veracity of my claim. He had lodged a claim for probate with the court on my behalf but, of course, it wasn't enough to keep bureaucracy happy. There have been endless requests for one more piece of paper; one more bit of evidence. I feel as though I have done nothing except sign forms since I arrived."

"Okay… but have you learnt anything about your origins, who your parents were, or whatever? Nathan must have found out quite a bit to feel confident about your claim getting up in court."

"Right, I'll start at the beginning. The first thing I discovered was the name I was given at birth was Kirsty Shelby McGregor. The Williamses only added their surname after my adoption went through. They left the rest of my original name unchanged, but didn't tell me or anyone else what it was, or use it in any way.

My birth registration told us who my mother was. Her name was given as Kate Shelby McGregor. We later discovered Kate was baptised as Catherine, but appears to have abandoned the name in favour of Kate when she was a teenager. One other important piece of information we gleaned from my birth registration: Kate was an unmarried mother. No father's name appeared on the birth registration. So, I discovered I was illegitimate."

"Given the era in which you were born, the rule was an unmarried mother could not name the father of her child, and the child was registered as illegitimate. The label probably didn't offer you the greatest start in life, but the Williamses taking you in does give you quite a lot to be thankful for. Who knows what your life might have been like if they hadn't adopted you? Apart from anything else, we wouldn't have met and been best friends at primary school, and again at university."

"Perhaps… or, perhaps I might have spent my entire life here in Millhaven. No, don't ask... all will be revealed as the story unfolds."

"Okay, you have me intrigued. So far, I haven't heard anything to suggest you might have spent your entire life in Millhaven. I thought you didn't arrive here until around the time we started primary school."

"Well, yes, I think it was my first encounter with Millhaven. So far, I haven't found anything to suggest I was here before then."

"Perhaps we should park the story of your life for the moment and return to the reason you came to see me in the first place: you found some bones. As I assume those bones are in Millhaven, maybe the first thing you should tell me is why you came back to Millhaven."

"Maybe things will become clearer as I progress with my story."

I nodded and invited her to continue as I dug around in my bag for a small notebook and pencil – and sneaked a look to check the conversation still was being recorded okay.

"The reason I'm here is part of the story of my life... but I get what it is you want to know. Okay... Nathan found the name of one parent and was content with that. I couldn't just leave it there and not dig a bit deeper. I had to know something about Kate McGregor. After finding out who my mother was, I was curious about whether I had a flock of aunts, uncles and cousins out there somewhere. After all, there might be a whole herd of relatives somewhere who didn't know anything about me ... or maybe they did know about me but, for all these years, wanted to pretend they didn't. The only way to find out seemed to be to do more digging. So, it is what we did. At least Nathan did – while I looked over his shoulder."

"Something tells me you did not find a herd of relatives, or you would not be here renting a unit in Millhaven."

"No. Research proved Catherine – I think of her as Kate – was the only child of Silas and Regina McGregor of Millhaven. So, no aunts, uncles or cousins roaming around anywhere, but it meant we now had the names of one set of my grandparents. And, from our research, we also knew Regina's maiden name was Shelby."

"...And you had discovered the origin of your Shelby middle name."

"Yes, so I then understood my mother's strange middle name, and probably why she passed it onto me too. But, it seems this is how this family history stuff works. You find one piece of information to answer a question, and all it does is pose another question. Anyway, one thing was obvious. Even in Nathan's earliest research there was a strong Millhaven connection. When he told me about it, I couldn't help wondering whether the Williamses also knew about my family connection to this place, and if it was why we moved here soon after they adopted me. While I know it's just speculation on my part, I can't help wondering whether they knew more about me than the official paperwork provided. Did we move here in the hope of finding family here who would take me off their hands before the adoption was finalised? I know it sounds ridiculous, but it's what not knowing does to you. It allows fanciful notions to develop."

"So, just to make sure I understand the story thus far, your possible connection to Millhaven is through your birth mother, and the McGregor surname. Am I correct?"

"Correct… Having discovered the McGregor connection, Nathan started digging around to find out what he could about my grandparents, Silas and Regina. His 'digging' turned up a lot more than either of us expected. The stuff he uncovered brought me back to Millhaven. It's funny the way Fate works sometimes. All this happened at just the right time in my life. It was when I was at my lowest ebb ever, and I was staying well clear of bridges… in case I found I couldn't control the urge to throw myself off one."

"After that comment, I'm not sure I should let you out of my sight in case you do something silly. And, now I don't know which part of your story I want to hear next: the part about why it was a bad time in your life, or more about what you discovered relating to your connection to Millhaven."

Before I could say anymore, my phone made its presence felt. "Damn! I do have to take this call. It's one I've been waiting for since yesterday morning." I knew the caller would hang-up without even leaving a message the moment he heard my voicemail cut-in. As I answered the call, I exercised 'restaurant courtesy' and made my way out onto the street.

The call was brief and terse. My caller confirmed a pending investigation he had asked me to undertake couldn't begin until sometime next week at the earliest. Not such bad news from my point of view, but he wasn't happy about it. I had intended to wrap up the case I was working on either today or tomorrow, and a few days off would be welcome after what had been a busy couple of months. I rushed back to our table to hear more of Kirsty's story, only to be disappointed.

Kirsty's phone played its tune as I dragged out my chair to sit down again. I heard her tell her caller she would call back in a few minutes. Damn… I sensed whatever her call was about, it was important enough to bring our night to an end.

"I'm sorry, Sonny," she began as I resumed my seat. "I didn't think before bowling into your office this morning. You have a business to run and, no doubt, plenty of work to do… and you would be out attending to some of it tonight, if it weren't for me and my problem. You don't need me taking up your time. It's not too late yet if you have something you should be doing instead of sitting here with me. Anyway, I am going to have to beg off the rest of dinner this evening. I must attend to the call I just received."

"There's no need to apologise. Let's just call it a night and arrange to continue whenever you are free… But, I hope it is soon. I will die of curiosity if I have to wait longer than tomorrow."

"I take it you are still as fond of eating as you used to be." She cocked an eyebrow at the remaining piece of bruschetta from our starter still sitting on the plate in the middle of our table.

"Well, I still do eat, and I do like good food but, these days, I'm more conscious of what and how much I eat... Ye-es, in spite of this morning's TimTams. We all are allowed at least one vice aren't we?"

"Good… how about we resume our meeting in your office first thing tomorrow morning? …Unless you have appointments or plan to be working then, of course"

"At the moment, I don't have anything booked for tomorrow morning, so I'll see you in my office at nine o'clock, if it suits you."

"Right... tomorrow morning at nine. Are you sure it suits, and you're not giving up work on my account?"

"Just in case something comes up and I can't be there, I'll call to let you know."

A few moments later, after leaving Kirsty still sitting at our table, I was on my way back to my office. While I was sure she was concerned about taking up my time, I had noticed her take a couple of surreptitious glances at her watch while I was out on the street dealing with my phone call. It was obvious I wasn't the only one with business to attend to this evening. Maybe, if I had heard a bit more of her story, I would have a better idea of what the rest of her night might involve.

As I walked back to my office, the only thing I was sure about was, I would not be working tonight. Kirsty was right about it still being early enough for me to spend an extra couple of hours on surveillance for the job I was about to wrap up, but it wasn't necessary. I already had enough without doing anything more tonight.

On leaving the restaurant, I had thought to go back up to my office to work for an hour or so. Instead, I walked around to the parking lot at the rear of the building, climbed into my car and drove home ... via a chicken-and-chips place on the way. After all, we hadn't eaten dinner yet when we left the restaurant – well, nothing other than a couple of pieces of bruschetta.

Any good intentions I had regarding transcribing the recording of tonight's conversation with Kirsty somehow managed to evaporate on the way home. Besides, the aroma of my dinner which filled the car had me famished by the time I arrived. Following dinner and a shower, I looked forward to a glass of wine to keep me company while I reflected on everything I heard from Kirsty today.

Maybe I should have done some surveillance instead of coming home. I might have slept better when I finally climbed into bed. As it was, sleep was a long time coming and, in the interim, my mind amused itself by conjuring up an endless list of questions about Kirsty, her life ... and those bones.

*****

After what felt like a short, restless night, I was awake early. It allowed me to be in my office by seven o'clock, well ahead of my advertised time of nine o'clock. With the routine admin tasks taken care of and the report on the case I was wrapping up ready to post, I put my feet up on the desk and embarked on a trip down 'memory lane'. I revisited different times spent with Kirsty over all those years now so long gone.

No matter how hard I examined those memories, or how clearly I brought images of people and incidents to mind, I couldn't find any evidence in my memory banks of any untoward behaviour in the Williams' household. I was certain there was nothing to support Kirsty's claim Fred Williams made his wife's life a misery. I didn't know where Fred was employed while here in Millhaven, but I had a child's vague recollection of his having been involved somehow with one or more of the large construction projects happening in the area at the time.

At university, Kirsty and I took different undergraduate courses, but we lived in the same share-house with a couple of other girls. I couldn't remember the name of Kirsty's course, but I seemed to remember it had something to do with agricultural science. She talked about testing plant varieties to try to produce better disease resistant strains. While it was all a foreign language to me, I could appreciate the importance of the work people in her field did and it's benefits for the rest of us. ... Note to Self: remember to ask her if she is still involved in the same work and whether she can continue it here in Millhaven.

Stiff from maintaining the same position for so long, I checked my watch as I tried to upright myself again. Time had slipped by almost unnoticed. I needed to fill the coffee machine in readiness for Kirsty's visit. I struggled to my feet and took a couple of steps away from my desk before my phone demanded

23

attention. Gut instinct told me it was Kirsty cancelling our meeting. My gut was wrong. It was Ben.

"Are you working again tonight?"

"No; wrapped-up the case."

"If you are okay with Chinese, I'll bring some with me … unless you would prefer something else."

"Chinese would be great. See you at the usual time? I thought you said you would be away for the rest of the week. What happened?" He told me his trip was postponed, confirmed the time for tonight, and ended the call.

Ben and I hadn't spent an evening together in a few days. Not since I started work on my last case and was out on surveillance every night. It would be good to slip back into our routine of dining together most evenings.

To fill in the twenty minutes or so until Kirsty was due to arrive, I decided to give in to the question niggling me since last night: why does the McGregor name seem familiar? I asked Google to look for 'McGregor' associated with Millhaven. No surprise… it came up with a whole heap of stuff for me to sift through. Rather than waste so much time and energy, I refined the search parameters by providing it with Silas and Regina's names.

This time, I struck gold with 'Regina McGregor', but it was not the information I expected to find. The most useful item was a newspaper article from about ten years ago. At first, I doubted it was going to be of much use, as it was too recent. I read the article anyway, and discovered my assumption was ill-founded. It was a story about Regina McGregor's disappearance around twenty years prior to when the article was written. *Disappearance* was not a helpful word in this context.

According to the article, an older resident (age not given) of the Millhaven district, one Mrs Regina McGregor, disappeared from her property under mysterious circumstances about two decades ago. It stated Regina had lived alone and, for many years, led a reclusive lifestyle. The article went on to suggest the woman might have been missing for some time before anyone became aware of the fact. When alerted to her possible disappearance, a full-scale investigation was carried out over several days. No trace of the woman was found, and no evidence discovered of foul play having been committed on the property. The article went on to claim the disappearance of Regina McGregor was one of the district's most mysterious unsolved cases. Over the ensuing years, the McGregor property had become a neglected wilderness.

"Christ, what had Kirsty let herself in for when she decided to take over the property?" I asked the universe. My only good thought was in relation to what Kirsty might find. There shouldn't be a pile of bones awaiting her following the police's investigation. If the investigation at the time of the disappearance didn't locate the missing woman, Kirsty was unlikely to do so when she started cleaning out the house. So... what about the bones she claims she found?

A brief glance through the other material on Regina McGregor which Google dug up didn't tell me anything more than I'd learnt from the previous newspaper article. Accepting I had hit a brick wall for now about what happened on the McGregor property, I closed Google. After retrieving the copy of the newspaper article from the printer, I was putting Kirsty's file away when she arrived.

I hoped the question now thundering around in the back of my mind wouldn't distract me while I engaged with Kirsty. Nevertheless, I knew the question would continue to nag me for the rest of the day... Should I mention the unsolved disappearance of Regina McGregor to Ben tonight, or wait until the McGregor name came up in conversation at some time? The latter option had the stronger appeal.

After ushering Kirsty to the lounge chairs in the 'interview corner' of my office and faffing about with usual niceties, I encouraged her to continue telling me her story. I encountered a further delay when she announced she needed a coffee first to fortify her for what lay ahead. With coffee and TimTams organised, I waited until about half the coffee was drunk before again encouraging her to get on with her story.

This time my efforts were successful, but I wanted to set the story's direction. "Before you go any further, tell me about this property you inherited, and how it all came about. Is it why you came back to Millhaven?"

"Yeah, I wanted to get out of Sydney and just lose myself somewhere. Then we discovered about this property. Well, I didn't discover it. First, my professional researcher found out about the deceased estate, and then Nathan discovered the property was part of the deceased estate."

"Oh, I see. Now, maybe we should return to your story from last night. We left off – thanks to interruptions from phone calls – at the point where you discovered Kate, your mother, was the only child of Silas and Regina McGregor of Millhaven. What happened next?"

For a few moments, she stared at some indeterminate spot across my office. Then Kirsty shook her head as if to clear her thinking and, with a sigh, continued her story.

"The next important event was when Silas died. He left his entire estate to his only child Kate ... and nothing to his wife. His wife, Regina, was allowed to continue to live on the property until such time as she remarried, or Kate assumed control of everything and made her own arrangements regarding her mother."

"So, you discovered your mother, Kate, inherited her father's estate here in Millhaven, and the estate included a property of some sort?" She nodded. "Then what happened?"

Chapter 3

"The property was left to my mother before I was born. I doubt she ever knew about it. I can't imagine someone ignoring the fact they inherited a property here in Millhaven. When Nathan called to say I might be able to claim my mother's inheritance, I didn't believe him.

My mother died when she was about nineteen. As I doubted she made a will beforehand, I couldn't see how I could inherit from her. But, Nathan persisted and came back to tell me he was confident my claim would succeed. So, once it appeared it might, he started the process to confirm the property had come down to me in turn. The timing was excellent. I left Sydney, came here, and have been working with Nathan ever since."

"Has the property come down to you now? I'm assuming it has or you wouldn't be still here."

"It's taken a while – and dozens of copies of official certificates and other paperwork. The process was ongoing when I left Sydney, but I thought I could hurry it along if I were here. When I arrived, Nathan told me he had applied for probate, and was confident the court would grant it within their normal timeframe of between two and four weeks. Having to wait only four weeks would be wonderful but, it seems the wait is much longer. Probate still hasn't been granted. The place still isn't mine. But, a call I received first thing this morning suggests it soon might happen."

"Well, it's not difficult to work out why it's taken so long. Before anything else could happen, they had to confirm you, and your mother before you, were who you claimed to be. Could you do anything once you arrived to help accelerate the process? What have you been doing since you arrived?"

"There wasn't much I could do to hurry things. Nathan was so confident about probate, he told me I was allowed to go onto

27

the property to look around while I waited. I wasn't to go into any of the buildings, or remove anything from the property, or make any changes on the place. Of course, I went out to see the place straight away … and discovered I could only view it from the road.

The overgrown track from the road to the house was impassable. I tried taking some photos from the road using the telephoto lens, but they weren't worth keeping. There is good news though. While I was standing there messing about with my camera, the farmer from the next property came past. Although he was in a hurry, we had a bit of a chat. He offered to clear the track up to the house for me. I didn't want him to go to any trouble, but he said it wouldn't take much more than putting the blade on the tractor and driving over to do it. I might've misjudged him, but he seemed a bit excited by someone showing some interest in the old place – *after all these years*, as he kept saying."

"When do you think you'll be able to drive up to the house to inspect it? Did the neighbour give you any indication of when he might deal with the driveway?"

"Well, he said he would do it that afternoon. I struggled with the temptation to race out there first thing the next morning, but common sense dictated I should wait until at least mid-morning before I checked whether he'd been able to do anything. If he had, I planned to inspect the property to assess how much hard work I had ahead of me."

"I'm imagining your frustration. Have you accessed the property yet, or are you still waiting to see it?"

"Oh, I was out there the next day. He had done a wonderful job of clearing the track. I drove straight up to the old house. Five minutes later, I decided it would be best if I lived on the place while the house and the property were being re-established."

"Kirsty, I've been thinking about the property. I have a vague recollection of a place outside town, which I think belonged to the McGregor family at some time. The property I'm thinking of has been abandoned for decades. I haven't seen it recently, and I don't know what the place is like now. I expect it is quite derelict after being neglected for so long."

"You probably are thinking about the right property. The neighbour told me the place had been abandoned for at least forty years. I expect there's a degree of inaccuracy in his estimation, but you are right about its being deserted for quite a while."

"So-o... Is it where you plan to reside ... And, what happens if you find it's not fit to be lived in?"

"I didn't go into the house not at first as I was told I wasn't to enter any buildings. I was worried breaking the rules might interfere with the probate process. But, I wasn't expecting any surprises when I did enter the house. I didn't dare hope it would need nothing more than a bit of a cleanout and a fresh lick of paint. When I was given permission to inspect the house, so I could start cleaning it out, I went to see about having the electricity reconnected as soon as possible. They told me it couldn't happen until I'd had a building inspection done by a registered builder – and I could provide proof of ownership of the place.

My only option was to talk to a builder with a view to using him to work on the house at some point in future. He then could seek permission to install a builder's pole close to the house and have the power connected to the pole. It wasn't what I would've liked, but it would get power to the premises, and allow me to use vacuum cleaners, high-pressure water cleaners and whatever else in the way of electrical equipment I might need when I started attacking the place."

"Kirsty, did it occur to you the place might be terrible inside? I'm not talking about the crud of ages built up in there. I'm talking about the layout. It might be a miserable rabbit warren of tiny dark rooms. After so many years, I have no doubt the kitchen and bathroom need replacing with something more modern. ...Which reminds me, is there a water supply connected to the house? You are going to need lots of water once you start cleaning the place."

"There are a couple of big rainwater tanks − at least, the farmer nextdoor told me they were for rainwater. Whether there is anything in them, and if it's fit for use, is something I haven't explored yet. So far, you haven't brought up anything I haven't thought about. I know there will be many things I haven't considered, but I'll deal with those as I encounter them. I'll be out at the property later today, and should be able to start preparing a schedule for the mountain of hard work I have ahead of me. There isn't just the house to think about. The whole property needs to be made productive again."

"Only too true I suspect. The downside of my business is: you don't have a life. Well, not one to speak of anyway." While it wasn't quite the truth, it was no more than a white lie. "While I can't do anything tonight, how about you come to my place for dinner tomorrow night? Of course, there's an ulterior motive. I'll want to know what else you've discovered."

"It's a deal. If it's not too early for you to be home, I thought, if I came at about six o'clock, we could have a drink before dinner. I have a feeling I will need to wind down a bit before I eat."

I noticed her surreptitious glances at the clock on my wall as we discussed dinner plans. It wasn't hard to realise her interest was in going to the property, not in sitting in my office being pumped for information. I employed a diplomatic ploy to allow her to leave, but also to allow me to return to my McGregor research.

"Gee, look at the time. I'm sorry, Kirsty. I've been sitting here chatting and asking endless questions when I know you are keen to be out at the property. Go and do whatever you need to do … and tell me all about it over dinner tomorrow night."

"Thanks. I do want to head out. There is so much to do; so much to get my head around. While it doesn't sound as though I've done much, I haven't stopped since I arrived. I admit a lot of time was spent talking to solicitors and trying to prove I am who I am. I'm hoping it's all sorted out soon. I have to check out of the unit I'm renting on Friday morning. I had planned to have other arrangements in place by then."

"You can always move in with me until you sort yourself out."

Once Kirsty left, I planned to continue my research into the McGregors of Millhaven, but it wasn't to be. Between my phone and 'walk-in' potential clients, the rest of the day morphed into a blur.

Ben, laden with a selection of Chinese take-away, arrived a little earlier than usual and almost followed me in the door when I arrived home. As he carried the food inside, he greeted me with, "Yeah, I know. I didn't think being early just this once would matter. I will be leaving early though. Something work-wise is happening a bit later, and I need to be on hand when it goes down. Shall we get stuck into eating straight away?"

As Ben's plan was to eat and run, no decision was required on the McGregor matter. For some reason, it felt like a relief, but I don't know why it should.

Later, I found myself heading for a shower and bed much too early for sleep to arrive soon. For the next couple of hours my mind continued at top speed as it tried making sense of the little I knew of Kirsty's story, and explored the memories I had of Kirsty and our friendship.

*****

A different feeling pulsed through me from the moment I opened my eyes this morning. I wasn't sure whether it was one of excitement or expectation. Whatever it was, I knew its cause was the prospect of hearing the rest of Kirsty's story. But, it would be another twelve hours until she arrived at six o'clock tonight. I just knew it was going to be a l-o-n-g day, and would require application of a large dose of creative thinking to help time elapse faster than usual.

Dawdling over breakfast and a second mug of coffee meant a later than normal start to my trip into my city office. The later start meant I didn't escape the tide of peak hour traffic also trying to crawl its way into the city. In spite of my best efforts, it was only a little after nine o'clock when I pounded up the stairs to my office. Attending to basic admin tasks didn't take long. Completing the documentation on my current file, and a trip to the Post Office to mail everything to my client, still managed to have me back in my office by about 10.30AM. Coffee, and a cake I bought on my way back from the Post Office, would help fill in a little more time.

Standing in my office's miniscule kitchenette waiting for the coffee machine to finish doing its thing allowed time for a terrible thought to develop. One way to fill in time, if I had nothing else to do in the office, was to go home and tackle some long-overdue domestic chores. I was saved from any further such foolish notions by the timely beeping of the coffee machine. I opened the box from the bakery and selected a tasty morsel from the several on offer. Well, there was no point in buying only one cake. I still had to fill in the afternoon as well, and cake and coffee sometime during those hours would help.

"Damn…," I muttered. Having just plonked my backside down onto one of the chairs in my 'interview corner', someone pounded on my door. It would not be a good look for a prospective client to find me about to tuck into cake and coffee; not professional-looking at all. Between their bouts of thumping on my door, I managed to hide the cake and coffee m in the microwave before attending to the door.

"Ben… What brings you here at this hour of the morning?" I asked in surprise at the sight of the district's top cop, Ben Richards, standing outside my door.

"I was in the area and realised I had missed my mid-morning coffee."

"So you thought you would come here and bum a free one from me? And, why are you still here and not in Brisbane?"

"Well why not…? Your car was in its usual spot behind the building, so I knew you were in your office. I reckoned you might rustle up a coffee and something to go with – even if it were only a TimTam or two. And, my trip to Brisbane might happen later this week, or not until next week. So-o… do I have to stand out here chatting, or are you going to invite me in to chat while you make my coffee?"

Stepping aside to let him pass, I waved him into my inner sanctum before following him across to my kitchenette. As we approached the kitchen, he exclaimed, "Now, that looks much like a box from the bakery. Could I be in luck today and have something more than a TimTam to accompany my coffee?"

By the time he finished speaking, he was at the kitchen bench and opening the box of cakes. "Oh no, wouldn't you know it? I have a choice this morning, and they are all the varieties I like best. Are you psychic and knew I would call in? Mind you, you could have made it easier for me and just bought one sort, so I didn't have to choose."

"As I wasn't buying with you in mind, it was never a consideration. I don't suppose there was a more pressing reason for your visit this morning – other than for free coffee, I mean?"

"Did you go out to work on a job after I left last night and maybe worked late? You are definitely prickly this morning. Anyone would think you didn't want me here today."

"No. No, you are a welcome distraction this morning. I was wondering how I was going to fill in my time until this evening. So, coffee and a chat with you will help."

"Terrific… great to see I'm useful for something. What's happening this evening that's so special?"

The next little while was spent telling him of Kirsty's unexpected arrival in Millhaven, and providing him with some background on our on-again/off-again friendship over the years. Kirsty's discovery of her birth name seemed to capture his interest more than anything else I told him.

"Why does the McGregor surname ring a bell for me? Do you recall a case involving the McGregor name here in Millhaven in the past? You were a part of Millhaven well before I first became connected with the place. The name would have to be something to do with a past case for it to catch my attention."

33

"It doesn't ring any bells for me but, until yesterday, I only knew Kirsty as 'Williams', not McGregor. I'm hoping to find out more of her story over dinner tonight."

"Hmm… Well, I suspect the McGregor name is going to keep my mind occupied for most of today. Enjoy your dinner. And, I will want to know what you find out about her background."

He left soon after, but only after I made it quite clear he was not welcome to join us for dinner tonight, and threatened dire consequences if he should 'just happen to drop in'. By the time he left, it was almost lunchtime. I abandoned my office in search of something for lunch and a newspaper with which to waste a little more time this afternoon.

Soon after I returned with the requisite afternoon timewasters, a spate of calls from potential clients kept me busy for an hour or so, and a bit longer by the time I emailed my brochures and other relevant information to those who requested them. Then, it was time to have lunch and put my feet up while I just about read the ink off every page of the newspaper. I had almost finished with the paper when a call came from Kirsty.

"Sonny, would it be all right if we had dinner at the restaurant in my building again tonight? A couple of things requiring my attention have come up. I'll need to go back to my unit when I leave the property. If it doesn't inconvenience you, could we meet in the restaurant at seven o'clock for dinner?"

"No inconvenience at all… I'll see you at seven."

She didn't offer any further explanation, and seemed in a hurry to end the call and continue whatever it was she was doing beforehand. The change of plans wasn't an inconvenience, but it did heighten the intrigue associated with Kirsty's presence in Millhaven.

A quick check on my emails and a few other minor admin tasks took me through to a little after six o'clock. It allowed me a few minutes before I needed to freshen up and head to the restaurant to think about the bones Kirsty claimed to have found. Did she actually find bones – real human bones – or was she speaking metaphorically about skeletons she was discovering in her cupboard? My gut and I agreed we were almost certain they were real bones she found. But, I had run out of time and needed to be on my way to dinner.

Kirsty McGregor was seated at the bar with her glass of wine already at half-mast. I spotted her as soon as I walked into the restaurant. A quick glance at my watch told me I wasn't late. It was just seven o'clock. As I hurried towards her, she looked up. I was shocked. She looked exhausted.

"You look as though you've been here for a while already. I could have joined you earlier if you called me. Is everything okay?" I climbed onto a seat beside her and indicated to the young bartender I would have whatever Kirsty was drinking.

"Yes. Why wouldn't everything be okay?" She seemed confused by my question, so I explained how exhausted she looked.

"Aw, I suppose I was feeling a bit wrung-out. So, I decided to come down and have a glass of wine while I waited. It's been a busy day, but I think I've achieved a bit." A brief interruption followed for the bartender to deliver my wine. Then Kirsty resumed. "Let's make ourselves comfortable at our table before I tell you about my day."

Our table was in the same quiet corner at the back of the restaurant and next to the windows overlooking the river. After the usual couple of minutes of faffing about getting settled, I encouraged Kirsty to get on with her story.

She stared out at the river for what seemed a long time. I followed her example and let my eyes drift out across the inky darkness. Lighting along the waterside esplanade was low, no more than a series of regular orange glows following the contours of the river. The inhabitants of a handful of small crafts moored out on the river all appeared to be 'at home' tonight. Their soft lights created fluid reflections rippling across the water. The moment was over all too soon, but the storytelling didn't begin. I prompted her.

"Good to hear you feel as though you achieved something today. What does tomorrow bring? I don't doubt you will be heading out to the property, but what do you plan do?"

"Of course, I'll stick with my now-established daily routine and go out to the property, but it won't be until a bit later; maybe not until mid-morning."

"So, if you don't want to go to the house until mid-morning, what are you going to do to fill in time until then? And what prevents you going there at the crack of dawn as you have been doing?"

"There is something I need to do first. Apart from other matters they want to talk to me about, the legal firm I've been working with left a message about having found a plan I might find interesting. Whatever it is, I'm sure it will be interesting. So, I'll call in there on my way to the property to collect whatever they have, and maybe talk to Nathan about progress with probate. Anyway, it looks as though I won't be at the property before ten o'clock; maybe not even until later."

"If probate still hasn't come through, you might not be able to start anything anyway. I don't imagine you want to spend time and money doing things, only to find you are not going to end up owning it. What will you do as an alternative, if you can't start on the house tomorrow?"

"Not a problem... I plan to attack the local newspaper archives again at some point in time. I spent some time there soon after I arrived in Millhaven, but I didn't have any idea of which years to search. After tomorrow, depending on what happens at the solicitors, and whether I manage to talk to Nathan or not, I might be able to better focus my research. So, if I can't explore the house tomorrow, I'll be back at the archives."

"Well, we should not make this a late night. You are looking exhausted, and it sounds as though you might have a big day ahead of you again tomorrow."

"I'm in need of a lot more of these," she said, and waved her empty wine glass at me. I caught the attention of the drinks waiter and gestured for the 'same again please'. While he fetched our drinks, Kirsty continued. "Tomorrow night is the end of my second week in the unit here, and I think someone else has it booked from Saturday." Whether it was due to her exhaustion, or having to vacate the unit, she seemed too depressed for my liking.

"Right... The offer I made earlier is still open. You are welcome to stay with me for as long as it takes for everything to be ready for you to live on the property. Check-out of here on Friday as planned, and move in with me. Bring your stuff to my place whenever it suits you."

"Thanks, I have thought about it. If you are sure it won't inconvenience you, I would like to take you up on your offer. I doubt it would be for more than a few days – hopefully. I could send some of my stuff home with you this evening to make things easier when I check-out."

The rest of the evening was spent revisiting memories of our days together at primary school and later at university. Given her apparent frame of mind, I figured it counterproductive to try for more of her story tonight.

As intended, it wasn't a late night. I was home by a little after ten o'clock. All the way home, a shadow of something I once knew tried to worm its way through from some dark corner of the far reaches of my mind. It didn't succeed but, by the time I was ready for bed, I could just about hear the distant tinkle of a bell associated with the McGregor name.

Before I left the unit block, we loaded some of Kirsty's belongings into my car. At home, I stacked her gear in the spare room she would be using until she moved out to the property. By the time I finished and had a shower, it was only just eleven o'clock and too early for bed, or so I told myself... But, what to do for an hour or so?

I now had plenty of Kirsty's story recorded and awaiting transcription. Try as I might, I couldn't persuade myself to make a start on it. After about an hour of 'navel gazing' and a glass of port, I called it a night.

Chapter 4

The morning was gloomy and heavy with the promise of rain. Humidity was oppressive. Somewhere between eight and nine o'clock, the sun managed to struggle through the heavy cloud cover for a brief period, before being obliterated again by the cloud. It wasn't a bad thing. Although brief, the sun had a nasty bite to it. Then, when I stopped for mid-morning coffee around ten o'clock, the heavens opened up and the rain bucketed down. I had no way of knowing how Kirsty's morning played out but, if she were able to start exploring the old house, she did not have a good day for it.

Escaping to Kirsty's property might not be such a bad idea, even if the rain had made a mess of the newly cleared track to the house. As I stood by my coffee machine waiting for it to finish filling my mug, my thoughts were about Kirsty. They were interrupted when my phone demanded attention. It was Kirsty. I felt my stomach tighten in preparation for the bad news I expected to follow.

"Sonny, have I interrupted anything important?" she asked.

"No, you haven't interrupted anything, but you sound a bit rushed. Is everything all right?"

"Rushed...? No... Well, yes, a bit maybe ... I can't believe what's happened." There was a brief pause, whether to gather her thoughts, or for theatrical effect, I wasn't sure. Then I heard her take a deep breath. Here it comes, I thought, but chose not to interrupt.

She rushed on to tell me her news. "Let me think. Right... I'll start from yesterday and the phone call from the solicitors' office. Then, in a later call, my solicitor, Nathan, agreed to come in early, so I met him at eight o'clock this morning. He had a couple of old documents and a map of the McGregor property they found in their archives to give me. And, there was one more little piece of the legal process to complete – just one more document to sign. I was bitchy about it, as I wanted to make a start on doing things on the property. He reminded me I could go and look around, but I wasn't to enter any building, or move or remove anything from the place, until the document I had just signed was accepted by some court or other."

"How long is it likely to take? Did he give you any indication?"

"Oh yes… according to him, it could take a couple of days – or a couple of weeks. I left him in no doubt how I felt about the way he was handling things. Then I headed out to the property, although I had no idea what I might do when I arrived, as I still wasn't supposed to enter any of the buildings. About an hour or so after I arrived out there, Nathan called me again.

He wanted me to come to his office straight away. I knew it had to be bad news. Almost sick with nervousness and worry, I took my time coming back into town. No point in hurrying to receive bad news, right? By the time I was ushered into his inner sanctum, I was almost a trembling mess. Then he delivered his news: *It's all through. Probate has been granted. The property is yours.*"

"Is it possible? You only signed yet another piece of paper for the court before you left town. It doesn't add up for me. Maybe you shouldn't do anything until you have something to confirm the news."

"I know. It seems surreal doesn't it? As it was explained to me, the court had approved my claim and the grant of probate was ready to go, but they needed just one last piece of paper. As soon as Nathan took it over to the court and lodged it, it was all done. They called him back as he was leaving the building to tell him the news and hand him a copy of the grant of probate document. He went back to his office and called me… and you know the rest."

Her words took a moment to register with me. Then I was congratulating her and gushing forth appropriate words to fit the occasion – and the big question. "So, what are you doing now?"

"I'm still parked outside the solicitors' office while trying to get my head around this latest development. It made sense to sit for a few minutes until I came down to earth again before I drove back to the property. Oh, and I was given the keys to the house. Are you coming out to have a look at the place?"

"Uhmm… maybe some time this afternoon, if I can escape from here. You said your solicitor had keys to the house? How could he have the keys?"

"When the police went to investigate Regina's disappearance, they found the keys and locked the place when they left. As Regina's solicitor, they gave the keys to Thomas Agnew for safe keeping. When he retired – only about five years ago – he handed the keys in to the court to be held in safekeeping as part of the McGregor estate. Now the estate is settled, the court handed the keys, along with the final documents, to my solicitor."

"When you came to my office last Monday, you said you needed my help because you had found bones. Did you find those bones on the property, and whereabouts on the property?"

"Yes, I found them hidden in the house."

"Kirsty, something isn't adding up. How did you find bones in the house, if you didn't have the keys to enter the place? … And, in any case, I thought you weren't allowed to enter any of the buildings?"

"Er, yes, I see your point. Look, it's a long story. If I don't see you before then, I'll explain everything to you over dinner tonight. But, right now, I have to drive out to my new home. I'll talk to you later. Bye."

The objection I was preparing to deliver went begging. She had ended the call and, no doubt, was on her way out of the city. As I flopped down behind my desk, only one question now occupied my mind: How did I feel about how the situation surrounding Kirsty McGregor and her property was shaping up? 'Confused' is the short answer, but my gut is telling me it isn't a strong enough word to describe the uneasiness I felt.

Yeah, I was uneasy about something… But why, and about what? If I felt this way about any other potential client, I would be demanding more information – and, more often than not, I would not be accepting the job. This was Kirsty, my friend for so many years. I couldn't treat her in the same way as I might any other suspicious-sounding case. The same question came back to nag me: why am I uneasy about it? Was it something she said? I pushed my chair back, put my feet up, and replayed my conversation with Kirsty as I sipped my coffee. I had no more than a few moments to reflect.

Within a few minutes of my conversation with Kirsty, my office felt as though it had a revolving door. A couple of potential clients made appointments for straight after lunch, and a number of unexpected 'walk-ins' came seeking information on my services and to find out whether their 'problems' fitted with the work I did. While it ended up being one hell of a day, by two o'clock, I had one definite new client and three potential ones. When the last of my visitors left, I was starving and suffering from caffeine withdrawal.

After dealing with lunch and the various tasks accumulated during morning, at last, I could relax for a few moments. Well, it was my intention until I remembered Kirsty was hoping to explore the old house on the property today. As I had nothing demanding attention for the rest of the afternoon, I could take a drive out to the property to see how she was getting on out there alone in a dark house on a miserable afternoon. It was the most inspirational thought I had all day, so I decided to follow through on it.

After grabbing the few things I needed to take home with me and snagging my bag off the back of a chair where I hung it when I came back from lunch, I was on my way down to my car, and heading out of the city a few minutes later. I had a 'sort-of' memory of where the property was located, and I hoped I was heading in the right direction.

Adjacent to the house in the distance, Kirsty's vehicle stood out against the otherwise drab background. "Why not – now

I'm here…?" I said aloud, as I turned off the road and onto the property. Although now muddy, the neighbour had done a good job on the track, and this morning's rain hadn't caused it any damage.

There was no sign of Kirsty when I pulled up. I called out to alert her I had arrived, and to avoid startling her. Having received no response, and working on the assumption she was somewhere in the old house, I set off to find her. I would not have risked life and limb on the derelict front steps had there been some other safer way of reaching the verandah about a metre above ground level. By placing my feet right against the runner on one side as I scaled the stairs, I managed to arrive on the deck without injuring myself or falling through the doubtful-looking stair treads.

Again I called out to Kirsty to alert her to my presence, and again there was no response. I felt my stomach tighten. Had something happened to her? I should have applied some common sense and not let her come alone. Standing outside worrying about it was not going to achieve anything, so I tiptoed across to the front door, which wasn't quite closed.

Why was it open? I checked the floor in the doorway and the door's hinges. Had Kirsty left it ajar after opening it, or had it been sitting this way for decades? My visual inspection didn't provide answers, so I put my shoulder against the door and pushed. The hinges were stiff, but I was surprised how easy it was to open it to almost its full extent. I stepped into the doorway and called her name again – and received the exact same response as to my previous calls. This had a bad feel to it. My stomach was now a squirming mass.

In spite of my trepidation, the dark timber floor looked solid. Apart from being dull and dusty, it looked as solid as if it had been laid only a few years ago. I tiptoed in, and found myself in a largish room. From what I could make out of the furniture under its patina of accumulated crud, the room had been a sitting room, and what I guessed was once referred to as 'the front room'. Still exercising caution, I tiptoed across the room and into a hallway leading towards the back of the building.

After taking only a couple of steps along the hallway, something occurred to me, and made me double back to the entrance to the hall. Today's only footprints across the sitting room floor were mine. While two sets of prints traversed the room, they were old. Kirsty had not been here before me today. I cast my eyes over the floor for the length of the hallway. The footprints there also were several days old.

Retracing my steps across the sitting room and out onto the verandah, I once more contemplated the level of risk to life and limb in again negotiating those front stairs. Not having found any other means of reaching the ground again short of throwing me over the verandah railing, I took a deep breath and negotiated the stairs in much the same fashion as I did on the way up.

"Okay, now I'm back on the ground," I muttered to the universe, "what do I do now?" As I knew Kirsty's prime reason for coming here today was to explore the house, why wasn't she in there? Why hadn't she been in there since she arrived? I placed my hand on the bonnet of her car. While it still retained some warmth, it was obvious it had been parked beside the house for a while. Right, what is around here for Kirsty to find more important, or interesting, than the house? Nothing I could see filled me with excitement.

A collection of old, rough buildings, which I assessed as being sheds or workshops of some sort, was the only significant thing visible from where I stood out front of the house. "Perhaps there's something more interesting out the back," I muttered. I picked my way around Kirsty's vehicle and strode out towards the rear of the house. I pulled up short when I realised I wasn't the first in recent times to tread this way.

The shin-high grass bore clear evidence of someone having tramped from the vicinity of Kirsty's car around to the rear of the cluster of outbuildings. Mystified, I followed in the footprints. Concentrating on following the track through the grass, I almost slammed into someone coming the other way as I rounded the corner of the first building.

"Kirsty…! Thank God… I was imagining all sorts of horrible things when I couldn't find you. What have you been doing… and why haven't you even been in the house yet?"

"Steady on, old girl. I've been checking out the area behind these buildings and looking for the water supply to the house."

"Why would you do that before exploring the house itself? I thought you were anxious to see inside the place."

"Yeah, I was. But, a few other things fell into place and my priorities changed. When probate was granted and I knew it was mine, other issues became more important. The house would still be there later, but there were other matters I needed to put in place first. As soon as I arrived, I called Bill Branigan, the builder I had engaged, to tell him we now had access to the house. I wanted him to install his builder's pole as soon as possible so electricity would be available on site. He might come out later this afternoon, or first thing in the morning, to identify a suitable location."

"Okay, but what has it to do with why you were wandering around out here?"

"As strange as it sounds, as I drove up to the old house, I realised I should be living on site. If I managed to organise power and water supplies, I could hire a caravan, or one of those small transportable buildings, to live in on-site until work on the house was completed. When Bill said it was possible power could be connected as early as the start of next week, I decided I should check out the water supply situation. Bill suggested a bloke who was a sort of expert, was the chap I needed for the water supply."

"The rainwater tanks behind the house look to be in good condition given the place's long history of abandonment, but I wouldn't be game to drink the water in them, or use it for anything else."

"No, the thought of it didn't appeal to me either, so I called the bloke Bill recommended. He was finishing off a job out this way somewhere and said he would call in to look at my situation on his way home late this afternoon. I thought it would be helpful if I could show him the existing water supply arrangement. So, now you know why I've been prowling around out here instead of exploring inside the house."

"Did you find anything?"

"I think I struck gold – so to speak. There is a well with a fairly unsafe looking cover over it. It looks as though it might have been redundant before the last residents abandoned the place. It was replaced by a pump at some time, which I suspect pumped water up into a tank sitting on top of the high tower beside it."

She showed me an ancient looking pump on a concrete block adjacent to a towering tank-stand which utilised ancient tree trunks as posts. "I don't suppose you found a tank which might have been on top of it in days gone by?"

"There is a rusted out bottom section of a smallish tank, which might have been atop the tower at some time in the past. I suspect it blew off in a storm after it became so rusted out it no longer held water. Anyway, I'm hoping Bill's 'expert' finds a simple solution to the water supply problem when he visits later today."

"In spite of everything you've told me, I still can't believe you've had sufficient self-restraint to ignore the lure of exploring the house today. …And, now I'm here, what about those bones you found. After all, they are the reason you came to see me; to ask for my help. Maybe you should show me the bones so I have some idea of what I can do, and whether or not I can help you."

"Okay, but we have to go into the house to see the bones. Come on."

"Kirsty, I've just been in the house – part of it anyway. While it was obvious someone had been there before me, no one had been in there earlier today. If you were only just given the keys, how do you explain the footprints I found? Whose were they?"

"All right … okay… they are mine … and Bill Branigan's. The house, just sitting there as it was, proved too much temptation. Although I thought they would be locked, jammed, or rusted shut, I couldn't resist just trying the front doors. They weren't locked and, with a bit of effort, they opened. Well, the one I tried did. Then, what else was I going to do, except explore the place."

"I understood you were not allowed to enter any of the buildings until the probate process was completed. Was I mistaken? Or, did your instructions change to allow you access?"

"Uhmm… no nothing changed. I wasn't supposed to enter the house … but who would know? Anyway, I couldn't help myself. I just had to see what it was like."

"But, I don't understand how your resolve can be stronger now you own the place. So strong, you've resisted the temptation to venture back in there today?"

"I knew, once I went into the house, I would want to keep working on it, and wouldn't be side-tracked by other distractions. I know it will take a lot of time and hard work to make the house liveable again. So, it will be easier if I'm living on site, and everything else associated with making it possible for it to happen is dealt with before I start on the house. I think I've identified an ideal site for my temporary accommodation, but it will depend on where Bill positions his builder's pole. My first thought was to utilise one of these old sheds as temporary quarters but, now I've walked around them, I think they are best left for another day."

"So what happens next?"

"That is your favourite question… but, okay, I'll answer it. Well, I thought you would want to see the bones and where I found them. So, that's what happens next. Come on. I'll show you what I found." As I followed her across to the old house, she explained, "Before I even started exploring the house, I knew it would be bad, but I wasn't prepared for what I found. Anyway, after my first quick look through the place, I called Bill Branigan, the builder I had contracted. I asked him to walk through it with me and indicate which walls were loadbearing, and which ones could be removed without it collapsing. Afterwards, I started removing a wall Bill said could go. In a cavity behind the wall, I found…"

"…You found bones."

"Yeah, I found a skeleton. There were no clothes, or anything else to help identify it, so I don't know what gender it is."

"So, what do you want me to do?"

"At least come and have a look at what I found, and then… oh, I don't know … maybe try to find out whose bones they are and how long they might have been there."

We had reached the front stairs. Kirsty skipped up the centre of the treads. Still not convinced about their condition, I stuck to my previous approached and kept my feet close to the stairs' left-hand runner as I picked my way up.

As I had left half the front door standing ajar after my earlier visit, there was no delay. I followed Kirsty into a cavernous 'front room'. With no electricity connected for the lights, and with the windows heavily veiled in the dust and grime of ages, it was akin to venturing into a dark cave. I stood still for a few seconds to let my eyes adjust to the darkness. It was a slow progression from darkness, to being able to make out shapes in the room, to at last being able to see quite well.

Having given the room a preliminary scan from all angles, I turned around to face the front doors. It was about then I remembered Kirsty. Where was she? Had she gone further back into the house? I called out to her.

"I'm over here," her voice came back from what seemed a good way off to my left.

I peered through the gloom in the direction of her voice, and saw her standing in front of a battered wall. Bits of the wall's sheeting were strewn on the floor around her feet, and a hefty-looking sledge hammer kept them company. It seemed I was about to view the hidden bones in their specially constructed repository. An idle thought about where the hammer had come from flitted through my mind. I doubted she packed it in her car with everything else when she left Sydney.

Chapter 5

An area of cladding almost a metre square was missing from the wall behind Kirsty. She beckoned me over with a previously unseen torch. As I approached, she shone the torch through between the studs and noggins of the wall to illuminate the cavity behind it.

"I hope you handle it better than I did when I first saw it," she said, as she stepped a little to one side to allow me to see into the space beyond.

"Not the first time I've seen bones," I assured her, "but it is more usual for them still to be sporting their flesh. No flesh this time will be a pleasant change." She didn't reply, but I thought I glimpsed her out the corner of my eye give a little shiver in response.

To see better, I took her torch and shone it around through the various spaces in the wall's structure. "Yep, even I can say with complete confidence, it is a skeleton and it is human. What I'm not prepared to hazard a guess about is its gender. I can't see it well enough, and I'm not an expert anyway."

After viewing the skeleton for another minute or so, I decided there was nothing more to be gained from peering through the hole in the wall. I turned off the torch and handed it back to Kirsty. A long list of questions was forming in my head, and I felt compelled to start looking for answers to at least some of them. "Come with me," I said, as I grabbed her by the arm and led her over to stand just inside the front doors. "Does the other half of this door open too?"

"Maybe… but I've never tried opening it. Is opening it important?"

"Well, apart from helping ensure we have a bit healthier air supply in here, it also might let in more light, so we can see what else there might be to find in this room."

By the time I finished speaking, Kirsty was positioning herself to try opening the door. "Hang on a minute. I'll give you a hand ... just in case it is not as co-operative about being opened as its mate was."

It did offer initial token resistance. Its hinges were stiff but, with both of us leaning against it, both halves of the front door soon stood wide open. While the move did allow in more light, it didn't make enough improvement to excite me. We sauntered out onto the verandah and leant against the railing. It was my opportunity to ask more questions.

Within no more than a few moments of seeing Kirsty's handiwork with the sledge hammer, I realised the wall she had attacked differed from the rest of the place both in materials and construction. The wall was an obvious recent addition – 'recent' being a relative term. No purpose for its existence was apparent, and there was no apparent means of entering the space behind it.

"Why did you decide to attack this particular wall?"

"Well, I was curious, and I felt entitled to know. So, I decided to remove an area of cladding so I could see what was behind it."

"Where did the sledge hammer come from? It doesn't look new. Do you always carry one around in your car?"

"Very droll... I knew I needed a tool, and had a pinch bar in mind, but I didn't feel inclined to drive back to town to buy one. So, I opted to explore the outbuildings for something suitable."

"You had a few buildings to search."

"In the end, I only had to look in one. I noticed some interesting-looking bits and pieces in the long grass outside the building furthest from the house, so I started there. I think it might have been a blacksmith's shop. There were no pinch bars, but there was a sledge hammer... and a lot of other interesting old gear. Now I can't wait to explore the other outbuildings to see what gems they might contain."

The sound of a vehicle making its way up the muddy track pushed all other thoughts from my mind, and curtailed further discussion. We made our way to where our vehicles were parked to await the newcomer's arrival.

"This is probably Bill's 'expert' come to look into my water supply," Kirsty said as we watched the truck pull in alongside her vehicle.

She was wrong. Signage on the side of the truck announced it belonged to Kirsty's builder, Bill Branigan. After the usual introductions and other necessary exchanges, Bill started strolling around in search of the ideal location for his builder's pole. I took the opportunity to leave.

"Kirsty, I will head home and leave you and Bill to get on with whatever you need to do. Are you still okay for dinner at my place tonight?"

"Ye-es, but I might be a bit late leaving here. Will it be a problem for you? I don't know how late the bloke who is coming to look into the water supply might be."

I assured her whatever time she arrived would be fine with me. In fact, it would be ideal if she were a bit late, as I still didn't have a clue what we might have for dinner. Somehow, I hadn't managed to give it a thought all day. As I drove away, I undertook a mental inventory of my fridge's contents. We wouldn't starve tonight, but whatever we dined on was unlikely to be an epicurean masterpiece.

A few thoughts vied for my attention as I drove into town. Being alone in the car allowed them to make their way to the forefront in whatever order they chose. While I wasn't sure about the substance of some of those thoughts, I knew Ben featured in at least one of them.

Ben's text earlier in the afternoon told me his Brisbane trip was on again. He was off to Brisbane at short notice to attend an important meeting and might be away until at least Monday night. I still wasn't ready to have Ben trampling all over my friendship with Kirsty. While such sentiment is worse than unkind on my part, I know him well enough to predict how things would happen from his first opportunity to meet Kirsty.

With Regina McGregor's disappearance still an unsolved case on the Millhaven Police files – and, if the old newspaper article remained correct – Ben would not be able to resist the temptation to reopen the investigation. ...And why not? It would do his career no harm to solve the riddle – although no further assistance seems required as far as his career is concerned. No, to be honest, not having him here in Millhaven for the next few days is something of a relief.

By the time I arrived home, I had decided on a quick and easy pasta dish for dinner. It had the added benefit of not being dependent on our eating at some pre-ordained time. Whatever time Kirsty arrived would be okay in terms of when to start cooking.

In the end, timing wasn't an issue. Kirsty called at a bit after five o'clock to beg off dinner tonight. The 'expert' had just arrived to start looking into re-establishing a water supply. She figured it would be late by the time he left, and she still had to pack up the rest of her stuff in the unit before checking out tomorrow morning. Although I insisted it didn't matter what time she arrived, she still refused. She sounded tired and eventually admitted she was not feeling sociable tonight.

"If it is still okay with you, I'll bring the rest of my stuff over to your place first thing in the morning before heading out to the property. It probably won't be too early as I have to check-out first, and I don't know what time it will be possible."

The change of plans for dinner allowed me to heat-up leftovers instead of having to cook. It also meant I would have time tonight to make a start on transcribing my recordings of Kirsty's story.

I ate my leftovers while watching the local evening news. Then, after detouring via the kitchen to add my plate to the dishwasher, I went into my office and booted up my computer. Good progress was achieved for about half an hour before momentum was lost. My mind took over and drowned out the recording. Some time elapsed before I realised I had been staring off into space while my mind wrestled with some of Kirsty's information. The unfortunate thing was, I hadn't turned off the recorder. It had continued in playback mode the whole time I had been lost in my own thoughts.

By the time I managed to find where I had been up to before I stopped listening to the story, I was fed up with myself and not inclined to resume transcription. About half an hour later, I was in bed. Tonight, sleep came easily.

*****

It was almost ten o'clock when Kirsty arrived this morning – and she was not in the best of humour. She hadn't been able to check out of her unit until the appropriate staff arrived at work at nine o'clock. Then she had to wait around until one of the housekeeping staff conducted an inspection of the unit to be sure it was being left clean and tidy, and nothing was missing. Although, she used the time to load the last of her gear into her car before finally checking-out, she hadn't managed to have breakfast.

"Well, you are not going out to the property until you've had something. What do you normally have, or what would you like this morning? Come on, tell me. The sooner you say, the sooner you have breakfast – and the sooner you will be on your way. "So, what would you like?" She settled for toast and coffee, and I joined her in another coffee while she dispatched her breakfast. While it might not be the best time, it was the first opportunity I had since yesterday to discuss the bones she found in the old house.

"Kirsty, I know you made a negative comment earlier about going to the police about the bones, but that is what must happen. It's the law."

"No, I am not going to the police. I don't want them involved. I've had enough of being grilled by everybody; enough of answering questions and being doubted. I just want to be able to move on with starting my new life here in Millhaven."

"As a licenced private investigator, I must report them, or risk losing my licence. Yes, they will need to ask you questions about finding the bones, but how you came to find them will be obvious. No one will suspect you of having put them there. I feel there is more to this. What else is bothering you about advising the police?"

"Bureaucracy and inconvenience... I just want to move on with setting myself up out there and clearing out the house. If the police become involved, they will take over the place. I won't be able to enter the house, and I might not be allowed back onto the property until they're finished. No, I'm not having it, not after all I've been through already."

"While I can't promise anything, I doubt that's how it would be. Yes, the police will have to inspect the scene and arrange for the bones to be removed for analysis. Once the bones are removed, and they have established how old they are, you will be able to resume whatever it is you want to do. Anyway, there are plenty of other things you could be doing if you are not allowed back into the house for a day or two."

"You just don't understand, do you? I wasn't supposed to enter the house – or any of the other buildings – until after probate was granted. As you might recall, I've only owned the place since yesterday. But, I was in the house and found those bones late last week."

"Unless you tell them otherwise, the police don't know when you found them. Kirsty, you came to me for help. How did you expect me to help you? What did you want me to do?"

"I don't know... I suppose I wanted you to help me get rid of them ... to get rid of them somehow so no one would find them again ... so no one would know where they came from and I wouldn't be involved."

"Well, that ain't gonna happen. I can't and won't be involved in such a harebrained and illegal exercise. You must report the bones to the police. At least tell me you will think about what I've said."

Chances of my message having been received and understood appeared somewhere between zero and none. Our discussion of the bones came to an abrupt end when Kirsty stood up and marched out to her car. So, what the hell do I do now? After thinking the situation over as I drove into my city office, I resolved to try one last time this evening to persuade her to go to the police. Of course, before I could, first she had to return to my place this evening. The mood she was in when she left this morning had me unsure I would see her again today. Had I scuttled a long friendship? Nothing to do but wait and see…

After buying lunch and a newspaper on my way up to my office, I spent the afternoon catching up on filing and emails. With nothing else demanding urgent attention, and feeling out of sorts, I decided to abandon the city early and go home. From the moment I left my office, Ben occupied my mind. I had to report those bones, and I knew the way I would do so was to tell Ben about them. No doubt it would make for an interesting conversation – and, would result in Ben meeting Kirsty.

Just after I turned onto my street, my phone chirped and interrupted further thought about Ben meeting Kirsty. It was Emily.

"I'm in desperate need of intelligent conversation and wine. Do you want me to bring something for dinner, and how many of us will there be? Oh, before I go any further, I should ask if you're working tonight."

"Not working tonight… Wrapped up my case, and don't start a new one until maybe early next week."

"Good. I'll see you around seven o'clock, or earlier if you feel inclined. It feels like ages since I had dinner at your place. Do you want me to bring anything… food, wine, anything?"

"The plan is to do a baked dinner, so just bring yourself – and a red wine if you have one." Another check on the time told me it was becoming critical for me to be home if I wanted to cook a baked dinner.

"Okay, I'll be with you by seven."

Now, how did I feel about Emily joining us tonight? After giving it a moment's thought, I decided it wouldn't be a bad thing for Kirsty to meet Emily but, if the evening wasn't to develop into a difficult situation, I would need to manage it with extreme caution.

Emily Ibbotson was a forensic scientist. As a friend, she (unofficially) helped out with my cases on occasion. The work she did for me often took her outside her comfort zone in her role as head of the region's forensic investigation unit. She was a talented investigator, a quick thinker, and had a mind like a steel trap. But, she was everything which might frighten Kirsty into refusing to talk to her. Kirsty's current fragility seemed to cause an adverse reaction to anything which suggested 'police involvement'. And, I still had some way to go with sorting out that situation.

My next call was from Kirsty. "The bloke who was coming to look at my water supply situation now won't be coming until tomorrow. There are a few things I want from the hardware store. As they stay open until late, I thought I'd take care of it this afternoon, but I need to do a couple of things here before I head into town. It means I might not be at your place before 7.30PM."

I told her not to rush as the timing for dinner wasn't critical. I was relieved the air between us seemed to have cleared since this morning.

Things might be starting to fall into place. Emily's presence at dinner tonight could prove fortuitous. If, as I hoped, I could manage to be alone with her for a few minutes before Kirsty arrived. There were a few things I wanted to talk to her about regarding the bones. Emily would appreciate the advance warning before she was called to play her part in the obligatory official investigation into the bones which would soon follow. And, I needed Emily to understand Kirsty's current reaction to discovering the bones. Emily and I would need to establish how to nudge the conversation around in a way which gave Kirsty an opening to discuss them.

As with all good plans, there is every chance they won't work. My plan to have time alone with Emily before Kirsty arrived was one which didn't. Kirsty arrived first. I explained the friend who would be joining us for dinner often helped out with some of my investigations, while avoiding any mention of Emily's 'real' job.

While I watched the clock's slow progress towards seven o'clock, I kept Kirsty chatting for a while before suggesting she might like to have a shower and relax in her room for a few minutes before Emily arrived. She jumped at the idea and disappeared off to her room... and I sent Emily telepathic messages to hurry up and arrive. They reached the intended recipient.

Before Kirsty emerged from the bathroom, Emily arrived a little earlier than expected. I made the most of the opportunity to have a few words to her about Kirsty and the hidden bones before having to introduce the pair of them.

"I'm sorry, Sonny. You should have said you had a guest tonight. I could have eaten at home instead of intruding here."

"Don't be silly. Kirsty is an old friend who is overnighting here, and she is someone I want you to meet – as soon as she finishes showering. But, I wanted a quick word before she joins us. Brevity is of the essence, so here it is pure and simple. Kirsty uncovered a skeleton in a wall cavity in a big old house on a property she inherited. For some reason, she is reluctant to go to the police about it, and came to me instead for help. I saw the bones today and, regardless of what she says, I will be telling the police about them. Or, at least, I will tell Ben about them. As they are likely to end up as something for you to investigate, I thought I would give you a heads-up beforehand."

"Are you sure you need a forensic scientist, and not an archaeologist and/or an anthropologist?"

"No, I'm not sure at all. But, instinct tells me the bones, although they have been hidden there for quite some time, are within the timeframe which merits a police investigation into their identity and everything else about them. Ah, here comes Kirsty now. I suggest you play dumb about the bones unless, and until, they come up in conversation."

As usual, the introductions were swift. I then took a couple of minutes to explain Emily and her presence to Kirsty. Contrary to my earlier thinking, I decided it might be a good thing if Kirsty did know about Emily's real job.

"Under normal circumstances, Emily and another friend usually congregate here for dinner. Sometimes they bring food, and sometimes I even cook for all of us. It's a nice social environment in which to unwind at the end of the day, and we inevitably end up talking 'shop'. Emily is head of the forensic laboratory here in Millhaven. She called this afternoon to check if I was working, or at home tonight. There are many occasions when one or all of us are working at night. It has been that way for Emily and me for more than a week now. At the moment, the other member of our dinner trio is in Brisbane for a few days. So it will be just the three of us tonight."

My comment about Ben's being in Brisbane was for Emily's benefit, rather than Kirsty's. I wanted to warn her we wouldn't be mentioning Ben by name or occupation in tonight's discussions, and none of tonight's discussions about the hidden bones on Kirsty's property would be relayed to Ben. One of the best quick thinkers I know, Emily understood and gave me a slight nod to indicate she did.

Kirsty appeared deep in thought for a few moments before asking, "Forensics... doesn't that mean working with the police?"

"Ye-es, we do become involved in a lot of their investigations, but we also work with other organisations such as the medical services. I suppose our work is best described as testing any samples from official sources, which arrive in our lab."

"So, if some human bones were found somewhere, your team would carry out tests on the bones?"

"If the police were investigating their discovery, we could be called in to assist. Even if the police decided the bones were so old they were more suited to investigation by another authority, there is a fair chance we might still become involved in carrying out various analyses and tests. I don't know if my explanation has answered anything for you. Is there a reason for your interest? If I knew, it might help me better answer your question."

"I've discovered some bones walled up in an old house."

"Well, no doubt I'll be hearing from the police once their investigation is under way. How long ago did you find them?"

"Only three or four days ago..."

"It's surprising I haven't heard about the bones from the police by now." I had to admire the way Emily was eliciting information from Kirsty.

Kirsty squirmed on her chair for a moment before commenting. "They haven't contacted you because they don't know about them – yet."

"As you say, it's probably why I haven't been contacted. Is there a reason the police haven't been notified? As a general rule in such situations, the people want the bones removed as soon as possible."

"Mine is a complicated story. After being told not to do anything on the property until I had been granted clear title to the place, I went ahead and did things – quite a few big things. I had just spent months going through the gruelling ordeal of proving I am who I claim to be, and I was not about to go through the exercise again. I didn't know what to do. I did want the bones gone, so I asked Sonny for help. When she suggested I notify the police, I refused. Apart from anything else, I imagined the whole house becoming off-limits while the police did their thing. I wanted to get on with refurbishing the place; didn't want to be locked out of it for however long."

"Okay... well, I suppose, if I had a quick look at those bones, I might be able to give you some idea of how old they are and what the process might be after they are reported. It won't change anything. You must report the bones to the police, and as soon as possible – like yesterday for instance."

"Argh... I know you're right. Maybe, after you have a look at them, I'll feel better about doing what I need to do."

"Right; how about I come to the property tomorrow for a look?"

We spent the next few minutes drawing mud maps of the property's location, and discussing what the place was like. Once the topic of how to find the place was exhausted, we moved on to discussing how Millhaven had changed over the decades since Kirsty left.

Emily left around ten o'clock and Kirsty and I weren't up much longer after we saw her off.

Chapter 6

Both of us were up early this morning. Kirsty's water supply expert, Les Stanley, said he might be at the property by eight o'clock. I walked Kirsty out to her car to see her off – and was stunned to see the amount of stuff she had bought from the hardware store. It almost filled every space in the vehicle.

"By the look of all the gear you have stashed in there, anyone would think you were planning a monumental construction job."

She grimaced. "I fear it will be just as much hard work. I'm off now, but don't you and Emily hurry out. Come out when you are ready. After all, it is Saturday morning, and both of you probably have a lie-in on Saturdays." Before she drove off, I assured her neither of us was so inclined.

Once she was gone, I sat down with another coffee to work out what I should take with me. There was no way of knowing how long we might be there, but our caffeine levels were bound to need a top-up sometime during the day. I scrabbled around in a cupboard and found the huge insulated pump pot I've often taken on stakeouts. It held a lot of coffee and kept it hot for at least six hours. Then there was what amounted to a picnic hamper to prepare.

Cold chicken, salad and bread rolls went into an esky, along with disposable plates and cutlery, and the various fixings to allow the construction of salad rolls for lunch. I stood back to consider my catering efforts. Lunch was organised but, by the time we were ready to eat, our hands would be in no fit state to handle food. A large container as well as another cooler of water, along with the coffee pot and the esky, went into my car. Just one more item was required. Instead of heading straight out to the property, I took a detour via the city to visit my favourite bakery for blueberry muffins to go with morning coffee.

Signage on a truck parked next to Kirsty's car told me it belonged to the 'expert' who postponed his visit until today. Les Stanley was here to sort out re-establishing a water supply. I assumed they would be somewhere in the area behind the string of outbuildings. On my way to find them, I met them coming the other way.

"Sonny, this is Les Stanley, a genius on all things to do with water supply. He has completed his inspection and is just about to leave." The introductions over, Les climbed into his truck and departed.

"It was good of him to come on a Saturday morning," I commented as he drove away.

"Yeah, and it's just as well I came early. It has been busy here ever since I arrived. Bill Branigan arrived soon after me, but stayed for only about half an hour. He dropped off some stuff for the installation of the builder's poles, and was leaving when Les Stanley arrived. His visit took quite a bit longer. By the time Les walked all over the area behind the buildings and checked out what remained from the past, I was beginning to think the situation might be more difficult than I imagined."

"Was it? And, is the prospect of a sound water supply now a possibility or not?"

"It was all good news. Les outlined what he considered my best option. I understood about half his information, but the gist of it amounted to 'no problems'. He confirmed there is a good supply available and the water table is high. It will mean installation of a new pump in the first instance so water is available immediately, and he recommended installing a tank on top of the old tank stand to have gravity feed increase pressure to the house when we connect it to the supply."

"Sounds expensive... have you made any decisions about it?"

"Yep; I told him to go ahead with both the pump and the tank. If all goes well, the new pump should be working by the end of Monday at the latest – if I have a power supply by then. His price for the whole job was good too; a lot less than I expected."

"From everything you've told me, it sounds as though, by the end of Monday, everything will be in place for you to live on-site – except for something to live in. Are you any closer to deciding what you might do?"

"Well, I was leaning towards a caravan but, after talking to Bill about how long I might be living in a temporary home, I think I'll look for a small transportable building instead. Discovering what is available and involved in getting it set-up out here are my challenges for tomorrow."

"Tomorrow being Sunday, I don't like your chances of achieving much."

"True… Maybe, if I go into town after lunch, I'll be able to make a start on sorting something out. If I have a spare moment this morning, I will check what is available in Millhaven and if they will be open this afternoon."

About half an hour later Emily arrived. "Sorry I'm a bit later than planned. I called at work first to collect some gear."

"Should we go straight over to the house so you can see the bones?" Kirsty asked.

"I suppose we should but, right now, I would settle for a coffee. Is it possible to rustle up something of that nature?"

"No hope… I'm not set-up…" Kirsty began.

"Not a problem; step this way, ladies." I led them to my car, and dragged out the pot of coffee, disposable cups and sugar and milk – and the box of muffins, and handed them to others to carry. "Right; three coffees coming up… before we go over to the old house to inspect some bones," I replied. "Now, where are we having this coffee?"

"Uhmm… perhaps we could sit on the verandah of the old house… There isn't anywhere else to sit," Kirsty suggested.

"Never fear; I have a better suggestion. How about we sit over there under the big tree?" I received nods from the other two. "Okay; you carry the stuff I gave you, and I will bring the chairs."

Almost as an afterthought, as I was packing the car, I threw in three folding chairs and a small table from my stock of camping gear. In no time, we were parked under the tree, drinking coffee and munching blueberry muffins.

Our coffee break over, we started towards the old house. "Wait. Wait a minute," Kirsty exclaimed. She rushed to her car, flung open the tailgate and began hauling out items. "We are not going to faff about with one piddling little torch today. If Emily is going to look at the bones, she should be able to have a good look at them. I bought an extra couple of torches."

"Thank you, but you shouldn't have gone to the trouble – and expense. As I said earlier, I was late because I called at work first to pick up some gear. Here, Sonny, give me a hand to remove this thing from its box and set it up."

She shoved a large box at me. Judging by the pictures on its label, it contained some type of work light on a stand. Once I wrestled the bits out of the box, Emily and I had it together in a matter of seconds.

"Aw hell, that won't be any use," Kirsty wailed. "There's no power to the property. There's nowhere to plug it in."

"Not a problem… a lot of the places I work don't have power. Bring the light with you," she called over her shoulder as she dragged another sturdy case out of her car.

Kirsty and I set off for the old house as instructed. A minute or so later, Emily joined us in the front room. "Right, let's get this light set-up and working," she said.

After positioning everything as close to the hole in the wall as possible, Emily opened the case she brought and plugged the light into whatever was in the case. "It's a battery pack," she explained. "As I said, a lot of my worksites don't have power. I can't work with a torch in one hand and instruments in the other … and I do need good lighting."

She switched on the light and I started adjusting it. After the initial gloom, the light was almost blinding. I angled it to maximise the light on the bones, and then stepped back and gestured for Emily to have a look. "Take your time," I told her. "Now there is a bit of light in here, Kirsty and I are going to have a decent poke about."

"Oh yes, human skeleton," Emily murmured a moment later. "Hmm... Let's see ... Yeah, female I think. Kirsty your bones have been here for a while, but not long enough for them to be of archaeological interest I don't think."

Kirsty gave me a confused look as she spoke to Emily. "What do you mean – in layman's language please?"

"Well, I would be speculating at this stage, but I think we are talking maybe a few decades rather than a century. Does it help you to work out who it might be?"

"It could be Santa Claus for all I know ... oh, but he wasn't female was he?" Kirsty replied.

Emily gave me a hard look. "Sonny, any ideas about a possible identity...?"

"Me? No, I've no idea who they might belong to. I don't even know much about the property or its ownership. I'm not going to be much help in guessing the identity of the person, or how or why they ended up walled up here." Emily cocked an eyebrow at me in a response I know so well from our years of working together. She didn't believe a word I said, and her assessment was bang on the money. But, this was not the time or place to congratulate her.

"So, ladies, what happens now?" Kirsty murmured. "I mean right now, this minute, today ... what happens next?"

"Sonny, use your phone to photograph the scene please. Include a shot of the wall and then try for a clear shot of the bones from between the wall's studs and noggins," Emily suggested. I started snapping shots of everything.

"Once she has photographed it all, then what do we do," Kirsty asked. Her voice was becoming high-pitched.

It was obvious she was uncomfortable with the whole situation and, in particular, with any possibility we might set about removing the bones here and now. Kirsty was beside me as we stood up close behind Emily while she peered in at the bones. But, when Kirsty asked her question, she seemed some distance away. I looked around for her. She now stood just inside the front doors, and looked ready to bolt. I felt compelled to rescue the situation for her as best I could.

"According to my watch, it is almost lunchtime. I suggest we discuss what happens next over lunch. Kirsty, could you clear away our morning coffee stuff, please, and then take the esky out of my car over to the table. Emily and I will join you as soon as we turn things off in here." Needing no further encouragement, she galloped across the verandah and down the stairs.

"Well saved," Emily murmured. "How are your photos?" I showed her and she approved them. "It's Saturday, and a certain person probably is sitting in a Brisbane restaurant having a boozy lunch with a bunch of his mates about now. How about we see if we can put him off his food with a few happy snaps of some old bones?"

"I think I should. While it might take more than a few photos to put him off his food, I am concerned about not having told the police about those bones before now. It is not a good look for a private investigator to withhold such information, even for this long."

"Do we need to try soothing Nervous Nellie a little before we break the news?"

"It might be a good thing to do, but I think I prefer to send the photos and then work on preparing her for the arrival of the police – probably at the start of next week."

While Emily and Kirsty availed themselves of my container of water to wash up, I remained in the front room of the old house to send the photos of the bones to Ben – accompanied by a note which might be construed as the bones having been found just now: *See attached photos of a skeleton found walled up in an old house on a property on the outskirts of Millhaven.* I added 'Talk to you soon' before changing my mind and deleting the comment. Then I went to wash off the grime and join the others for lunch.

Lunch was a tense affair. Kirsty was more than a little uptight, and I was nervous the recipient of the photos might call me. I would not want the others to hear even one side of such a call when it came. Emily picked up on my tension and, having guessed what it was about, made a move to ease the situation.

"As much as I hate to eat and run, I do have to head back into town. I have things to do this afternoon." She gave me a hard look as she came over to dump her disposable plate and cutlery in the rubbish bag I brought for the purpose.

Her message was clear, and I followed through on it. "Yes, I have a bit to do this afternoon as well and, Kirsty, you were hoping to go into town to look into temporary accommodation options. Maybe, we should just throw all this stuff back into my car. All of us can then head off to do whatever we need to do."

The rush which ensued almost knocked me off my chair. Within minutes, everything was back in my car and Emily was heading off along the track. I told Kirsty I would see her at home after she finished in town ... And received a short, terse reply. Yep, she was not happy about the way the morning had played out.

As I pulled into my garage, my phone chirped. I didn't need to check the caller ID. I knew who it would be. No time was wasted on niceties.

"And, exactly how were these bones discovered?" was Ben's opening comment.

"A wall was going to be removed as part of refurbishing the old house. As soon as a bit of the cladding came off, it revealed a narrow cavity behind the wall – and the bones in it."

"And how did you come to be involved in all this?"

"The current landowner is my friend since primary school days, and she invited me to have a look at the place."

"Where are you now? Are you still there?"

"No, I'm home again."

"Okay; I'm booked on the first available flight on Monday but it doesn't arrive in Millhaven until late afternoon. I'll see you Monday night. In the meantime, you might print out those photos for me, and take any more you think relevant to an investigation. And, if you happen to be talking to Emily, you might mention she'll have some old bones land in her lab within the next few days."

'Smug' would just about describe how I felt as I walked inside. Throughout my whole conversation with Ben, I had managed not to give any indication Emily knew anything about the bones. She can make her own decision about whether to tell him otherwise, but I felt it safer not to mention her today. While I was putting away everything from today's 'picnic', Emily called.

"I assume you have received THE phone call you were expecting."

"Oh, yes, I received 'The Call'. He was a ball of business as usual. If I should be talking to you between now and when he returns, I am to warn you some old bones will land in your lab in the next few days."

"Should I come for dinner tonight so you can mention it to me?"

"Perhaps you should. You can help me deal with the situation I think will blow-up here later. Kirsty has all afternoon to stew over everything from this morning. She was not happy at lunchtime. I suspect she will be worse by this evening."

"Right you are; dinner at you place. What time do you want me there? Should I arrive at seven o'clock as usual?"

"If you don't have anything else happening, come at six o'clock. I don't know what time to expect Kirsty this evening, but it won't hurt to have a quiet drink before dinner."

To fill in time until the others arrived, I took myself out onto the deck to sit and stare off into the distance. I let my mind wander through the part of Kirsty's story I'd heard so far. Still amazed and confused by Kirsty's reluctance to inform the police about having found the hidden bones, my mind revisited an earlier thought: Did she know more about the McGregor family than she admitted? It was hard to believe her solicitor, Nathan Jones, hadn't discovered more than Kirsty shared with me. A moment later a realisation slammed in from left field. Now I think on it, how much had I learned about the McGregor family since Kirsty came asking for help at the beginning of the week?

I dashed into my office and dragged out my case file... my *slim* file. So far, the only facts residing in it were the name of Kirsty's mother, Kate, or Catherine to be more precise, and the date of Silas McGregor's death. I had noted Silas' wife's name. Was her name a good place to start further research? Was it important in any way to understanding the story of the McGregor family and their property? While it probably wasn't so important, it was an easy place to start my research.

A few minutes of muttering to my computer later, I had confirmed Regina McGregor, prior to her marriage, was Regina Shelby. 'Shelby'... now there was something else which rang a bell in the vast dark distant corners of my mind. When no recollection of the surname – other than as Catherine McGregor's middle name – came to the fore after a few moments of concentration, I turned to Google for assistance. I typed in the name 'Shelby', and then, on second thought, added 'in New South Wales'.

Surprised by the volume of hits Google offered me, I toyed with the idea of trying to refine the search parameters. A closer look at the list of hits told me a number of them appeared to relate to the same family. Okay, it's worth a look before I do anything else I suppose, I told myself as I clicked on the first hit. During the brief moment while I waited for it to open, I realised I knew one other connection to the Shelby name. It was Kirsty McGregor's middle name. So, Kate had given her daughter her mother, Regina's, maiden surname as a middle name. "Not an uncommon practice back then," I acknowledged aloud.

Before long, I realised there was more to Regina's surname than I imagined. The Shelbys were a big name as pastoralists in the north of the state. But it seems they dabbled in various other industries in the area, including early coal mining. The name graced all the social pages on a regular basis. After a few minutes of scanning only what I judged to be the most relevant hits, one thing was clear: the Shelbys were wealthy – and in a big way. When he married Regina, old Silas McGregor must have congratulated himself on snaring the only child of the last generation of the Shelby family. It will be interesting to learn what she was worth on the death of her parents. But, it was something to pursue at another time.

In spite of my high hopes, I added little to my file on the McGregor clan by the time Emily arrived. Without wasting time, I poured a couple of glasses of wine and we took them out onto the deck. Most of the heat and humidity of the day had disappeared, replaced now by a light, cool easterly breeze. There was little conversation as we watched shadows lengthen and twilight darken into night. It was a time for being as one with nature and allowing it to help establish some semblance of equilibrium in our psyches... akin to 'recharging our batteries' after today's events.

Emily startled me back to reality when she asked, "Do you think the damage we caused today can be repaired?"

"I have no idea. Today's performance was so far out of keeping with the Kirsty I knew. She could have been a complete stranger. Still, we haven't seen each other for some years now. It's reasonable to expect we both changed during those years. If I knew what was behind her current attitude, I might be able to intervene in a more effective way."

"It's sad to think of a friendship spanning decades maybe ending in such a way. Are you okay with it?"

"Uhmm … 'Okay' is a relative term. If you are asking if I can cope with what happened, my answer is 'just about'. I'm hoping I can dig up something to help explain what underlies her behaviour. Regardless, I had to comply with legal requirements and notify the police. My conscience is clear about having done so. The problem is in her mind, and she is the one who has to deal with it. By the way, as I mentioned earlier, Ben remains ignorant of your presence on the property today. So, when he tells you about the hidden bones, you will be able to act as though it's the first you've heard of them."

"Thank you. By being there today and seeing the bones, I didn't contravene any professional or ethical protocols, but it will be tidier if Ben doesn't know about it. Is Kirsty likely to mention my presence to him, do you think?"

"Who knows? Somehow, I don't think so. I suspect she will be uncooperative and not volunteer any information at all. Although Ben can be quite 'persuasive', I think Kirsty's determination is every bit his equal."

"Should we be concerned about Kirsty? It's long gone seven o'clock when I thought she was supposed to be here for dinner. Given her darkening mood today, do you think it might have boiled over in some way?"

"Good questions… but I don't know the answers. I suppose we should do something about food before too much more of the night slips away, but let's give her another ten or fifteen minutes, shall we?"

A couple of minutes later, my phone broke the silence on the deck. "In case you haven't noticed, I won't be there for dinner or anything else tonight. I've made other arrangements." With that, Kirsty ended her call. It left me with my jaw hanging down at knee level.

After sharing the 'good news' with Emily, we spent a few minutes discussing possible ways of repairing the friendship sometime in the future. We agreed I should let the matter run and allow it to decide its own course until Kirsty was more settled on her property.

"In the meantime, I think it's time we did something about food," I announced.

Chapter 7

Our steak and salad dinner was accompanied by the excellent red wine Emily brought, and a detailed post-mortem of our time at Kirsty's property. As soon as we packed the dishwasher and I set it to do its thing, Emily suggested we take our coffees through to my office to do more work on uncovering the McGregor family's story.

While I waited for my computer to boot up, Emily wiped over the large whiteboard attached to the wall opposite my desk. "Right... tell me what we already know so I can put it up on the board," she said. I looked up to see her poised, marker in hand, ready to write the facts as I called them to her.

"Don't become too excited. All I *know* so far will take no more than a couple of seconds to scribble on the board. By the way, have you ever heard of the Shelby family from New South Wales?"

"No, not from New South Wales, but I know the name as belonging to a Queensland family. Why do you ask?"

I explained discovering Kirsty's grandmother was a member of the Shelby family. "The family appeared to be involved in a wide variety of enterprises in their day, moved in all the 'right' circles, and were not short of a bag or two of cash."

"So, you think old Silas McGregor did all right for himself in marrying Regina?"

"Good question, isn't it? We don't know his background. Was he nobody with nothing more than a few shillings in his pocket, or was he from a comparable background?"

"And, was it a marriage made in heaven, or one arranged over a handshake by a couple of men, and without any involvement of Regina?"

"I hadn't thought of the possibility of an arranged marriage between two empires, but it can't be discounted. It's only a gut feeling, but I suspect Silas might have been a bit older than Regina. Argh, hell… it sounds like I might have to dive into the family history research caper again."

"If it were an arranged marriage, who gained what from the deal? The question in my mind is more about the Shelby family's gain, rather than how Silas McGregor benefited. The simple answer might be that he won the girl, but I can't help thinking it must have been something more than so fundamental."

"We are taking wild stabs in the dark. A few more details of the people involved might provide a better view of the situation back then. Emily, do you have any bright ideas about what else we might look for to help better understand these people? My gut tells me it was something about those early days which led – perhaps many years later – to those hidden bones."

"No clues at all… It's best if I don't develop any half-baked ideas about the people or what happened out on the property. I don't want false thinking to impact on the investigation I am bound to be involved in once the police begin looking into those bones."

"Yeah, fair enough; you're going to have enough hard work ahead of you without anything we do now complicating matters for you. I think I'll spend time tomorrow researching anything and everything relating to the McGregors in the hope of having a bit more on the whiteboard before Ben descends upon me. Best not to do much tonight. Today's events might be having more effect than I thought."

Emily was on her way home before nine o'clock, and I intended to spend another hour or two on research. It didn't take me long to realise an early night might prove more beneficial tomorrow than slaving away at the computer tonight. I was in bed by ten o'clock.

*****

Up early this morning, and no time wasted over breakfast. Before Ben Richards arrived, I was determined to know, if not everything, a whole lot more about the McGregor mob and the property Kirsty now owned.

If my expectations were correct, Ben's visit would be a torrid time, which included a 'third degree' about the hidden bones. The more I had on my whiteboard, and the more background information I could give him, the sweeter his visit might be. I already planned to make his favourite pasta dish for dinner. So, with any amount of success, it might help sweeten his disposition.

He is entitled to feel a bit put-out about the way things happened. I knew the way I 'notified the police' about the bones did not follow 'proper protocols', and I would hear all about it. As the district's top cop, Ben Richards doesn't expect the discovery of old bones to be reported to him directly... especially when it interferes with his post-conference weekend with his mates in Brisbane. Yep, it is unlikely to be a happy copper who visits me.

Pushing Ben and last evening out of my mind, I settled down in front of my computer. Now, where to start? I decided to adopt the same approach as for my earlier research, and called up Trove, the National Library of Australia's newspaper archives site. After typing in a variation of the search parameters used previously, I waited. A list of about a dozen hits came up. "Start at the top of the list and work through it," I reminded myself aloud.

The first couple of hits were from the 'Social Jottings' pages of a major tabloid. They confirmed the McGregors were of sufficient standing on the social scene to merit mention in a major tabloid. The first snippet told of the couple's visit to Sydney to attend the wedding of the socialite daughter of a state politician, while the next mention was about one of Silas' animals taking off the Grand Champion prize at the Royal Easter Show. Interesting though they were, it was not the information I wanted. Further down the list of hits was a notice of the death of Silas McGregor.

All it offered was confirmation of what I already knew: *He is survived by his wife, Regina, who continues to reside on the Millhaven District property, and a daughter, Catherine.*

Disappointing but predictable... I took a moment to consider the brief Death Notice before moving on. It referred to Silas as a 'well-known landowner and grazier in the Millhaven District', so I interpreted it as Silas' still being prominent in social circles at the time of his death. Comment about Regina told me nothing new and, at first, nor did the brief mention of Catherine. After some thought though, I suspected the way in which Catherine was mentioned did tell me something.

There was no comment regarding her marital status, so the reader might be led to assume she was single. And, no comment regarding where she resided might also suggest she lived at home with her mother. After a few moments' consideration, I fast came to the conclusion mention of Catherine was out of necessity, and its brevity out of respect for her parents. I felt certain whoever worded the death notice was well aware of the situation within the family regarding Catherine.

Apart from what I thought I detected in the careful wording of it, the death notice posed a new question for me: How old was Catherine when her father died? A second question slid in from out of nowhere. Regardless of how old she was, where was Catherine living at the time of her father's death? I suspected she was not living at home. If she were, the wording of the notice might have said something like 'a daughter, Catherine resides with her mother' ... or maybe more like 'his wife, Regina, and daughter, Catherine, who continue to reside...'. Of course, it was pure speculation on my part, but I was almost convinced the death notice was a fine example of 'newspaper jargon' designed to tell the reader the important fact (Silas was dead) while blurring the rest of the details.

After scanning the next few hits, and finding they didn't relate to the family I was interested in, I decided to change tack and set a more precise search parameter. "Good thinking," I muttered to myself. "So, what do I ask it to look for?" A few moments of thought later, I was asking Trove to find me all it could on Catherine McGregor. "Well, that's not long," I snarled at the list of three hits.

Yes, I knew about the first one. It was the mention of Catherine in her father's death notice. The remaining two hits related to the death of an elderly woman some years before Silas died and, therefore, were nothing to do with my Catherine. Nothing even suggested she might be a close relative. Okay, time to try a different approach. Perhaps Regina was a better target for Trove to explore.

The search produced a longer list of hits this time, but still not a substantial one. A particular entry caught my eye. I expected to find lots of snippets from the gossip columns, but this one was different. It was the article I found previously. The one featured in the local newspaper about ten years ago. I couldn't remember ever reading the article at the time it appeared in the paper. And, I couldn't remember the event when it occurred over twenty years ago. When I did the maths, I realised I would have been away at university at the time – and not showing much interest in the Millhaven newspapers. As a result, I didn't know anything about Regina's disappearance when it happened, or when the article appeared in the paper ten years ago. After scanning the article on the screen, to confirm it was the same article I printed out previously, I dug the earlier copy out of my file. I hadn't realised the length of the article until I flicked through its several pages.

A quick scan to develop an understanding of the context of the article sent me back to the beginning to make notes as I read it again. This was not an article about some socialite's high life, or of a merry widow's life stuck on a property outside Millhaven. It told the story of a widow who disappeared more than a decade before the article was written. The widow was Regina McGregor.

While the usual sensational speculations about where she was and what happened were dotted throughout the story, there was no conclusive ending. I returned to the headline and started reading again. This time, the name *Thomas Agnew* jumped off the page at me. I had noticed the name when I first read right through the article, but somehow it didn't excite my synapses.

This time his name did, and it demanded I pay more attention to what he had to say back then.

Engrossed in reading Agnew's part of the story, I didn't hear a vehicle arrive and park out front. I remained unaware of my visitor until the doorbell alerted me. I scrambled out from behind my desk, and threw a folder over the printout of the newspaper article before galloping to the door.

Speech almost failed me. I managed to croak 'good morning'. Standing on my doorstep was none other than Kirsty McGregor... A downcast and apprehensive looking Kirsty McGregor. Oh joy... now what, I asked myself. Nevertheless, common sense and courtesy dictated I should invite her in. So I did, but perhaps not as graciously as I might.

"Kirsty... This is unexpected ... Did you want to come in? Has something happened?"

"Thank you. I won't take up more than a couple of minutes of your time. I only came to apologise for my behaviour yesterday. I don't expect you to forgive me, but I felt I must at least apologise. Maybe we can have a coffee again sometime when all this other stuff blows over."

"Nah, come in. We can have a coffee now. Maybe while we have a coffee you might be able to explain what happened yesterday. It would help me understand what went wrong."

A few minutes later we were sitting on the deck with our coffees and leftover muffins from a couple of days ago. As Kirsty began to peel the paper from her muffin, I warned, "They are not the freshest but, if they are too dry, we can always dunk them."

"It will be fine. If I thought I was going to be having coffee with you this morning, I could have brought the ones you left with me yesterday. I'm pleased I didn't though. Now I will be able to ruin my waistline with them over the next couple of days."

Conversation was stilted. A definite awkwardness existed between us. Not surprising I suppose, given yesterday's events, but I couldn't help wondering whether the friendship was repairable and might one day return to what it had been. After a moment or two of soul-searching, I decided I didn't need to apologise for anything. I hadn't done anything wrong; quite the contrary. I had complied with the law and my legal obligations as a private investigator, when I informed the police of the discovery of the bones. Nevertheless, I was aware I could have handled the situation better.

After a few awkward moments of reflection, Kirsty broke the silence hanging over us. "I know you did the right thing, and I should have advised the police about the bones as you told me to after you saw them on Friday. But, the very thought of it created a feeling of terror. I don't expect you to understand, but I'll try to explain what the last few months have been like for me. It doesn't excuse my behaviour, I know, but hear me out please."

I nodded. After all, talking through yesterday's events was the only way to clear the air between us and allow our friendship to resume. She took a deep breath before continuing.

"While nothing physical was involved, I feel as though, for the last few months, I have been prodded and probed from every imaginable angle. I suppose it left me psychologically traumatised in some way. It was the whole process of trying to prove my identity. Sometimes I felt as though I had reached the end of my sanity. Yes, I know I could have walked away from everything and saved myself the mental anguish. But, I was entitled. I knew we had proved it. The more people questioned it, who I was, and everything else, the more determined I became. My response to the process might have been influenced by my vulnerability at the time."

"Vulnerability…? In what way? It is not a word I would have associated with you in the past."

"…Long story, Sonny. I will tell you about it, but not today. I'd lost the woman I thought of as my mother, discovered she had lied to me – by omission – about being adopted, and I had a disastrous break-up of a long-term relationship with a bloke who was ripping me off while cheating on the side. I had to sell my house, and I already had Dulcie's home on the market. On top of everything else, I almost went to court to achieve an equitable dissolution of a business partnership. Somehow, discovering I was adopted and illegitimate seemed like the final straw.

When Nathan contacted me to say they believed I might the rightful heir to the McGregor estate, I was determined my claim would triumph. It would be the only positive thing in my life for months. Then the process of proving who I was and my right to the estate left me feeling I'd been stripped bare of every shred of dignity. I still haven't recovered from all those months of scrutiny and humiliation. I just wanted to be left alone to work through it and heal in my own way. Having the police tramping all over the place wouldn't allow it to happen."

"You're right, I don't understand… not fully anyway. But I do understand the loss of someone close; a loved one. I can't offer you much advice, other than to recommend you give the cops your full co-operation when they arrive. It will help ensure they do what they need to and are gone and out of your way as quickly as possible."

The thought still gnawing away at the back of my mind related to how much Kirsty had discovered about the McGregor family. If all she told me was the extent of it, she hadn't been as curious as I would expect. If she does know more than she's told me, why is she withholding information? What can she gain by not sharing it with me? Although I've asked the question before, it appears the only way I will extract anymore from her is to ask it again.

"Kirsty, you told me about discovering who your birth mother was, and your grandparents and the McGregor estate. What else do you know about the McGregor family?" She started to shake her head, so I rushed on. "I can't believe you weren't curious to know more about them and the estate you might inherit. Weren't you tempted to dig further into the McGregors?"

"Yes, I was… I am. But, there was so much going on – so much to take in, I couldn't cope with anymore. I suppose I decided to deal with one thing at a time. My first priority was to move out of Sydney, and it meant sorting out the McGregor estate inheritance. Once I was settled on the property, I thought I would have the headspace to take on more of the family's history. It would be the best time to return to digging into the past."

While her explanation wasn't inconceivable, I remained sceptical about its truth. If nothing further was to be forthcoming from Kirsty, I needed to return to my own research into all things McGregor. My priority was to persuade Kirsty to leave. I took a not-so-subtle look at my watch; making sure she noticed. It worked.

"Anyway, I should be going," she said, before pushing her chair back and standing. "I only came to apologise, and I don't want to hold you up, if you're working today."

As I walked her to her car, I confirmed I was working today and had a mountain of stuff to get through. After agreeing we would meet again soon for a coffee or a meal, I watched her drive away. It was obvious she was reluctant to leave, and probably was looking for company. And, yes, I did feel a tad mean about encouraging her to leave. But, seated at my desk with a fresh coffee beside me, I was happy to return to my McGregor research.

I removed the folder covering the printout of the newspaper article from ten years ago, and started reading it again. Ah, yes, Thomas Agnew. I had just encountered his name when Kirsty's arrival halted further progress. According to the article, Thomas Agnew was Regina McGregor's solicitor for many years. His comments highlighted his concern the police's investigation into Regina's disappearance failed to shed any light on the matter. He also spoke of his concerns for the future of the substantial McGregor property and other assets. Regina's disappearance left everything in limbo, and he predicted the situation would not be resolved any time in the near future. Thomas Agnew...? Was he still alive? If he were, where was he, and hold old would he be now?

"There's only one way to find out," I confided to the universe, as I turned my attention to my computer... and came up empty.

Suffering a hefty dose of frustration at the time wasted on fruitless interrogation of my computer, I took a break to think about how else I might find Thomas Agnew – if he were still alive. A few minutes later, the fog cleared. I remembered the copy of the Local Government Electoral Roll for this area I managed to acquire after the last Local Government elections. "Worth a look..." I told my empty office.

There he was! At least, there was a listing for one *AGNEW, Thomas Reginald*. Was it the right bloke? His residential address was at a large retirement complex on the north side of the city. It looked encouraging, but the elections were two years ago. Was he still alive? He must be old to be living in the retirement facility. Invoking the 'nothing ventured, nothing gained' principle, I called the Millhaven Retirement Village.

Just as I was coming to the conclusion the office must be unmanned today, a none-too-happy woman answered with a snarled, "Yes...?"

Adopting my sweetest and most apologetic tone, I asked if Thomas Agnew still was a resident. She told me he was and demanded, "And, as he has his own phone, why didn't you call him instead of calling the office?"

I started to apologise. And thought, bugger it, and ended the call instead. Back on my computer, I checked the White Pages listing, and found his phone number. After a couple of deep breaths to steady my nerves (or was it excitement?), I keyed the number. When the phone kept dialling for longer than expected, I thought my luck had run out. I was about to end the call, when a man sounding out of breath answered.

"Good morning ... ah, yes, I suppose it might be still morning ... This is Thomas Agnew."

My response opened with confirmation that, while it was a bit after eleven o'clock, it was still morning. He chuckled, rekindling my excitement. I rushed to explain who I was and why I was calling. When he suggested I call on him, his excitement level sounded as though it matched mine. I asked if he were allowed out of the place, and if I might take him to lunch somewhere while we discussed our topic of mutual interest. He assured me the retirement village wasn't a prison – in spite of what some of the staff might believe – and he would be delighted to have lunch with me.

About half an hour later, I collected him from his cottage and took him to a little restaurant overlooking the marina. His eyes lit up as he assured me a seafood lunch was fine by him. Over a chilled white wine while we waited for our meals, I assessed how much he knew of the events which led to my call.

"Before we begin, I wonder if I might ask you if you are familiar with Nathan Jones, a solicitor with Truman & Parsons."

"Yes, I know Nathan. He is my nephew. What has he been up to… and do I want to know?"

"No, he hasn't been up to anything as far as I am aware. Have you spoken to him lately – about any of his recent cases I mean?"

"Perhaps it might help if I tell you about Nathan and give you a potted family history lesson along the way. Before I do, what do you know of the legal firm of Truman & Parsons?"

"Well, it's a short answer. I know nothing, other than Nathan Jones is one of the solicitors in their 'stable'. Is it important for me to know more about the firm?"

"My learned opinion is it would help. If you would be so kind as to pour a little more from that bottle into my glass, I will begin your history lesson."

As I finished replenishing our glasses, our meals arrived. After the initial few moments of faffing about making room on the table for the platter, and a few more moments of oohing and aahing over the array of seafood placed before us, it was agreed it would be criminal to let it spoil for the sake of a history lesson.

The next few minutes demanded all the concentration we could muster to peel prawns and free oysters from their shells. Between us, we made a considerable dent in the platter of seafood before our attention returned to Thomas Agnew's threatened history lesson.

"If you are hoping to learn about happenings – cases I mean – dealt with by Truman and Parsons' solicitors, you are in for a disappointment. Was it your intention?"

"No, of course not. I wouldn't dream of asking about anything so sensitive and, if I were silly enough to do so, I wouldn't expect you to share such information. He nodded his approval and cleared his throat.

Then, he opened his story by announcing, "The first thing you should know is, while Nathan Jones is my nephew, I do not discuss cases with him – present or past. In fact, for a few years, we didn't speak at all. Are you still interested in hearing my story?"

"Silly question, Sir…," I said, and gestured for him to get on with it.

Chapter 8

"I suppose, before I begin, I should ask what you know of the Truman & Parsons legal firms' background. It will save me boring you with stuff you already know. I must admit your interest in Nathan does intrigue me."

"To claim my knowledge of Truman & Parsons is scant is being generous. I know the practice has existed in Millhaven for decades, but not much more. Never having had anything much to do with solicitors puts me at a disadvantage in this discussion." It was a bit embarrassing to admit to my lack of knowledge. I felt guilty about not having read up on the firm before talking to Thomas.

"Right... Well, a bit over a hundred years ago Old Truman, my grandfather, set up practice here in Millhaven. In those days, legal firms in regional areas tended not to be major establishments, and Truman's followed the trend. It started with just the man himself and a young woman to do the typing and run the front office."

"Okay, so no Parsons involved at the outset, but the firm prospered and grew to become the well-established entity it is in the community today."

"Old Truman did all right after his move to Millhaven. Against his wishes, his only daughter trained as a solicitor and, against what he considered his better judgment, he took her into the firm after she was admitted to the bar. But, she remained mainly confined to not much more than producing various documents for his cases, or undertaking research on his behalf.

A couple of years later, he took in a young, upcoming solicitor named Reginald Agnew and, a few years later, Reginald married Truman's daughter. They went on to have a daughter, and then me. My sister did not want a bar of the legal profession and chose a different career for herself."

"There's been no mention of Parsons so far. When did he happen?"

"The world was changing and those changes intruded on the Millhaven community as well. Up until then, the firm mainly dealt with what might be described as family law: wills, probate, conveyancing, and basic contracts such as share farming agreements. But, crime was on the increase everywhere, including Millhaven, and big-city firms were keen to move in to handle the cases here.

Around this time, Old Truman died, leaving the firm to his daughter, my mother. She made my father a managing director or something of the sort, and he ran the practice for her. It became obvious the firm had to expand to take on criminal cases as well. They needed to bring in appropriate expertise from the city and Oliver Parsons was keen to move out of the city and into a more regional area. He drove a hard bargain and wanted nothing less than a partnership."

"It seems he had your parents over a barrel."

"Yes, he had the upper hand, but it was obvious, if the firm was going to expand, it needed expanded accommodation as well. The upshot was, my father and Oliver Parsons put up their own cash, and with a bit of help from my mother, they erected the building which still houses the firm. Their buy-in to the new setup gained both men a partnership, and added 'Parsons' to the name of the firm.

And, so the firm continued from there. I suppose it was inevitable I would join it not long after being admitted to the bar. I stayed with them until my retirement about five years ago. During my time, I married, but my wife died a handful of years later and we had no children. My sister married, and produced a daughter and a son. Her son is Nathan Jones, which makes him my nephew."

"It appears he came into the firm via the family connection, much as you did, and has remained there."

"Don't get it wrong. Nathan was a bright lad who topped his course at university. He also is an astute, intuitive, operative, and came into the firm on merit, not on connection. In spite of everything else, Nathan was lazy – is lazy. He thought he was in for a comfortable ride, but found it not quite as expected. I inherited my mother's part of the firm when she died, and I was tasked with 'educating' Nathan on work ethics. I rode him hard and, in all honesty, I can say he performed well.

While still quite young, my father died leaving me his share of the firm and, a few years later, Oliver Parsons died. Oliver, for various reasons, left no close family. His share of the firm came to me as well. I left the name as it was and we continued from there until I retired about five years ago. I still own the business, but I have two directors who run the place. Nathan is an associate director."

"So, although you retired, apart from meetings with your directors, Nathan would also keep you up-to-date with what was happening within the firm."

"No, not so... I soon found, every time I turned around twice, Nathan came to visit me. It didn't take me more than a few weeks to realise his visits were due to nothing more than his laziness. He came seeking advice and information on clients in past cases. I soon put an end to it. I told him I would not discuss clients, cases, or any other aspect of legal matters with him. If he wished to see me, I would welcome his visits but such topics were forbidden."

"Oh dear, how did he react?"

Thomas chuckled. "It seems he took offence. I never saw him again for a few months. In spite of the potted history I've given you, our extended tribe is quite numerous, and there is a constant flow of weddings, funerals, anniversaries, and christenings to attend. At first, Nathan avoided me; refused to talk to me. But, with such an array of family gatherings featuring on our calendar, he couldn't maintain his stance for long. We now speak at such family get-togethers, but without mentioning anything of a legal nature. From the reports I receive, I believe Nathan is performing well within the firm. It's just as well.

When I drop off the twig in probably the not too distant future, he will become one of the partners.

So endeth my story. Now perhaps it's your turn to tell me why you were interested in my association with Nathan."

"Before I begin, thank you for your patience, and sharing so much background information. My reason for asking might seem strange after everything you've told me. In simple terms, there were two things I wanted to know: whether Nathan discussed his cases with you, and what sort of operator he is. As you have answered both of those questions, if you can spare me a bit more time, I'll endeavour to explain my interest."

"I'm at your disposal. I mean, I'm here with you until such time as you choose to take me back to my bungalow at the retirement village. But, you almost have me sitting on the edge of my chair and bursting with curiosity. So, please tell me your story."

"A friend of mine since our primary school days has lived in Sydney for quite a few years now. Over the last little while all manner of drama has almost torn her life apart. In the midst of it all, a few months back, she discovered she had an interest in a matter here in Millhaven. A genealogical researcher found a connection to Millhaven and initiated discussions with Nathan before she ended up in a coma in hospital. When information she promised to provide to Nathan didn't materialise, and he couldn't contact the researcher, he contacted my friend directly.

After working with Nathan for some months, and while still living in Sydney, she found the frustration, coupled with other dramas in her life, about to tip her over the edge. Two weeks ago, she relocated to Millhaven in a bid to expedite the matter Nathan was handling for her."

"I hope you're not going to tell me something is amiss with the process."

"No, quite the opposite but, what has been happening fits well with what you told me about Nathan. Within about ten days of arriving in Millhaven – and after a few terse words to Nathan – the matter was wrapped up.

You probably wonder why I needed to talk to you about something already done and dusted. I'll try to explain. My friend remains psychologically fragile from the various happenings in her life over the last little while. Another incident has occurred and I am concerned about its possible outcome, and how it will impact on my friend. By discovering as much as I could beforehand, I hoped to be in a position to help her through what might lie ahead."

"So, how might I help you to achieve it?"

"An old newspaper article I read suggested, on your retirement, you might leave behind one piece of unfinished business. My interest lies in that 'business'. Due to its uniqueness in a sense, I thought Nathan Jones, as the legal representative involved, might have informed you of its resolution. I have to admit to being surprised it hasn't happened."

"There was only one matter I could not close before I retired … And with which I am still involved in a roundabout manner. Apologies for interrupting; please continue."

"Well, I suspect you realise the matter referred to is the unclaimed deceased estate of Silas McGregor. Perhaps, more important even for me, is the apparent disappearance of his wife, Regina Shelby McGregor. Probate of the McGregor estate was granted a couple of days ago. My friend is now trying to come to terms with the outcome. I fear, as things start to settle down around her, her attention will begin to focus on Regina McGregor's disappearance."

"It's interesting you tell me probate has been granted. I have heard nothing of it, but I now want to know everything about your friend, her connection to the McGregor's, and everything involved in the granting of probate. Although possible, it seems unlikely the McGregor's daughter is the friend you mention. I base this on the fact she would be a fair bit older than you, rather than of a similar age group. But, as the McGregor estate was left to her, my assumption could be wrong."

"Nope, your assumption was correct. I never knew Catherine, and never will. She died in Sydney when aged about nineteen.

It's doubtful she knew anything of inheriting her father's estate. She seems to have kept her background well hidden. The friend I speak of is Kirsty McGregor, Catherine's daughter, who was born when Catherine was about seventeen."

News of Kate's death seemed to hit him hard. Conversation stalled for a minute or so. Then, without looking up from his plate now littered with the shells of our seafood lunch, he nodded and murmured, "So... Regina ... had a granddaughter. Life can be a bitch when it chooses."

Unsure how to respond, I allowed a few silent moments to elapse. The ambiance was broken by the arrival of a waiter to clear away our plates. The interruption jarred Thomas out of his reverie.

"Sorry... I was thinking how sad it is, not only for your friend, but also for Regina, they will never know one another. Pour a little more into my glass please to help drown my maudlin thoughts."

As I obeyed, I attempted to bring the conversation back to the deceased estate. "So, you were the McGregors' solicitor for quite a few years?"

"No. I was Regina McGregor's legal representative. I never dealt with Silas McGregor at all. His legal dealings were through a different firm. In fact, I'm not sure who his solicitor was in the end. As I said, I only dealt with Regina."

"Oh, I see. I hadn't realised Regina had needed her own solicitor. Was it commonplace back then? I formed the opinion married women had little say or governance over their lives, their lives being the dictate of their husbands."

"Maybe it was not so far from the truth as a general rule. In some ways, Regina's life was very much the same as most other married women's lives at the time: generally disregarded as independent agents of their own lives. In another way, she was an exception to the rule. There was a side of her life which nobody, particularly Silas, knew about except Regina and me."

"Okay, now it's my turn to be intrigued. I am desperate to get to know Regina McGregor, all about her life, and what happened to her."

"I can help you with some of it, but what happened to her remains a mystery. A mystery I hope is resolved before I drop off the twig… In which case it probably should be soon."

Twice in the last few minutes I had noticed him sneak a look at his watch. I didn't need to be too bright to work out my time with him today was approaching its end. "I hope the retirement village isn't organising a search party for you. I've had you out and about for quite a while, and I realise I could be denying you your regular afternoon nap. While my selfish desire is to pursue all you can tell me about Regina, I suspect it might have to wait until another day"

"I do have to be home soon to take some medication which seems to require precise timing if it is to be effective … But I can spare you a little more time. So, let's make a start, shall we?"

"I didn't know whether you were aware of recent developments regarding the McGregor estate, but it appears you are not. My friend, Kirsty McGregor, now owns the property. She had a rugged time achieving clear title to the place, so hasn't had much time to dig into the family's background. Aware not knowing was bothering her, I decided to undertake some research for her. Your name featured in an old newspaper article regarding Regina's disappearance. Who better to talk to than someone with such a close association with the family?"

"Before we proceed much further, I would remind you of one minor point. My association was with Regina McGregor only, and not with any other member of the family."

"Okay; I understand, and I suspect there is much to be gleaned from your comment. For the moment, I will interpret it to mean you did not act for Silas McGregor. May we proceed on such basis?" He smiled and gave me an enthusiastic nod. I half expected him to tap the side of his nose in a conspiratorial gesture. "Did your representation of Regina begin before or after her husband's death?"

"Before… She first came to see me about five years before he died. So, it was nearly fifty years ago when this young, green, solicitor was allocated Regina McGregor as a client. Prior to coming to me, she had no legal representative. I suspect her motivation in seeking representation was because she knew she would need it in the future."

"Did you see her often, and for what purposes? I'm trying to get my head around what purposes a well-heeled lady of her era might have. If I'm honest, I would have to admit to a stereotypical idea of women of her circumstances back then as having husbands who took care of all the 'important' issues affecting the running of the business and the household, while the wife managed the household staff."

"Yes, such division of roles as you describe still predominated in some quarters in the era in question. In the McGregor household, there was only one staff, a housekeeper, who did most of the cooking and helped with the laundry. Silas didn't see the need for an idle wife. He believed an idle wife would soon become bored and ruin the ambiance of the household."

"So, on what types of issues did Regina seek your advice?"

"She had nothing when she married and had to fight and scrimp and save. Silas was tight-fisted, often leaving her short of cash to buy food. To make ends meet, she raised chickens, grew vegetables, made her own butter, and kept a couple of pigs for meat and bacon. Then her grandmother died and left her some money. She managed to hide the news from Silas, and came to ask my advice on how to manage it so Silas couldn't get his hands on it. I set some up as a trust fund, and invested a portion of it. Later, she saw it as a way to give her young daughter the best start in life."

"Am I right in thinking there was only the one child, their daughter, Catherine?"

"By the time Regina had Catherine, she was getting on a bit and another child might have been risky. Anyway, she had done her duty and provided an heir, albeit not the one he wanted. As it turned out, it wasn't an issue. Silas doted on the child, and the marriage had deteriorated to the extent where another child was never a possibility."

"After you set up her inheritance to protect it for Regina, did you see her often?"

"Not at first but, after a while, I saw a lot more of her. Whenever she came to town, she would call in to see me. I often required her instructions relating to her investments. I suppose it's when I started noticing the signs. The signs of how dreadful her marriage was. He wasn't always careful about where he inflicted the bruises. Sometimes they were there for all to see." Thomas paused for a moment, and shook his head as if to clear the memories from all those years ago before continuing.

"Then, one day, she came to me in quite a distressed state. Via a friend-of-a-friend process, Regina discovered Silas had made a will. It left everything to Catherine, but Regina would be allowed to continue to reside on the property until she remarried, or Catherine asked her to leave. The other galling feature was for his existing cash assets, and any income from the property subsequent to his death until Catherine assumed ownership, to go to Catherine … not to Regina. It would leave Regina in a perilous financial state."

"He intended leaving Regina without an income? Had he found out about her grandmother's inheritance?"

"No, I don't believe he ever knew about her inheritance. His intention to leave his wife destitute in the event of his death was clear to everyone who knew. But, as he had left her with a roof over her head – for at least some period of time anyway – there would be little she could do about it. Further compounding the horror of it all was the fact Silas was almost thirty years older than Regina. His death was likely to leave her facing a long widowhood, or forced to seek another husband."

"What a bastard! I had developed a dislike for Silas without knowing the first thing about him, but my assessment seemed accurate. All the while he was abusing his wife, he was being mentioned in the social pages as a fine upstanding pastoralist and entrepreneur. I suppose the only good thing was, he died while Regina was still a young woman. At least then she could use her own money to bring up her daughter the way she wanted."

"If only it were true…" I shot him a startled look. He held up a hand to forestall any questions and continued with what he was about to say.

"Regina was in a terrible state one day when she came to see me. For the best part of a year, I had suspected something was amiss, but she always assured me everything was fine. Then she could keep it from me no longer. For some time, she believed her husband was guilty of 'improper behaviour' with their daughter – to use her words."

"He was molesting his daughter? Incest…? Christ, what kind of monster was he? Was there any evidence, or was she just suspicious of his behaviour?"

"At first, I believe it was quite covert, but he became more brazen about it as time went on. Regina noticed her daughter becoming withdrawn at the same time as she observed other more overt behaviour on her husband's part. As for what kind of monster he was, I believe he was one of the worst kinds imaginable. Although Regina did all she could to protect her daughter – and paid a heavy physical price for it – in the end, she couldn't prevent what was happening.

The day came when the situation resolved itself, albeit not in a way which suited Regina. Catherine ran away from home. There was no warning, no note, and no further contact with the girl. Regina was in a terrible state when she came to tell me about it and, of course, she held Silas responsible for it."

"Tell me about Regina. What was she like?"

"Regina was a real lady in every way. She was brought up to be one, and came from that sort of family. She was an attractive, well-educated woman, who was warm, gentle and kind. It was a pleasure to serve her, and to talk to her. In spite of everything happening at home, in public, she remained dignified and polite."

"Okay… then why did someone like Regina – someone from her background –choose to marry someone like Silas McGregor?"

"She didn't choose. In fact, she had no say in the matter."

"What…? It was an arranged marriage? I thought arranged marriages were long out of fashion by the time Regina and Silas were married. Do you know how it came about?"

"Oh, yes. I know, because I asked her the same question as you just did: why choose Silas McGregor? Although, at first, she was embarrassed about the story, she told me anyway. You might not be aware, but Regina was getting on in age by the time she married Silas, who was nearly thirty years her senior, and she was considered likely to spend the rest of her life 'on-the-shelf' as the saying goes."

Although he hadn't checked his watch lately, I noticed Thomas was looking tired. Thinking he might need an afternoon nap, I suggested he might like to return to the retirement village. He admitted he often took a nap in the afternoon, and he was to take the critical medication around the time I collected him to take him to lunch, but he had forgotten to take it. He didn't want our meeting to end, but agreed it would be best if I took him home.

"No doubt, we have a whole lot more to talk about, and I hope we may continue our discussions. What was the next thing you were going to ask me about? If you tell me now, I'll have time to think about it, and to have the sequence of events straight in my head before we meet again."

"While it is nothing which can't be left for another day, I was going to ask you about your last few meetings with Regina. As you suggest, having some time to think about it before we meet again is a good idea. Come on, I'll take you home now so you can take those medications you need."

On our way back to the retirement village, we agreed to meet again tomorrow at three o'clock at his home. He promised to have coffee waiting for me when I arrived.

After dropping Thomas at his place, it was still only three o'clock when I arrived home. As I had recorded my whole meeting with Thomas, I decided it would be wise to transcribe as much as possible of the recording before Kirsty arrived this evening. By working at breakneck speed, I managed to complete the transcription and was adding a couple of notes to my whiteboard when I heard Kirsty arrive at about 6.30. The curry was simmering and all I had to do was to cook the rice.

Contrary to what I expected, she suggested we have a drink and then eat before aiming for an early night. I offered no argument.

Chapter 9

Kirsty left my place early this morning. It would be a big day on the property ... if everyone followed through on their promises. The builder's pole was to be installed, Les Stanley was to have the water supply up and running by this evening, and the transportable building Kirsty bought was to be delivered and installed on the base they prepared for it yesterday. There would be one helluva disappointed girl tonight if anyone reneged on their promise.

With complete faith in the various entities involved in making the above list of events happen today, Kirsty loaded her car with all her gear. By the time she finished, there was barely enough room for her to slide in behind the wheel. Although I knew it was a waste of time, I suggested leaving the move onto the property until she knew all the necessary work was complete ... or, at least until tomorrow.

As I anticipated, she had every confidence in the contractors, and she was determined to spend tonight in her new accommodation.

"I don't know why you thought I'd leave everything here," she confessed. "It makes more sense to take everything out to the property so I can start setting up where I'm going to be living. So, I might as well take all the stuff I've had stored in my room." A small bag of cold foodstuff from the fridge in her unit remained in my fridge. "I hope it only needs to be here until tomorrow, but I can't be sure they will connect the power early enough for my new fridge to be cold soon enough to prevent the food spoiling. If they do, I'll either come back here to collect it later this afternoon, or sometime tomorrow. Regardless, I will be starting my new life on my new property tonight."

Almost as a last minute thought, before she left this morning, she borrowed one of the camp stretchers from my camping gear in the shed and somehow managed to find room to slide it into her car along with everything else.

With mixed feelings, I waved her off. As I watched her disappear down the driveway, a whole raft of questions flowed through my mind: did she have basic cooking and eating equipment? Did she have towels and bedclothes? Did she have food; basic groceries? I couldn't help but wonder how long it would take Kirsty to realise she didn't have the basic essentials to set up her new accommodation … and how soon she would be back looking to borrow more gear.

More out of habit than anything else, I went into my city office at my normal time. After taking care of all the usual first-thing-in-the-morning routine chores, I found myself with a clear schedule until three o'clock when I again was to meet with Thomas Agnew. To fill in the available time until then, I returned to transcribing the tape of Kirsty's story. It kept me busy until a few minutes after two o'clock.

Several times during the day, I marvelled at how Fate appeared to be in my corner today. As I switched off the recorder, the same thought returned once more, and again I thanked Fate for arranging matters as it had done. While I was concerned about how Kirsty would manage to spend her first night on the property, it suited me not to have her with me tonight.

With Ben coming for dinner and to find out all there was to know about the bones, the situation would be more than a little tense – and possibly counterproductive if Kirsty were there too. Until this morning when she was emphatic about not returning to spend the night at my place, I intended to call Ben and change our arrangements for this evening. I was going to suggest we met at his place rather than mine. Now a change of plan wasn't necessary. But, it was time to put such thoughts aside and concentrate on the next phase of today. After a quick dash to the bakery to buy a cake, I returned to my office to freshen up before heading for the retirement village and coffee with Thomas.

"Aah, clever girl," he cooed as I opened the box to reveal the strawberries and cream filled sponge cake. "I had intended to make a batch of muffins or pikelets, but I have been inundated by visits from the neighbours today ... and it left me feeling more than a little embarrassed about having nothing to go with our coffee this afternoon."

A few minutes later, when well into the business of dispatching coffee and cake, conversation returned to Regina McGregor and the reason for my visit.

"Thomas, when we left off yesterday, you just told me Regina Shelby's marriage to Silas McGregor was an arranged one. And, from the way you tell it, not a happy one. How did this arranged marriage of hers came about, and why?"

"As a twenty-something year old, Regina became involved with a workman on her family's property. It was a brief affair. Although they kept it secret – for obvious reasons – their secret came out when the chap left in a hurry and, a couple of weeks later, Regina announced she was pregnant. The family promptly locked her away on the property until after the child was born. It was a boy, but he only lived for a few hours.

You might expect, once the child was no more, and with no one outside the family aware of the whole event, life would return to normal for Regina and the family except... it wasn't how the family saw it. She was now a 'fallen woman', tainted for life, and a stain on the family's name. She continued to be confined to the property, essentially hidden from the world. Their prevailing attitude was, no man in his right mind would want such damaged property and, therefore, she would never marry. She would continue to be a burden on the family for the rest of her life."

"So, the family took it upon themselves to find someone prepared to become her husband...? And, what did he receive in return for his noble act – apart from someone to keep house for him?"

"Ah well, the offer he received was too good to refuse. After all, she was a good looking woman, and the compensation offered was more than adequate. I was given to understand, as Silas was the lesser son of a long-established pastoral family in another state, it meant he had no chance of taking over the family business, and was forced to strike out to make his own way in the world. He had been a foreman of some kind on the Shelby property when he was presented with a chance to improve his lot.

McGregor was considered an ideal candidate for marriage to Regina. In spite of his age, he had never married, and only imbibed and smoked a cigar on the odd occasion. Over a handshake to seal the deal, apart from a wife, Silas received a good-sized block of land and a small amount of cash to help him establish his new property."

"The whole event speaks volumes about the type of man Silas McGregor was, although I suppose, for someone with no prospects of bettering himself, it was an offer too good to resist."

"Silas made no secret of his ambition in life: to have earned enough by the time he was too old to work to be able to buy a small piece of dirt on which to grow a few vegetables and raise a couple of sheep or cows. There he was, being offered his life's ambition with a couple of bonuses thrown in for good measure."

"It still makes me angry and frustrated to think about Regina's acceptance of the arrangement, even though I know she probably had no choice."

"Well, she did have a choice: marry Silas McGregor, or be thrown out onto the street. She claimed it was made clear, if she didn't marry Silas, the family would no longer support her and she would be thrown out and disowned."

"Okay; so, in reality, there was no choice. I assume a hasty, low-key marriage occurred."

"No, it didn't play out as you might expect. As soon as the betrothal was announced, Silas went off to make a start on establishing his new property, and was away for about three months before returning for a quiet family wedding. Forget the notion of a honeymoon. This was a business arrangement. As soon as the wedding was over, the couple left on a wagon for Silas' new property. There was no house at all. Silas spent those months prior to the wedding concentrating on installing fencing, not accommodation. So, for the first eighteen months or so of her marriage, Regina's home was a tent. After the tent, they moved up to living in a tiny slab hut."

"I hope it was where they lived for a while because, at last, he had provided a proper home – of sorts – for his wife."

"You are in for a disappointment I'm afraid. Nothing so wonderful happened. Although the slab hut was primitive, they only lived in it for about four or five years. Although the area of land Silas was given wasn't a bad size, it wasn't great agricultural land and it struggled to carry even a small flock of sheep. It seems the property was a jagged protrusion from a much larger area of land. The particular area of the state where the properties were situated was considered by most people to be unfit for grazing, but it was rich in coal deposits – and much sought after by mining companies."

"Maybe the deal he struck wasn't as good as he thought it would be. Eking out a living off a low grade block of land wouldn't be easy. Did the situation there have something to do with their move to Millhaven?"

"Yes… or so I was told. It seems at the same time as the deal involving the parcel of land was being struck with Silas McGregor, Regina's father had another deal on the boil. He was in the process of selling to a mining company the much larger tract of land adjoining the block he gave Silas. Shelby was a major shareholder in the mining company and, when they discovered coal on his land, he was keen to unload it. It wasn't paying its way as a grazing property. If he sold it to the mining company, he would not only do well from the sale but, as a shareholder, he would receive ongoing dividends from the mining company's profits."

"It seems Regina's father and Silas McGregor were of one and the same kind: unscrupulous. I suppose, if I were feeling a tad more generous, I might describe them as 'opportunists'… but I don't think it's an accurate enough descriptor."

"Well, maybe 'opportunist' is as good a description as any. Silas made the best of the next opportunity when it came along. The mining company needed extra land on which to erect supporting infrastructure such as offices, workers' accommodation, and machinery and equipment workshops. Silas' block was an ideal location. He held out for a while before driving a hard bargain. An enormous purchase price gave him enough to buy land he had already looked at near here. The Millhaven land became the home block of *Westbrook.* By the way, it remains the name of the property your friend now owns. After their move to Millhaven, the couple returned to living in a tent again for quite some time.

Over the years, Silas bought up smaller surrounding blocks, which by themselves were too small to be viable. By amalgamating them with his home block, he soon had a valuable property. Regina struck a deal with Silas. There would be no heir until such time as she had a decent home to raise it in. The central portion of the house was built, and Regina kept her side of the bargain by producing Catherine. The central part of the building still there today was completed just in time for the arrival of the baby."

"Good for her. It was about time something went her way for a change. At least then she and the baby had a proper roof over their heads."

I wanted to ask Thomas about his last meetings with Regina before she disappeared. I wondered whether there was anything to suggest something was amiss, or if anything out of the ordinary had occurred. But, it was getting late, and I already had taken up a couple of hours of Thomas' time. Also, I needed to be home to prepare for Ben's visit tonight. It wasn't so much about having dinner ready, as having my head in the right place to deal with what I knew was to come.

"Thomas, it's late and I think we both need a break from questions and answers. I am anxious to know about Regina's life after Catherine ran away, and how she seemed in the time just prior to her disappearance. If you can spare me a bit more of your time, may I schedule another meeting with you for some time soon?"

"Quite a bit of the story remains untold and I'm sure you and your friend want – need – to know it. Did you want to meet again tomorrow?"

"Er… no, maybe not tomorrow ... I'm likely to be busy all day. Do you have time for a meeting on Wednesday?"

Having agreed to meet at ten o'clock on Wednesday morning, I was on my way home to prepare for Ben's arrival. As I drove across town, I felt my stomach tightening at the prospect of what tonight might bring. It became worse as I wrestled with the question of whether to share what I had learnt so far of Regina's story, or to wait until I knew the whole story before sharing it with him. Although I wasn't aware of having arrived at a definite decision, by the time I was preparing the pasta sauce for dinner, I knew Ben would not be hearing Regina's story tonight.

Ben arrived at 6.30PM and, from the way he strode in coupled with the set of his jaw, I knew this evening would be memorable for all the wrong reasons. Although my stomach had been a roiling mass from the time he arrived, it settled quite fast once we took our glasses of wine out onto the deck.

"Dinner is almost ready," I told him as we settled down to watch the sunset. "I've only the pasta to cook just before we are ready to eat."

"There's no hurry. I seem to have been on the go all day. A quiet few minutes watching the sun set is what I need now."

About fifteen minutes later, I left him alone on the deck while I went into to finish preparing dinner. Conversation was light and inconsequential all through dinner, and I have to admit to being lulled into a false sense of relief. I felt this evening was not going to be as rough as I had expected.

It was as I packed the dishwasher, the inquisition began: What was the name of my friend; how did I come to know her; where is she living? The rapid-fire questions were delivered without pause between them. Although it made it impossible to answer any of them, until I finished dealing with the dishwasher, the situation suited me. I wanted a more structured and logical approach to how tonight's session was conducted.

So, as soon as the dishwasher was dealt with, we relocated to my office. Ignoring Ben's earlier questions, my first move was to drag out the photos of the house and the bones hidden behind a wall there. After studying each of the shots for a few moments, he returned to his earlier line of questioning.

"Right... so I might begin to develop an understanding of this whole business, perhaps we should start with some information about your friend... Kirsty, is that her name? How do you come to know her? As best you can, tell me what you know of her background."

"I knew her as Kirsty Williams until a couple of days ago." I saw Ben's eyebrows shoot up towards his hairline, but he didn't interrupt. "Although she didn't know it at the time, her full name back then was Kirsty Shelby McGregor Williams. Since discovering 'Williams' was her adopted surname, she has now dropped it in favour of her birth name: Kirsty Shelby McGregor."

The next few minutes were taken up by my version of how I came to know Kirsty and the couple who adopted her, the subsequent deaths of the only parents she ever knew, and of her discovery she had been adopted when she was about two years old. While it was a précised version of the story Kirsty told me, it gave Ben enough information to satisfy him and allow me to move on to the more recent – and more relevant – chapters of Kirsty's story.

"Having discovered she was adopted, it's easy to understand how driven she was to discover more about herself; starting with who her mother was. With the help of a professional researcher and her solicitor, she learnt about her start in life, and her solicitor went on to discover her connection to the McGregor estate at Millhaven. It was the start of what has been a harrowing process for her.

She had to prove she was who she claimed to be. If you think about yourself having to prove who you are, it is not as easy to do as you might think. Anyway, in Kirsty's case, the journey of discovery, and everything else associated with it, has left her a bit fragile psychologically."

"Was the requirement to prove her claimed identity a necessary first part of the process to confirm her claim on the local deceased estate?"

"Yeah, and having confirmed her identity, her solicitor was able to apply for probate of the estate – her grandfather's estate. Now, as the rightful owner of the property, she is setting herself up in temporary accommodation on the place while she works her way through refurbishing the big old house. It was amongst the first blows struck in the process, which uncovered the bones hidden in a compartment behind a wall of more recent vintage than the rest of the house."

"Why did she come to you instead of going to the police in the first instance?"

"Her current frame of mind seems to have her almost terrified of any further encounter with bureaucracy. She just wanted to be settled and to be able to start rebuilding her life. If the police became involved, she feared she would become excluded from the place and, for some reason, the prospect terrified her."

"What a load of nonsense! Of course the house will have to be a crime scene until all the evidence is collected, and then any structural changes will need to be postponed for some period of time. How does she think the police can do their job if she is stomping about all over the site?"

"And that is the exact attitude I hope you manage to lose before you go to talk to her. As I said, she is fragile. You will do much better with a soft approach, than going in with all guns blazing and throwing your weight around."

"Throwing my weight around…? Are you talking to me, Ben Richards, the bloke you have known for how many decades? When have I ever thrown my weight around?"

"I don't have time or inclination to remind you of them all right now, but you know what I mean. If you adopt an officious approach, you are likely to be stonewalled, and suffer a complete lack of co-operation. So, go gently ... please."

"Okay, message received. I'm not expected back in my office until Tuesday. It allows me a little leeway for tomorrow. I want to see those bones first thing tomorrow morning. I am assuming you don't know of any reason why I can't do so ... and, I suppose you will insist on being there too."

"...Right on both counts. What time do you want to be there?"

"It's more a case of what time do you want me to pick you up. I assume you are coming out to the property with me and want me to collect you on my way out."

"No, I do not. I will make my own way out. Then, whenever I am ready, I can come home again, or go into my city office to do some work, while you do whatever it is you do out there."

"I see. Then I will meet you out there at ten o'clock. What does the situation require?" Confused by his question, I responded with a shrug and a shake of my head. "Okay, is there power?"

"Possibly... there should be electricity connected in some way after today."

"Uh huh... right; take a powerful torch. What about water – fit to drink I mean?"

"Maybe... there should be a water supply after today. Do you still carry bottles of water in your car?" He nodded. "Make sure they are topped up before you leave home."

"Just in case...?"

"Yes, just in case the new water supply isn't a goer yet. If you plan on spending any length of time there tomorrow, you could be dying of thirst by the time you leave."

"Anything else I need to consider before setting out?"

"No... Oh, yes. Wear work clothes. I don't mean your normal work clobber. I mean heavy duty, get-dirty-type clothes. The house is filthy."

"Have you had any contact with Emily since we last spoke?"

"Yep, she was here for dinner last night. As you suggested, I mentioned she might have some bones to look at in the near future."

"What did she have to say about them?"

"Nothing… She just said 'okay'."

"You gave her all the details of where they are and how they were found, didn't you?"

"No. Why would I do your job for you?"

"Aw, right; I see. Not to worry, it's okay. I will give her a call and fill her in on all the details after I inspect the site."

I spent the next few minutes drawing a map and making sure Ben knew where to go and how to get there. Although it still was early, Ben was looking wrung out, probably as a result of a heavy weekend with his mates in Brisbane. As soon as we finished our coffees, he was on his way home.

An early night suited me too. I needed an early start in the morning to take care of a few things before I headed out to the property … And I intended to be there well before ten o'clock.

Chapter 10

During the wee hours of this morning, the heavens opened up to vent their pent up vindictiveness on Millhaven. It continued bucketing down when I scrambled out of bed at five o'clock. Damn; the old house where the bones are hidden is dark and gloomy enough on a bright sunny day. If this keeps up, it will be a lousy day for exploring hidden cavities. Overcoming the temptation to flop back into bed, I dragged myself out to the kitchen.

As Kirsty hadn't felt the need to spend the night at my place, I assumed the various works went according to plan yesterday and her new abode was rendered habitable. If my assumption were correct, power was connected and would prove convenient this morning. With Ben's impending arrival at the property at about morning tea time, it would be as well to top up our caffeine levels before any friendships might disintegrate. Now power and water were available, coffee could happen without too much fuss and bother, but something to go with it was another matter.

It was the reason for my earlier than usual scramble out of bed today. The little extra time allowed me to produce a batch of cupcakes to take with me. It didn't take long for a batch to be in the oven. As I loaded the array of bowls and tools into the dishwasher, another problem occurred to me. There would be at least three of us for morning tea – and possibly more if workmen were still around. It was unlikely Kirsty's kitchen ran to sufficient coffee mugs for all of us.

While I waited for the cakes to bake and then cool enough to be iced, I put together a basic hamper to take with me. It included disposable cups and plates, and containers of coffee, sugar, and milk. I remembered the bag of foodstuff from Kirsty's unit still sitting in my fridge, and made a mental note to throw it in the esky before I left.

Then, there was nothing to do except to have breakfast, decorate the cakes, load up the car, and head out. I was about to wreck any plans Kirsty had for a lie in this morning. I would be out at the property by soon after 7.30AM. Although it was something of an uncivilised hour to arrive on someone's doorstep, I wanted time with her before Ben arrived. I wasn't naïve enough to expect things to progress in a smooth and civil way once Ben got down to business. But, the optimist in me hoped my early-morning efforts might help smooth the way and avoid too much stress and trauma.

The deluge continued and the track to the house was awash but, thanks to the neighbour's earlier efforts, it seemed to be holding up okay. I crept along it to avoid causing deep wheel ruts in the now soggy ground. Changes about the place were evident from the moment I pulled up in front of the house. An area of soil had been disturbed beside the house and this now sprouted a builder's pole. A short distance away from it, and behind the start of the row of outbuildings, another similar pole had been installed.

I squelched my way through the soggy long grass from my car and around to the second builder's pole. About three metres from the pole, Kirsty's new transportable building sat resplendent on its low foundation piers. The other thing to catch my eye was a brand-new tank atop the ancient, tall tank stand. As I climbed the two steps to the small landing outside the front door, no lights were visible, and no sounds came from inside the building.

My rain jacket was not great at coping with the heavy rain. From my knees down, my jeans were soaked. As were my trainers which squelched noisily as I climbed the stairs. And, my shirt was becoming soggy as I sweated under the rain jacket. I grimaced at the muddy footprints I'd left on the stairs and across the landing, and then watched the heavy rain obliterate them. Turning my attention to the job I came to do, I thumped on the door.

A bedraggled, bleary-eyed Kirsty eased open the door a fraction and peered out. "Sonny, what the hell are you doing here at this ungodly hour of the morning?"

"Ungodly...? It is eight o'clock already. The day is fast away... and I am sure I am starting to dissolve out here. Is there a backdoor I can use to come in without making a total mess of your new digs in the process?"

"Hang about while I find a towel to put down for you to use as a mat."

While I was removing my sodden shoes, I wondered how successful she might be at finding the promised towel. She did have a car full of stuff she brought with her when she moved in, but I doubted it ran to more than the one bath towel for her own use. I was wrong.

Moments later, an enormous, brightly coloured beach towel was thrown on the floor just inside the door. Leaving my shoes on the landing, I took one step inside onto the towel – just far enough inside to have me out of the rain. I removed my rain jacket and, with reasonable accuracy, threw it out over the landing's railing. Although the lower part of my jeans was soaked, minus the soggy boots and jacket, I wasn't nearly as wet as I expected to be. Nevertheless, I continued to stand on the towel for a minute or two to avoid the possibility of dripping water all over the floor.

"I see you have moved in, so I assume everything went according to plan with all the work yesterday. From the bit I've seen so far, this place should be quite comfortable."

"Yep, although I haven't added much to it yet, it feels good. While it is compact, it does have three bedrooms and all the usual amenities... and it is airconditioned."

"What are you planning to do about setting it up – I mean about furniture and stuff?"

"Before I left Sydney, I put anything I wanted to keep into storage. As soon as I saw everything was coming together yesterday, I made a few phone calls. The removalist company should be picking up my stuff from the storage facility sometime today. I expect it will be here within the next couple of days, and I'll be able to set up properly then."

"Well, we will have to have a housewarming soon after your stuff arrives."

"Funny you should suggest it. I was thinking much along the same lines last night. If everything goes to plan, next weekend might be a good time. Now, what brings you to my door so early? I'm sure it wasn't curiosity about my new home."

"No-o, well, not entirely anyway. I came early to give you a bit of advance warning. A friend of mine, the top cop in the area, will be arriving around ten o'clock. He will want to see the bones, and I guess it will kick off the process of doing whatever they need to do to remove the bones from the old house. But, I wanted to see how you had set yourself up, as well as warn you about your impending visitor."

"Damn; does it have to be so soon? I was hoping I wouldn't see anyone for a few days. It would give me time to settle in and feel at home here."

"Yes, I hear you. But, the sooner the police make a start on this, the sooner you will have the whole place back to yourself again. I know the house has been your focus since your first visit, but what else have you looked at? Have you looked at what's in those outbuildings, or taken a tour of the property to see what work needs to be done to bring it back into production again?"

"Not really; I suppose, if I'm honest, I haven't really looked any further than the house."

"Look at it this way, now you have somewhere comfortable to live, the house should become less of a priority compared to what else needs doing on the place. And, yes, the police probably will exclude you from the house for a day or two, but it will be an ideal time for you to look at other things… investigating those outbuildings… inspecting the property… There are plenty of other things to be done, and you could be doing them while you can't enter the house."

"I suppose you're right... No, I know you're right. I do want to know what's in those outbuildings, and I do want to know how much work I've got to do on the property. But, something is stopping me getting on with it. I think maybe the prospect of what I will find is so overwhelming, I'm not game to tackle it."

"You don't need me to tell you, but it will still be there waiting for you next week, next month, or whenever you get around to it. It's not going to go away, and nothing is going to happen if you don't make it happen. The property won't get any better unless you start work on it. You've never been one to back away from a challenge or an awkward situation. And yes, I know you've had a rough time lately. But, getting stuck into things here might be just what you need to help heal the damage you've suffered over the last few months. At least think about what I've said."

"Nothing you've said is news to me. It's all stuff I've thought about already. Look, Sonny, I know you have a business to run, and I've no right to ask this but, if you do have a bit of spare time in the next few days, would you think about spending it here with me... please. Even if it was only few hours here and there, I think it might help me make a start on those things I need to do."

"Let's see what the world looks like after ten o'clock this morning. After Ben sees the bones, we might be in a better position to know what will happen, and when."

"If he's coming at ten o'clock, will he expect coffee? I'm set up okay for myself for the next couple of days or so, but I wouldn't be in a position to offer him coffee – or anything else other than a drink of water perhaps."

"It's just as well I figured it might be the case. I threw some stuff in the car before I left home. If the rain would just ease up for a moment, I'll bring it in. You're right. I thought he probably would welcome a coffee, so I brought the wherewithal to accommodate it."

About half an hour before Ben was expected to arrive, the rain eased off to a light drizzle. I donned my soggy shoes and jacket again and sprinted to my car to retrieve the morning tea provisions. After handing everything in to Kirsty, I went through the process of leaving all my wet stuff on the landing before following her inside. A few minutes later, Ben arrived a bit earlier than expected ... And yes, he would love a coffee before we made a start on the business of the day.

After the introductions were done, a tense Kirsty hurried to make coffee while I set out cupcakes and everything else we needed. Full marks to Ben, he kept conversation light and friendly all through our morning tea.

"So, Miss McGregor, how long...."

"Kirsty, please; I'm still adjusting to being McGregor."

"Okay, Kirsty, how long since you were last here in Millhaven."

"Not since we left at the end of my primary schooling. Then we moved about a bit for three or four years before settling in Sydney."

"You would hardly recognise the place after being away for so long. So, what happens now? Are you planning on staying here – I mean living here on the property?"

"Yep, that's my intention. Well, my initial thought was to do up the old house and live in it. But, it will take a while before the old place is liveable so, for however long it takes, I will be living in this, my new little bungalow."

"It looks as though you should be comfortable here, but from what I saw of the property as I drove in, you have a big job ahead of you out there as well as trying to do up the old house. Will you hire workers to deal with the paddocks?"

"No, I don't think it will be necessary. I have an agricultural science degree and spent much of my university days gaining practical experience in paddocks looking a lot like these."

Ben seemed impressed with the concept of Kirsty working the place herself. But, morning tea had dragged on long enough. It was time to attack the real reason for Ben's visit.

"I'm sorry, ladies, but I'm afraid duty calls. Kirsty, perhaps you would show me those bones you found. Shall we adjourn to the old house?"

"Hang on a minute while I collect some stuff. There is now power to the builder's pole adjacent to the house, but it is so dark inside, we probably still will need torches to see well enough."

A few moments later, Kirsty emerged from a back room carrying torches and a new looking long electric lead. "Sonny, if you carry the torches and the lead, I will bring the work light," she suggested.

"Here, give them to me. I can carry them… oh, and I already have a torch, which I will grab out of my vehicle on the way past," Ben offered.

There were a few wasted moments while we sorted out who would carry what, before our procession set off to see the bones. Kirsty, carrying the long lead, led the way. She was followed by Ben carrying his torch and the work light. Carrying a torch each for Kirsty and me, I brought up the rear. On her way past the builder's pole, Kirsty paused just long enough to plug in the lead. After feeding it through under the railing, she threw its remaining coils through onto the verandah floor.

Again, Kirsty led the convoy as she bounced up the front stairs. Ben hung back, allowing me to pass him. Sticking to my now familiar approach to climbing those stairs, I kept my feet close to the left-hand runner as I picked my way up to join Kirsty. Ben eyed off the stairs with ill-concealed suspicion. While still unsure about the whole exercise … and while I held my breath … he followed my example and soon arrived safely beside us. He is a big lump of a lad and much heavier than me. I had half expected the steps to give way under his weight.

"Right; lead on, Kirsty. Let's have a look at these bones of yours," he announced.

Kirsty uncoiled the lead as she went. Although we couldn't move it into position yet, I helped her connect the work light ready for Ben to use. Ben was using his torch to view the bones through the studs and noggins of the wall and prevented us moving it closer. A couple of minutes later, he stuffed his torch in his back pocket, and moved the work light to suit him.

"That's better," he murmured as he took another look into the cavity behind the wall. Then, turning to where Kirsty and I stood off to one side, he asked, "How much has been changed here? Have there been any changes to the bones, or anything else in this hidden chamber, since this cladding was removed from the wall?"

We shook our heads in unison and Kirsty replied, "No. The only thing that's changed here was I took that bit of sheeting off the wall. We've only looked at the bones from out here. Nothing behind the wall has been touched or impacted in any way."

"Okay. Well, thank you, ladies. You may leave me to it now while you go and get on with the rest of your day. I have photos to take and phone calls to make. Don't leave anything behind. The house now officially is a crime scene, and entry will be prohibited until our investigation is completed."

"And, how long is that likely to last?" Kirsty demanded.

"Hard to say at this stage, but at least a couple of days I would think," Ben replied.

I could see Kirsty was reluctant to leave, and I feared a situation might develop between her and Ben. It would not be a pretty thing if it happened. I grabbed Kirsty by the arm and tried dragging her towards the door. She resisted, and tried to shake me off.

"Move...," I hissed at her. "Let's get out of here as we've been told to." My tone suggested she shouldn't argue, and the hefty yank I gave her arm almost pulled her off her feet. It was an effective move. When she half stumbled, I pulled her towards the door. I had her moving in the right direction. Once we were out on the verandah again, she shook my hand off her arm.

"What do you think you're doing? I wasn't finished in there. Who does he think he is telling me I can't enter my house?"

"Pull your head in, Kirsty. You know who he is ... And, more importantly, he knows who he is. As the top cop in this area, he has every right to order us off his crime scene. You knew it was going to happen, so what are you carrying on about?"

In a huff, she strode off and bounced down the stairs. I followed at a more cautious pace, and then had to hurry to catch up with her as she strode towards her new abode. As I followed her up the stairs to her front door, I asked, "Do you happen to have any bread?"

"What? Why are you asking me about bread?"

"Well, if you do happen to have some bread, we could use some of the stuff I brought with me this morning to make something for lunch. It's the stuff out of your unit's fridge which was at my place from when you moved in with me."

"Do we have to feed him as well?" She directed a sharp flick of her head towards the old house.

"No, I shouldn't think so. I doubt Ben will stick around long. As soon as he's taken his photos and made a couple of phone calls, I would expect him to leave. I'm sure he doesn't want to be hanging around out here, although he may be back later today after others arrive to begin the investigation."

"So, does your mentioning lunch mean you might be staying for a while, and don't need to rush back to your office?"

"Yep, I am planning to stay until about four o'clock… unless you tell me you don't want me to. While we have lunch, I thought we might work out what we are going to do after Ben leaves."

With no argument or any other suggestion forthcoming, it's what we prepared to do. As we were about ready to sit down to second-rate salad sandwiches and coffee, Ben came looking for us.

"Are you two going to hang around here for a while?" he asked. We confirmed we both would be in the general vicinity until about four o'clock. "Good. Emily Ibbotson and her forensic team should be here around two o'clock, and a couple of my blokes should arrive around the same time. I'll leave now, but I should return around the same time as the others come to start work. If I'm not here when the others arrive, please point them in the direction of the crime scene."

We agreed and, a few moments later, we heard him drive off. "Right," Kirsty began, "if we don't hurry up and eat these sandwiches, we are going to need a spoon. They are becoming soggier by the minute."

After we dispatched the sandwiches, I brought out the rest of the cupcakes for dessert. Once we were sitting back with cake and coffee, it seemed an ideal time to plan our afternoon.

"Kirsty, do you have any ideas about what you might like to do after lunch?" She shook her head. "As we can't go into the old house, I thought it might be a good time to see what treasures are hiding in those outbuildings. If we are careful, we should avoid having one of them collapse on us."

She jumped at the chance. We hurried ourselves to finish lunch and clean up so we could make a start on our forthcoming adventure. Something occurred to me while we were clearing away our lunchtime rubbish. "Perhaps you should be aware, Kirsty," I began. "Ben doesn't know Emily already has seen the bones. While there was nothing illegal about her seeing them before Ben did, it is not good form for it to happen. Neither Emily nor I have told Ben about her previous visit. It would be best if he remains ignorant of the fact."

"So, are you suggesting, at no point should I allude to her earlier visit to view the bones?" I nodded. "Okay; I'm pretty sure I can manage it without too much trouble. Now, if you still have your torch, shall we attack those outbuildings? I'm beginning to feel quite excited about what we might find."

I knew what she meant. I felt the same way. But, we were forced to curb our excitement for a bit longer. As we walked around to the first outbuilding in the row, a vehicle picked its way carefully along the still muddy track. I recognised Emily's work vehicle, and apprised Kirsty of the situation. We went and stood by our cars to await her arrival.

"Am I the first?" Emily lowered her window and asked. "I thought Ben would be here." After scrambling out of the car, she looked back along the track. "This will be my team arriving now. I don't want to waste their time while they wait for Ben."

"Ben instructed us to point you in the direction of the crime scene if he wasn't here when you arrived," I told her. "So, I took it to mean you should go over to the house and get started. After all, it's not as though you need him to tell you what to do. He and a couple of his detectives will be here soon enough I expect."

"Fair enough; what are you two going to be doing while we are busy in there?"

"We are about to embark on a journey of exploration," Kirsty said, and dropped Emily a knowing wink. Emily's eyebrows shot up in response. "We are off to explore those buildings," Kirsty added, and accompanied it with a grand sweeping gesture towards the outbuildings.

"Good luck ... and give me a shout if you come across any treasure. We'll decide whether we'll tell Ben about it, or split it up between us before he finds out." She returned Kirsty's wink as she opened her vehicle's hatch and started pulling out her equipment.

Chapter 11

The recalcitrant double doors of the first building refused to yield to a couple of bouts of brute force. "It's no good," Kirsty said. "We'll need to use my new pinch bar to gemmy it open. I don't want to use the sledge hammer on it. Hang about while I fetch the bar."

"No, don't worry about the bar just yet. Let's try some of the other doors first. With nothing more than a bit of persuasion, one or more of those might prove more willing to open."

As we moved along the row to the second building, Ben's car arrived. "Do we need to talk to Ben now he's here?" Kirsty asked.

"Nah; he is in work mode now, and will just get on with what he needs to do. We can ignore him and any others working in the house. Cops working a crime scene are none of our business. Besides, he will know where to find us if he needs us – although I doubt it is likely."

Although the second door we tried did spring open, we didn't venture inside. Kirsty was keen to open as many doors as possible before exploring the interior of any of the buildings. She suggested, "Let's work our way right along the row to open as many as we can without having to resort to more violent means. Then, the exciting part can come later when we have a better idea of the condition of those buildings … and are more aware of which ones are going to collapse on us."

"Sure, if it's how you want to proceed. But, remember, I intend leaving here a bit before four o'clock, and won't be back here today. In which case, you will be treasure hunting on your own."

"I don't intend entering the buildings today. They can wait until tomorrow. As you would have noticed, at the moment, my larder resembles Mother Hubbard's cupboard. I need to visit the supermarket, and do a couple of other things in town, so I will follow you when you leave. I need to go today. As the stuff I had in storage might arrive as early as tomorrow. I don't want to be off the property when it comes. No doubt the old house festooned in crime scene tape will grab their attention as they drive up. I think I would prefer for them still to be wondering about it when they leave."

This sounded so much like the Kirsty of old, the tease I had known all those years ago. While it wasn't a significant thing in itself, it was enough to give me a hint of hope for her return to normal soon.

Later, after spending an hour or so in my city office, I headed home with the intention of spending the evening going over my notes from my two meetings with Thomas Agnew. I wanted to spend some time thinking about the questions I would put to him tomorrow. Five minutes after I sat down at my desk in my home office, Ben called.

"Are you home for dinner tonight, or are you working?"

"Home tonight; my new job was supposed to start early this week but, as I haven't heard anything further from my client, I'm now not sure when, or if, it will start."

"Okay, I'll see you around seven o'clock for dinner, and I'll pick up something on my way there. By the way, have you spoken to Kirsty since she left the property this afternoon?"

"No. She said she had shopping to do and she would follow me in to town, but I haven't heard from her since I left. Why, has something I should know about happened?"

"Emily caught up with Kirsty just as she was about to leave the property. To facilitate the removal of the bones, they needed to remove part, or all, of the wall for easy access. While it is a crime scene, and there was no need for Emily to discuss it with Kirsty at all, I suppose out of courtesy, she told Kirsty about their plan to remove the wall. It seems Kirsty wasn't too impressed. Do you know what it was all about?"

"Did she explain why the prospect of it might have upset her?"

"Not as far as I've been able to find out. By the time I made it back there this afternoon, Kirsty had already left for town. I only have Emily's side of the story. I don't doubt what Emily told me. I was just trying to get a handle on what might have been behind Kirsty's reaction. Do you have any ideas?"

"I only can hazard a guess. It might be rooted in her trauma over the last few months and her psychological state as a result of it. I suspect she would have seen the removal of the wall as usurping her newly found ownership of the place. Yes, I know she had started attacking the wall, and intended removing it, but that is just the point. *She* wanted to remove it. It would have been her first positive move as the owner establishing her new life on the property."

"But, she knew we had to get the bones out somehow. She wanted the bones removed so she could get on with doing whatever else she needed to do to the house. If anything, Emily's team did her a favour by removing the offending wall. I thought she might have had something to say to you about it."

"Yes, she knew the wall had to be removed, or some part of it did, and yes she did intend removing it anyway. But I don't think that's the point. I think it was more about somebody else coming in and taking over ... And robbing her of the opportunity to strike the first blow – so to speak – towards establishing her new life on the property. Anyway, how did it all end?"

"Women...! I'll never understand them. How are we ever supposed to know how they think? Here we are doing her a favour and she gets all bent out of shape. As for how it ended, I think it was okay. Emily said it was sorted out, and it must've been all right given how Kirsty left and went into town. If you do hear anything about it, please pass it on to me. While it doesn't matter now the wall is down, it might help me better understand how women think."

"If the wall is down, I assume the bones have now been removed from the site. What more is there to do in the house before you hand it back to Kirsty?"

"Emily took the bones to her laboratory last thing this afternoon. As for how much more there is to do out there, the forensic team and my blokes will be combing the place for evidence all day tomorrow and possibly the next day as well. Even if they finish going over the place tomorrow, we might hold it as a crime scene for an extra day or two – just in case we need to come back and look for something else. I can't give you anything more definite at the moment and, to be frank, Kirsty is just going to have to be patient. I'm sure she can find plenty more to occupy herself on the property without worrying about not being able to enter the house."

"You're right, there's plenty to do out there. I probably will go out there again sometime tomorrow just to help her stay focused on doing other things until house is no longer a crime scene. Now you have the bones, are there any indications about what happened out there, or when it happened? … Or, whose bones they might be?"

"At this stage of proceedings, it would be guesswork. Emily suggested the bones had been there for several decades, but not centuries, and they weren't of archaeological interest. I don't think there's any more I can tell you. What time do you think you might go out to the property tomorrow?"

"Oh, I didn't have any real plan, and I didn't give Kirsty any definite indication of when I might arrive, but I doubt it will be before lunch. The best I can tell you is it will be sometime during the afternoon before I'm free to leave my office."

Ben didn't stay late. After being away for the best part of a week, and due back in his office tomorrow, he was keen to make an early start in the morning. I almost breathed a sigh of relief when I saw him off a bit after nine o'clock. It allowed me to devote an hour or two to planning for my next meeting with Thomas Agnew, and imagining what the next instalment of Regina McGregor's story might bring.

Gathering Regina's story episode by episode was frustrating, and not the way I usually work. Thomas is an old man. But his mind still is sharp, and I want to know the whole story; to

119

collect every minute detail of Regina's life. I figured the best way to do it was over a series of short meetings, rather than one long marathon session. It would allow Thomas plenty of time between our meetings to dwell on the story and dredge up all those tiny, sometimes insignificant, details of her life.

*****

Once all the usual admin tasks were dealt with this morning, I opened my Regina McGregor file and read through the story I'd collected so far, making notes as I went, of further questions I might ask about some of the details. Time slipped away unnoticed. It was 9.30 by the time I realised how late it was. A feverish few minutes of stuffing things in my tote bag, and dashing to the bakery downstairs for something to take with me for morning tea followed, before galloping out to my car. Somehow, I managed to knock on Thomas' door right on the dot of ten o'clock.

"Aha, good girl; I see you've brought something to sustain us through the forthcoming ordeal," he said, and nodded towards the cake box I was carrying. "Come in, come in. I've just fired up the coffee machine, so we'll be fuelled up and ready to go in a few minutes." I followed him through to the kitchen and suggested it might be as good a place as any for us to sit this morning.

As he indulged in his second slice of cake, and I sipped my second mug of coffee, I felt myself growing impatient. I wanted to get on with the story, but was loath to rush him or be rude in any way. I needed him onside and wanting to tell me everything. With only a mouthful or two of cake left on his plate, he paused and put down his fork. When he looked up at me, his brow was furrowed and his eyebrows were drawn almost together across the bridge of his nose. He shook his head as if to clear away some unhappy thought. I almost went into panic mode. Had his memory let him down today, or worse, is he suffering a touch of Alzheimer's. Within a few moments, my panic subsided and my breathing returned to normal.

"Now, I'm afraid you're going to have to prompt me today. Where did we get to with Regina's story when we last left off, and did you want to continue from there today, or were you hoping to pursue some specific different line of enquiry?"

My relief was almost overwhelming. I wanted to race around the table and hug him. The thought of what the shock might cause an old man stopped me … and I didn't want to find myself applying CPR instead of hearing the rest of Regina's story.

"You were going to tell me about the last few times you saw Regina. I can't help wondering if there was something going on in her life which might help explain her sudden disappearance. Hmm…; maybe I should ask if her disappearance was sudden. Did you detect any warning signs something was amiss?"

"Oh, yes. Yes, I knew something was not right for a while before she disappeared … and, yes it was sudden. Of course I pressed her about what was wrong. It became obvious something serious was troubling her. She lost weight and looked drawn and haggard for a couple of months before she disappeared. We had established something of a ritual. Whenever she came to town, she always called in to see me, and not because she had a problem. The official reason for her visits was to check whether I had anything I wished to discuss with her. As I looked after her money and investments, her visits were out of courtesy; to see if everything was okay and none of her accounts were the cause of any concern for me."

"She sounds like a caring person who sought to avoid causing others problems."

"Regina was a true lady and, as you say, caring. I looked forward to her visits, however brief they might be on occasions. And, towards the end, they became brief, quite brief."

"No doubt her changed appearance alone was enough to prompt you to question her about the cause. Do you think she might have been ill, seriously ill, I mean? Something along those lines would have been my first conclusion about what was going on in her life."

"It was mine as well, but she insisted she wasn't ill. She did seem distracted whenever I saw her, and it persisted for at least a couple of months. In the end, I did manage to get her to open-up a bit to me about what was happening. A man had arrived on her doorstep some months previous to when she told me about it. He said his name was Raymond Clifford, and he claimed to be her son... the one she believed died shortly after birth. His story was along the lines of being adopted when he was only a few weeks old, and having found out about it just before his 'grandmother' died."

"Did she believe his story? Whether she did or not, his appearance must have been a terrible shock for her."

"You're right. He was a shock and, at first, I don't think she gave his story much credence. But, having experienced how ruthless her family could be towards her, she couldn't discount it without more information. Over the following couple of weeks, he appeared at the property on numerous occasions and went to great lengths to convince her of his identity. After his dying grandmother told him of his adoption, he challenged his parents about it.

His father point blank denied it, and was supposed to have given him a hard time for even suggesting such a situation. According to his story, he worked on his mother when the father wasn't around, and berated her until she finally admitted he was adopted. Although, she always maintained they never knew anything of his real parentage."

"God, I can't even imagine the turmoil his appearance must have caused her. You say she was sceptical at first, but it sounds as though he stuck around. And, in a similar way to how he worked on his adoptive mother, he worked on convincing Regina she was his birth mother."

"Yes. You see, there was so much about his story which was plausible – I mean, that is if Regina's son hadn't died, but was spirited away and put up for adoption by the family. While he appeared to be about the right age, his colouring made her suspicious. After she thought about it for a while, she realised she and her son's father were very different, both in build and colouring. In the end, I think she conceded that, although the man resembled neither of them to any great extent, it was possible he resulted from such a union.

When he first arrived and initiated his campaign to convince Regina he was her son, he found accommodation somewhere here in town. But, he showed up at the property just about every day. Without first seeking Regina's permission, he began helping out on the property – assisting the manager Regina employed to keep the place productive."

"His 'helpfulness' would have been a major part of his campaign to win her over; to have her at least like him a little, even if she didn't believe he was her son."

"I also believe it played a major part in the process ... And it seems to have worked. After only two or three months, Regina let slip to me that the man was now living on the property. While I don't know the details of how it came about, or how and where he was accommodated, I know it was only a few months later I learnt he was living in the big house. It's possible he was there from the outset, but I like to think it took her at least a while before she allowed him to live in her home."

"This is the first I've heard of this *prodigal son*. I found no mention of him in anything written about her disappearance. And, if he had embedded himself so neatly in the fabric of the place, how come he wasn't there when they were investigating her disappearance? How come HE didn't report her disappearance at once? As I understand it, Regina was gone from the property for some time before the police became aware it."

"The simple answer to those questions is: he wasn't there. He wasn't there for a little while before the last time I saw her, and I might well have been the last person to see her. I have to give him credit. His campaign seemed to be working to perfection. Not only was he living in the house with Regina, but he took over running the place. Oh, a manager was still employed, but he was 'manager' in name only. In reality, he was reduced to being nothing more than a worker. I never could determine whether Mr Clifford's elevation in the order of things was Regina's doing, or a self-assumed promotion."

"Regina strikes me as strong person, and I don't imagine the former manager of the place took too kindly to his virtual demotion. Surely Regina must have approved of what was going on."

"She was made of stern stuff but, as was evident in her earlier life, she also was intelligent enough to work out when 'swimming with the tide' – so to speak – was, if not the only option, the best option. When I quizzed her about it, or criticise the setup, she was reticent to discuss it, but never spoke favourably in support of it."

"Was this a case of some form of pressure being brought to bear; some form of control over Regina? Did Raymond Clifford threaten to reveal the skeleton hidden in Regina's and the Shelby family's cupboards for all those years?"

"It's possible I suppose, but I never heard anything to suggest it might be the case. All I know is, once he settled in on the property and seemed to take over the running of the place, I saw Regina less often. There were occasions when I saw her, or her vehicle, in town but she never came to see me."

"How unusual was it compared to the frequency of her visits prior Raymond Clifford's arrival?"

"Extraordinary... we became quite close after Silas McGregor died. Not only was I looking after her personal assets for her, but I like to think she valued my opinion on other matters as well, especially in regard to the running of the property. Then, over a period after his arrival, the frequency of her visits dropped off until they became at best sporadic. But, in the last few months before she disappeared, Regina's visits picked up again. I still didn't see her ever week, but she did visit my office two or three times a month. She was troubled. I sensed she wanted to talk to me – to tell me something. But, it seems I never asked the right question to force her to open up to me."

"If you were so close, and she valued your advice on running the property, I wouldn't have thought it so difficult for her to talk to you about whatever was bothering her. Was the situation showing any signs of resolving itself before she disappeared?"

Thomas nodded and stared off into the distance for a few moments before answering. "About three months before she disappeared, things improved. She started coming to see me again every week when she came to town. She still looked drawn and tense. Although her visits lasted as long as half an hour sometimes, our conversations were stilted somehow. It took a while for her to become more open with me."

"Were you aware of anything which might have brought about the change?"

"Well, it took me a while, and although I don't know what it was, I did manage to discover something had happened between Regina and Mr Clifford. The upshot of it was Clifford shot through. Just as he had appeared from out of nowhere, he disappeared again. At least, it is what Regina wanted me to believe. If I'm honest, our friendship had taken a beating in the early days after his arrival."

"Are you suggesting he somehow turned her against you – or at least against talking to you?"

"Oh, no, it was all my doing. My initial response to his presence was just to warn her to take care, and not to disclose too much to the man. Then, I noticed she had weakened and was starting to believe there might be some truth in the story he spun her. I became alarmed and counselled caution. In fact, I berated her about exercising the greatest caution possible until she found evidence to confirm his claims. I pushed too hard. She became annoyed with me, and accused me of treating her like some mindless adolescent. It led to a huge row on one occasion before I woke up to how my tactics were being counterproductive. I pulled back, but I think the damage was done, and I don't think I ever had the chance to undo it – not really."

"So, Raymond Clifford had rolled up his tent and vanished into the night, or somewhere equally mysterious. Damn! It's ruined a nice little theory I was developing. If he no longer was around, he couldn't be responsible for her disappearance... *Or could he?* Oh, now that is an interesting thought... I'm sorry. I was thinking aloud then. An idea just slid in from out of nowhere."

"Do you intend sharing it with me?"

"No, not just yet... It needs time to grow and develop before it is fit for exposure to others. Apologies for interrupting your story, we were at the point where Raymond Clifford vanished from Millhaven again."

The moment was lost. My stomach growled loudly, causing me to check my watch. It was after twelve o'clock already. There was every chance Thomas Agnew was feeling just as starved as I was. Just as I was about to apologise for having taken up so much of his time, a siren shattered the peace of the Millhaven Retirement Village. I looked at Thomas and shouted, "What's that all about?"

He didn't have to reply. I had no sooner asked the question than a tinny voice shouting *'evacuate, evacuate now'* filled the air. I shot Thomas a look, which I'm sure did nothing to hide my alarm. He shrugged and pushed himself up from the table.

"It's probably a drill – or maybe a false alarm. They spring surprise drills on us every so often, and it's a while since we had one. It's either that, or someone has burnt the toast again and set off a smoke alarm on the control board in the main office. I'm sorry, but I do have to be at the evacuation point before they start calling the roll – and find me missing. You should jump in your car and get out of here before life becomes complicated."

I threw my bag over my shoulder as I followed him out the door. As he shuffled away from me along the footpath, he called over his shoulder, "Call me to set up another meeting so we can finish the story."

Bemused by what had happened, I drove out of the village and headed for home and lunch.

Chapter 12

I was halfway home when Kirsty called. "Are you still intending to come out here today?"

"My concern was I would be in the way when all the stuff you had in storage arrived. You don't need someone else around when you're trying to work out where to put everything."

"The truck arrived just after eight o'clock this morning. Unloading it was a lot faster than I expected. Last night, I drew a plan of the building and worked out where the furniture was to go. When the truck arrived, all I had to do was show them where to put the various pieces as they unloaded them. The place almost looks lived in now, and it feels good having some favourite things around me again. So, are you coming out or not?"

"Well, right now, I'm on my way home to have lunch. Maybe after I have lunch, I'll take a drive out your way."

"No, don't do that. I haven't had lunch either. Come out here now, and I'll have lunch ready for both of us when you arrive."

With no room to argue and, as I had nothing else on my calendar for this afternoon, all I could do was to turn off at the next intersection and head for the property.

As I drove off the road, I noticed the track was showing some signs of all the traffic over it in the last few days. It wasn't in a bad state, but it had deteriorated since the first time I drove along it. Various vehicles were parked out front of the old house. I recognised both the forensic team's wagon and Emily's car. An obvious police vehicle was there, along with an unmarked sedan which I felt sure also belong to the detectives. I eased in to park beside the wall of the first outbuilding.

True to her word, Kirsty had lunch ready and waiting. The place looked so different now her furniture and other bits and pieces were added. We ate our lunch at a light-stained timber dining suite in the dining area adjacent to the kitchen. As soon lunch was finished, Kirsty was keen to show me through the rest of the place. The transformation was amazing. It now looked and felt like a home. I had no doubt she would be comfortable here for as long as it took for the old house to be refurbished and liveable again.

"If we can remember to load it into your car before you leave, you can take your camping stretcher home again. While I appreciate your lending it to me, I think I'm going to be happy sleeping in my own bed again tonight, as opposed to your creaking stretcher. Now, unless there is something I haven't shown you in here, let's see what treasures those outbuildings might contain."

Armed with torches and Kirsty's new pinch bar, we skirted around my car to the double doors on the first of the outbuildings. A bit of brute force applied via the pinch bar soon had the doors ready to be pushed open.

"Let's see if we had enough Weet-Bix today to be up to the job in hand." Kirsty shot me a wry grin and commented as she placed a tentative shoulder against one side of the door. When nothing happened, she added, "I knew this wasn't going to be easy, but I suspect it's going to be harder than I anticipated."

With a bit of effort and the two of us pushing and shoving, we managed to push the door in just far enough for us to slip inside through the gap. "These doors need to open out, not inwards," I told Kirsty. "They are big doors and, if they opened inwards, most of the internal space of the shed would need to be left empty. Now we are inside, we can push the other half of the door out. Then, this door we just pushed inside might be able to be pushed out too."

Opening the doors outwards required a lot less effort than pushing the first one inwards. After only a few minutes, both of the big doors stood wide open, and we were about to embark on the first of our treasure hunts.

We didn't have to go too far to find our first 'treasure'. Occupying centre stage in the shed was a large tractor. Although I don't know much about tractors, I suspect it was top of the range when it was bought. Kirsty, who knows a lot more about tractors than I do thanks to her degree in agriculture, seemed over the moon about our discovery. She walked around it peering into its workings at various places, poking and prodding things as she went.

"This is a gem – if it still goes. I suppose it might take a bit of work to get it running again after all these years, but it is in good condition and doesn't look like it's done a lot of work in its day. I wonder how hard it will be to get a diesel mechanic to come out to have a look at it," she added almost as an afterthought.

A deep workbench running across the end of the shed held various substantial looking tools, including a now caked-solid grease gun. "It might be easier to buy a new one than try coaxing it to work again," I suggested, gesturing at the grease gun.

"Hmm… Maybe… Leaving it outside in the sun on a couple of hot days might do the trick," she replied. As she inspected the offending item, she gestured towards the tractor and said, "Getting that beast going again will be my priority, not fussing about with the grease gun. I wonder if there are implements lying around somewhere. I can't say I've noticed any, but they could be hidden in the long grass."

All this was good to hear. Kirsty was shifting her focus from the old house and onto what was required to bring the property back into production. I couldn't help feeling it might be the first step in re-establishing the Kirsty I had known for all those years. After spending several minutes poking about in the shed, I was growing restless and was keen to move on. Kirsty wasn't done with this shed yet and continued to raise clouds of dust as she picked up just about every object on the workbench.

Attached to the wall at one end of the bench was a rack containing a number of 'pigeon hole' small bins, and affixed to the underside of the bench below the pigeon holes was a small drawer. Of course Kirsty wanted to open the drawer, but it was less so inclined. After a bit of tugging and a couple of rude words directed at it, the drawer conceded defeat and, grudgingly, ground its way to about half open.

Kirsty threw up her hands and sprung back. Judging by the look on her face, I expected to see a rat – or something worse – jump out at her. Instead, she thrust both hands into the drawer, pulled out its contents, and brandished it in the air like a winner's trophy.

"Look at this! I don't believe it. But I'm holding it, so it must be true. It's the workshop manual for the tractor. It's in pristine condition … well, apart from the dust. But, it's not been eaten or affected by the weather or anything else. It's amazing. This is like finding the pot of gold at the end of the rainbow." She added the last comment after noticing the bemused look on my face. I found it difficult – impossible – to muster an equivalent degree of excitement about a grubby old book. But, in the true spirit of supportive friendship, I didn't admit to it, and tried for an appropriate, and at least half-plausible, response to the find.

To my relief, at last, it was time to move on to the next building. I did see Kirsty casting longing looks back into the first shed as we exited and moved towards our next challenge. "I'll bring the pinch bar, just in case we need it again," I said as we moved off.

As I half expected, the pinch bar again was required, but the single door offered less resistance than the previous ones. Even with its door wide open, dust and cobwebs obscured the contents. We relied on our torches as we picked our way through equipment stored everywhere, some hanging on the wall, and other bigger items parked wherever there was free floor space. I recognised some of the tools: shovels, rakes, axes, an old-fashioned scythe, and what I thought were reaping hooks. Most of the rest of the equipment was beyond my ken.

A strange, large item propped against the wall had me intrigued. It looked like a corkscrew on steroids. "What on earth is this thing?" I asked.

"Postholes augur... You use it for boring postholes when you're working on the fences. It's an old-fashioned manual model you're looking at. It was driven by hard yakka and required a lot of grunting and sweating. The one over here [she shone her torch on it] is a more recent model. It's driven by a petrol engine, so less grunting required."

My lesson about posthole borers complete, I moved over to a pegboard attached to the rear wall, and took down a strange looking pair of pliers. I didn't know Kirsty was watching.

"Fencing pliers...," she informed me, "used for twitching the ends of the strands of wire together when you're fencing."

If I was to be educated about every strange looking object in this shed, we could end up spending the rest of the day in here. I felt compelled to attempt to rectify the situation. "Kirsty, fascinating as this tool shed might be, I'm in desperate need of a caffeine fix. Is it possible we might go back to your quarters for a coffee?"

With the aroma of freshly brewed coffee filling the building, and a plate of TimTams on the low table in front of us, we sipped our coffees in Kirsty's recently furnished sitting room. It had a relaxing, almost stupefying effect on me, and I suspected it was much the same for Kirsty.

As expected, our conversation centred the contents of the two sheds we explored. Kirsty remained almost euphoric about our finds so far, especially the tractor. Then, we turned our attention to speculating about what the rest of the buildings might contain. Time slipped away before we realised the end of the day was almost upon us.

"Should we try opening one more of those buildings before we call it a day?" Kirsty asked.

Of course we should. While I wasn't excited by the prospect of poking about in another dust and cobweb filled old building, I knew Kirsty was dying to do so. Armed with our trusty torches, we again skirted my car on our way around to the front of the line of old buildings.

The third building in the row looked much the same age as all the others. But, as we stood out front of it to conduct a visual assessment of how safe it might be to enter, I realised it differed a little from its fellow buildings. This one looked more… more rustic somehow than its neighbours. For a brief moment I wondered whether I should mention my thoughts to Kirsty, or if it would be best to keep my fanciful notion to myself. In the end, it wasn't a decision I needed to make.

Just as Kirsty announced, "Right, let's find out what this one has to surprise us," the sound of a vehicle and a cloud of dust making its way up the track caught our attention. "It looks like a farm quad bike," Kirsty said as she watched the machine take shape as it approached. "Whoever this is, I suspect they're not here because they're interested in the bones. Come on, let's go to meet them."

A wiry bloke with skin the colour and texture of old leather jumped off the bike the moment it stopped. He was dressed in what I suspected was typical farmer's uniform: high visibility shirt, jeans and work boots. He grabbed the battered felt hat out of the basket on the back of the bike and slapped it on his head before striding towards us with his hand outstretched to Kirsty. While I looked on oblivious to who or what was happening, Kirsty greeted the new arrival like a long lost friend. Then Kirsty remembered I was there.

"Oh, I'm sorry, Sonny. This is Neil Walker, my next-door neighbour. He is the good Samaritan who cleared the track up to the house for me." After completing the obligatory introductions, Kirsty continued. "So, Neil, what brings you here today? Is everything okay?"

"We-ell… that is the question I was going to ask you. Is everything all right over here? I couldn't help but notice the police were regular visitors over the last couple of days, and it got the better of me. I couldn't help myself. I had to come to see if you were okay. And, of course, I wanted to check on the condition of the track given all the traffic in and out of here since the heavy rain the other day."

"I appreciate your concern. As you can see, we are both alive and well. Don't worry about the cops being here. I think someone living here again has reminded them someone disappeared from here quite a while ago and has never been found. I imagine they'll have a bit of a poke about, and then lose interest again. How did you find the condition of the track? I thought it held up pretty well."

"Yeah, it's not bad. If the coppers are likely to be finished in the next day or so, I'll leave it until after they're gone before I run over it with the blade again. Apologies for interrupting whatever it was you were doing. I'll be off now and leave you to it."

"Truth be told, I think we were about to call it a day when you arrived. You don't happen to feel like a cold beer or a glass of wine, do you?"

Minutes later, the three of us were seated at the dining room table with our drinks and a platter containing crackers and a tub of dip. Conversation focused on Kirsty's achievements so far: power connected via builder's poles, new water supply installed, and her new 'temporary' accommodation which could be 'home' for quite some time to come. No mention was made of the bones found in the old house.

As we walked Neil back to his quad bike, Kirsty asked, "Neil, do you happen to know any good, reliable diesel fitters in Millhaven?"

"Why do you want to know about diesel fitters?"

Kirsty gave him a brief explanation of finding the tractor in the shed, and Neil asked if he might have a look at it.

"Sure; step this way please. You're not going to tell me you are a diesel fitter are you?"

"No, I wasn't going to do say that but, after all these years, I do know my way around a tractor quite well... And, I do know an excellent diesel fitter. I'll have a word to my son, Angus. If he can't make it before then, he might come over on the weekend to have a look at it."

After lifting the cover, moving various levers and pedals, and checking the tyres, Neil announced, "It looks in good nick after sitting around in here doing nothing for so long. Might not need much more than a full service to have it up and running again... I'll mention it to Angus at dinner tonight."

"My gratitude would know no bounds if he did take a look at it. But it would be a paying job. I'm not looking for favours. Please make it clear to him," Kirsty said.

We watched Neil head home along the track. As we turned to go back in to clear away after our drinks, I noticed those who had been working in the old house were preparing to leave. Emily came across to speak to us.

"A couple of people might be back in the morning to finish up here, but it's likely everyone will be gone by lunchtime. The police might continue to designate it a crime scene for another day or so. After that, everyone should be out of your hair and you should be able to go back into the house."

Kirsty invited her in for a drink before she left. Emily declined. "Tempting though it is, it would not be a good look for me to be fraternising with the landlord on whose property we have a crime scene. I'll take a raincheck though, and be back to collect on it after the crime scene tape comes down."

"I should be going too," I told Kirsty as I followed her inside to help clear away after our drink with Neil. It was almost five o'clock. Although I hadn't heard from Ben all day, I expected him to call soon to check on tonight's dinner arrangements. For some reason, I thought it would be best not to take his call in front of Kirsty.

Ben called as we were adding the last of the glasses to the dishwasher. I took the call on the landing outside the front door. He wouldn't be joining me for dinner tonight. After being away last week, he was still trying to catch-up on everything which had piled up on his desk in his absence. Eating alone tonight suited me fine. I could transcribe today's meeting with Thomas Agnew... and it meant I didn't have to make a rushed departure to be home on time.

When I went back inside, Kirsty asked if I was working tonight, or if I could stay to have dinner with her. The temptation was to lie and claim I would be working. Transcribing the recording of today's meeting was 'work', but I sensed Kirsty's invitation wasn't just out of politeness. She wanted company. So, I agreed to stay. After all, I could try to leave early and still do some work afterwards.

"Would steak and salad be all right for dinner?" she asked. I could do something else if you would prefer. I just happen to have a couple of nice looking steaks I'm keen to try."

"Steak and salad will be perfect. I could do with a bit of a clean-up before dinner though. I keep a set of clothes and a towel in a bag in my car. In my line of work, you never know when you might need them. So, if I could borrow your shower...?"

The water pressure was so good, it felt like being bombarded by thousands of needles, and left me feeling scrubbed clean and invigorated. When I returned to the kitchen, Kirsty had the steaks out on the bench to come to room temperature, and fresh glasses on the breakfast bar.

"I thought we might have another drink before worrying about making dinner. It would be great if this place had a deck, or some other outside area. Somewhere to relax, have a drink, or just watch the sun go down. In the absence of anything of such nature, we will have to make do with the sitting room."

About half an hour later, the steaks were sizzling and I was making the salad. "You were lucky to have the power connected so soon," I commented. "People complain about having to wait weeks – even months sometimes – for the utilities company to do anything."

"Yep, I picked two good operators. Both Bill Branigan and Les Stanley seemed to be able to make things happen without appearing to expend much effort while about it."

There were so many questions I wanted to ask, but it was time to put questions aside and start eating. As I carried the salad to the table, I felt my stomach rumble in anticipation, and the smell of the steaks had my tastebuds up and paying attention. Minutes later, done medium-rare and finished with a dollop of garlic butter on top, the steaks were living up to my expectations. The salad and crusty bread were perfect accompaniments. Bowls of fruit salad topped with a scoop of ice cream rounded off our meal. Then, we took our coffees and glasses of port through to the lounge, along with a platter of cheese and crackers to help fill any gaps left after our meal.

After about half an hour of revisiting old memories, and catching up on recent news of names associated with those memories, it was inevitable talk would return to recent events in Kirsty's life. Events which saw her return to Millhaven. I admit to being responsible for reintroducing the topic

"At the risk of stating the obvious, Girlfriend, this lifestyle change you've embarked on sounds a mammoth undertaking, and a hell of an expensive one. Your inheritance didn't include a bucket of cash too did it?"

"There wasn't anything quite so useful as far as I know, but I am aware of a little cash involved. Although I still don't know the full extent of the bequest, I doubt there would be a lot of cash. I'm sure someone would have told me about it by now if there were. Anyway, within reason, the cash thing isn't a concern. I sold two properties in Sydney. The current Real Estate market saw them sell for eye-watering prices, and allowed obscene nett amounts to be added to my bank accounts."

"Burning your bridges, so to speak, on leaving Sydney was a brave move. Do you have any second thoughts about making such a rash move before you fully understood what might lie ahead for you in Millhaven?"

"None at all… I knew I wanted out of Sydney and, regardless of what happened, I did not want to live there again. In reality, it didn't matter where I ended up, I would need to spend money on somewhere to live. So, it might as well be in Millhaven. Don't look so shocked. By the time I decided to sell, I already knew I might inherit this property. It wasn't as though I didn't think about my future and having nothing to support me."

"Did your relationship break down as a result of your desire to escape Sydney, or was it one of the deciding factors?"

"Have you ever experienced the end of a long-term relationship you thought would last forever?"

"I am a widow, and have been for a long time now. So, yes, I think I do know what it's like."

"Sorry; I didn't mean to open old wounds, but I didn't know you were married."

After reassuring her about my husband's death having been so long ago, I didn't have a problem with its being mentioned, she seemed more at ease and open to discussing her relationship breakdown. She took a deep breath before launching into it.

"My situation was a bit different. We had been 'an item' for about nine years, and lived together for about seven of those years. Marriage was not something we discussed. Perhaps I was naïve enough to believe the relationship was so solid, we didn't need a legal contract to keep us together. Oh, don't get me wrong, those years weren't all sweetness and light. If I'm honest ... and I find I can be honest these days ... there were occasions when I loathed having him around. But, apart from all the emotional stuff, we were partners in a business we set up. Escaping was never going to be easy to achieve."

"If my memory serves me correctly, you studied agricultural science – or something along those lines. Was he an agricultural scientist too?"

"Your memory is spot on, and I continued to work in my chosen field right up until I left Sydney to come here. But, early in my career, I managed, part-time, to complete a degree in Information Technology. It's how we met. He was working in IT and I encountered him during some of the work placement I did as part of my degree. The business we set up together was in IT. He specialised in hardware, while my particular area of expertise was software and programming – although we both could work in each other's area if we had to."

"So, when you left Sydney, you left behind, a long-term – now defunct – relationship, a business, and your long-held employment. I'm not sure I could be so brave as to throw it all away without a well-thought out plan for my future."

"You had to be living it to understand it. It was the only decision to make, and it was the right decision." She gave me a wry smile as she finished speaking. I wondered who she was trying to convince: me or her.

Our conversation had opened up old wounds. Kirsty fell silent and kept her eyes on her hands clasped in her lap, where one hand was attacking the cuticle of the thumb on the other hand. Whether out of cowardice or because it presented as an ideal opportunity, I made noises about needing to take myself home to attend to some work before tomorrow. It wasn't a complete lie. I did want to revisit today's meeting with Thomas Agnew to work out what more I needed to know, and to develop a list of appropriate questions to ask to elicit the details I wanted.

It was about nine o'clock by the time I arrived home, and I almost had to physically drag myself into my office to start work. Once I made a start, I became engrossed in Regina's story. Speculating about what else there might be to learn about the lady's tragic life saw time slip by unnoticed. It was after midnight when I fell into bed.

Chapter 13

My first priority today was to arrange yet another meeting with Thomas Agnew. Should I aim for morning coffee with him again, or take him to lunch somewhere? With nothing pressing to deal with this morning, coffee might be the better option, and would then leave the rest of the day free. I made a mental note to call him between eight and nine o'clock.

Everything was a struggle this morning. After a disturbed night's sleep, I wasn't firing on all cylinders. The same nightmare returned to wake me three times. All night, I was chased by the same driverless tractor and being attacked by a rampant unmanned posthole augur. As I don't recall yesterday's time at the property being so confronting as to cause my rough night, I'll file last night away as just another psychological mystery.

Thomas was available this morning. I arranged to collect him at ten o'clock and bring him to a new little coffee shop in the city heart. While it did involve a bit more messing about, it seemed the least I could do to make up for my continued demands on his time. He was standing at his door waiting for me.

As soon as we ordered, I initiated what I expected would be the last episode in the Regina McGregor story. "Thomas, yesterday you said you felt your constant counselling of Regina to be cautious of Raymond Clifford might have strained your relationship with your client. How did it manifest itself, and did it inhibit your ability to act on her behalf? Or, did it become so bad, she felt compelled to dispense with your services?"

"Oh no, it was not so cataclysmic as to require such drastic action. It was more a case of… I'm not sure how to explain it other than to say she stopped treating me as a friend, and started treating me as her solicitor. I'm not sure it makes any sense to you, but it's the best explanation I can manage."

"Did the 'strained relationship' persist, or was it resolved at some point?"

"After a few months, things seemed to return to normal. At first, I thought, thanks to the solid underlying friendship we shared, the situation had resolved itself. A little while later, I discovered I had help from strange quarters to re-establish the *status quo*. On one of her visits, she looked haggard. Although she insisted she was fine and there was no need for concern, I saw the bruises, and challenged her about them."

"I suspect this story is going somewhere I wished it didn't. Did she open up to you about the bruises? Were they Mr Clifford's handiwork?"

"With persuasion, she did admit to what had been happening. Yes, you were correct. It appears Mr Clifford had been trying to take over the property… not just to manage the place, but to wrest control of it from Regina and assume ownership. When she discovered what he was up to, she took measures to prevent it, but not through legal channels via me. She stopped the bank and suppliers accepting anything bearing his signature. Life became difficult for him and his grand scheme was unravelling. He resorted to physical abuse to force her to comply."

"Not again…! It was bad enough when her husband belted her about, but you couldn't standby and do nothing while a supposed son did the same."

"There wasn't much I could do, I'm sad to say. The moment I saw the bruises and she admitted what was happening, I attempted to call the police. She stopped me. He had gone. Raymond Clifford had gone; vanished in much the same mysterious way as he had appeared. My concern was he would return with a vengeance, and I didn't like to think about the outcome of such a situation."

"What did she tell you about his departure? Was it a sudden thing, or was there some 'arrangement' involved?"

"She said there had been an almighty row late one afternoon. She told him she knew what he was up to, and he could either provide some evidence to prove he was her son or leave the property and never return. He screamed abuse at her, and was angrier than she had ever seen him before. Frightened, she started moving towards the door in a bid to escape the kitchen where the argument happened. He grabbed a frying pan off the sink and came at her with it. She ducked and sidestepped, and his blow with the frying pan fell on air.

Although she wasn't injured, she found herself jammed up against the end of the kitchen cupboards and unable to get away… and standing next to the rifle she left there after shooting a hawk trying to steal her chickens earlier in the afternoon.

As he came at her again with the frying pan, she raised the rifle and fired. The shell hit the frying pan and ricocheted off into one of the walls. He wasn't injured, but the shot stopped him in his tracks. She sent him packing but, as it was dark by then, she allowed him spend the night in one of the outbuildings. But, made it clear he had to be off the property first thing in the morning."

"I'm not sure allowing his to stay the night was a wise move. If he were so violent towards her, anything could have happened during the night."

"My understanding was she left him in no doubt what would happen if he came near her or the house again before he left. And, if he were still there in the morning, she would call the police to have him removed. He seems to have understood the message. The next morning, she was cautious about venturing outside in case he was still hanging around. She waited until her workman arrived and she saw him at the shed before she ventured out.

After calling him over to the house and explaining she had told Clifford to pack his bags and be gone, the workman checked all the outbuildings and anywhere else he thought someone might hide. There was no sign of Clifford. They believed he departed sometime during the night."

"Good for her. She was doing okay before he arrived, and I'm sure she would do so after he left. How long after his departure was it when Regina disappeared?"

"Well, no one is sure about when she disappeared. The workman, who resumed as the farm manager after Clifford left, didn't see her every day. It was more a case of only seeing her if he had a problem, or she wanted to speak to him. The rest of the time, he just got on with his work without needing to check-in with his boss."

"Tell me about how Regina's apparent disappearance was discovered, and how long after Clifford's departure it was before anyone discovered she was missing."

"To answer the last part first, it might have been up to six weeks after the incident with Clifford. How it was discovered was tragic. Prior to Clifford's arrival, the property manager was paid in cash, and Regina placed his pay packet in a particular place in one of the outbuildings for him to collect. After Clifford left, payday reverted to the original arrangement.

When payday came round at the end of the fortnight, and his pay packet wasn't there, the manager was concerned. Rather than confront Regina about it, and in the belief she simply had lost track of the days, he decided to wait a couple of days to see if his pay turned up. From memory, I think he waited four days before going to the house to ask Regina about it. She wasn't there and, when she still wasn't there a couple of days later, he raised the alarm."

"Is that when the police were called in to investigate?"

"No, not right away... I made up the manager's pay for her. When I realised Regina hadn't collected the manager's pay from me to take home to him, I assumed she had forgotten or lost track of the date. So, I took his pay out to the property and gave it to him. While I was there I was going to check if Regina was okay. The manager told me she wasn't at home, and he hadn't seen or heard her about the place for a few days. I remembered she spoke of maybe going to visit someone she knew years ago. Later, I realised the trip occurred sometime earlier. She already had told me about it. Anyway, the upshot was we agreed to wait a few more days before becoming too concerned.

142

Nevertheless, the manager knew Regina supplied places in town with eggs and vegetables on a weekly basis, and went to speak to them. They told him, when their usual deliveries hadn't arrived for the second week in a row, they tried calling her. Their calls continued to go unanswered. The manager went to the police."

"So, Regina could have been missing for a couple of weeks at least by the time the police went to investigate."

"While we expected they would follow-up on it straight away, the police didn't consider immediate action necessary. It was several days later, and only after considerable hounding by a few concerned people – including me before the police decided the situation was serious enough to investigate. They believed there was some logical explanation for Regina's absence. Perhaps she went away for a few days without telling anyone. But, when they went to investigate, she wasn't there, and was never there again."

I saw Thomas swallow hard a couple of times after I noticed the tide rise in his eyes. After all these years, Regina's disappearance remained hard for him to discuss. Quite a close friendship must have existed between them over the years for him still to feel her loss. I allowed him a few moments of silence to collect himself before continuing.

"Were you satisfied with the police's response – their investigation – once they saw fit to take action?"

"Argh, I think they were thorough and efficient. You know how it is. When the outcome isn't the one you wanted, you blame someone for it. The police came in for a lot of criticism when they reported they found nothing conclusive to explain her disappearance. In the first instance, I was as vocal as anyone about it, but I soon realised they did all they could."

We appeared to have reached the end of Regina's story. Nothing had changed. Regina McGregor was still missing, and her disappearance remained a mystery. The only change was, I had joined the ranks of those friends and associates who struggled with the loss of a fine lady all those years ago. While

I fought to control my frustration, there were still questions I needed to ask. After signalling for fresh coffees, I resumed the interview.

"Thomas, one thing has me curious. A wall was erected at one end of the front room of the old house. Do you know when or why it was built?"

"Oh yes, the unfinished wall…"

"I'm sorry; the what…?"

"Yeah, Regina mentioned the wall to me. It would have been a little while before Clifford left. She came home from a visit to town one day and found he had started building a wall across one end of the room. He claimed he needed an office and, while it would be smaller than he wanted, it would be his office. She was not happy about it. I gather she told him to take it down and not to do anything similar in future without her permission.

A right royal argument followed, but the upshot was the wall was never finished. As I understood, the framework remained in place but it had never been clad, and the space had never been used as an office."

"Do you know if it remained unfinished, or if the framework was still standing, after he left?"

He appeared to give it some thought before answering. "Uhmm… I believe so. I recall asking her if the eyesore were still there. She said it was, but she was going to ask the farm manager to take it down. I remember she giggled, and said the wall seemed to be of such shoddy construction, she could probably take it down herself if she attacked it with a hammer."

"Okay, now I know about the wall." The argument raging in my mind was whether to tell him about how we found the wall, or to let him go on thinking the wall was never completed. I opted for the latter. But, Thomas' comments about the wall opened a whole new can of worms.

If there was nothing but the framework in place when Clifford left, at what point, and by whom, was the wall completed. My gut suggested the wall was part of a plan developed long before

Regina threw Clifford off the place. Did he return? Thomas hadn't mentioned it. Maybe I should jog his memory.

"Would you mind if we return to Regina's story for a moment?" He agreed and I continued. "Is there any chance Clifford returned to the property at some time after Regina ran him off? I mean, could he have come back onto the property with or without Regina's knowledge?"

"It's an interesting question. My answer has to be, I don't know. And, it would be the truth because, while there were some grounds to believe he might have come back, I don't *know* he did."

"Perhaps you might share what those grounds in support of his return were."

"Once the news of Regina's disappearance broke, speculation was rife throughout the community. Although most of it was rubbish, some of the stuff I heard made me wonder. A couple of the business people in town who knew Clifford (the postmistress and the manager of the hardware store) claimed to have seen him in town just prior to the time when Regina most likely disappeared. I know they told the police about their sightings of the man, and I'm sure the police looked into it during their investigation, but nothing came of their claims. It's an unusual question for you to ask. What is behind it?"

"While I'd love to give you a considered and logical explanation for my question, I'm afraid it stems from nothing more than my speculation about the incident. And, as you say, there has been enough of it in the community already without my adding to it."

Thomas had glanced at the clock on the wall a couple of times over the previous few minutes. I didn't have to be a genius to work out there was somewhere he needed to be.

"Goodness, look at the time... I do apologise, Thomas, I hadn't intended to take up so much of your morning. But, it has been wonderful to hear the last of Regina's story ... And frustrating to know there is no more to be told. As it's almost lunchtime, we could stay and have a bite to eat here, or I could take you home. Whichever you prefer is fine with me."

"Thank you for your most generous offer of lunch, but I do have another luncheon engagement to attend back at the village. So, if you don't think me too rude, would you mind taking me home?"

It was with some degree of relief I dropped Thomas at his front door. Although there was so much more I wanted to know, I had run out of questions – and I don't think he had anything further to offer. This must be how those close to Regina, and probably much of the community, felt after her disappearance. It wasn't hard to understand how speculation ran rife after the police investigation failed to find any answers.

After engaging the parking brake, I looked around in surprise. I was parked behind my office building in the city, and had no recollection of a conscious decision to come here after dropping Thomas at his cottage. Nevertheless, I'm here now, so I should grab some lunch and go up to my office to do some work. The blinking red light on the answering machine welcomed me.

Kirsty had left a message not long after I went to collect Thomas for coffee. I thought it strange she didn't call my mobile, and dug it out of my bag to check if I had missed her call. No call, and no surprise – I turned my mobile off before I started interviewing Thomas. I turned it back on and waited. Yes, there was a missed call from Kirsty and a voice message. The same message as she left on the answering machine.

"Where are you today? Will you be coming out to the property, or are you working?"

Damn; did I promise to go there again today? I couldn't remember, but I did not feel in the least bit inclined to do so. Not only did I have the recording of today's meeting to transcribe, but I wanted to spend a large slab of quiet time digesting all I learned from Thomas this morning. And now I felt guilty about letting her down. I heaved a sigh and reached for the phone.

"Hi, I just picked up your messages after coming back to my office. I could come out this afternoon, but only for a couple of hours. Was there anything in particular you wanted to do today?"

"No, nothing urgent; I thought we might investigate the rest of those outbuildings. But, if you're working and can't make it, don't worry about it."

Now the guilts really kicked in. Of course, I was going to the property and would see her in about half an hour. It gave me time for a quick check on my emails before I was in my car again and heading out of the city. From the moment I turned onto the track, the lack of vehicles parked out front of the old house caught my attention. Kirsty's car was the only one there. The sound of my vehicle on the track brought Kirsty out to meet me.

"Have you had lunch," she asked as I climbed out of the car. I nodded. "Good; so have I, but I was going to indulge in a coffee before we started work. Can I interest you in one too?"

Of course she could, so I perched at the breakfast bar while she made it. When I left the place yesterday, Kirsty was quite upbeat. I felt finding the tractor and all the other equipment might have been a turning point, and she now might be starting to come to terms with her new situation. The absence of police and forensic personnel today also might be assisting with her renewed outlook on life.

The coffee was good ... I was a bit braindead and exhausted after the couple of hours spent interviewing Thomas ... and, Kirsty's lounge chair was comfortable. She didn't appear in a hurry to go exploring sheds, and perhaps it was just as well. If she decided to dash out and start work, I would struggle to drag myself out of my chair. I think I almost achieved semi-stupor state as she nattered on about how great it would be to have the tractor serviceable again and be able to do something on the property herself – like grading her own track instead of depending on others to do it.

Some part of my mind noted silence had descended over us. I realised Kirsty had stopped speaking ... and probably was waiting for me to contribute something to the conversation. I said the first thing to float through to the front of my mind.

"I noticed you are alone out here today, but the crime scene tape is still in place. Did anyone come today?"

"Yep, they all were here again – all except Emily. Police and the forensic team blokes were here from about eight o'clock this morning. I'm not sure what time they left, but the last of them was gone by eleven. One of the police came to tell me they had completed their investigation and it was unlikely they would be back. The site remained a crime scene though for at least another day or two in case they needed to do more work. Someone will come to remove the tape when they are satisfied there is nothing more to be done here."

Although quite a bit of time had been wasted, the caffeine was starting to work its magic and my synapses were starting to fire again. "If we are going to look at sheds, we should make a start on it. I need to be away from here by four o'clock at the latest, I announced.

Kirsty glanced at her watch. "Let's not bother. It's almost three o'clock and hardly worth getting filthy for about an hour's work. You look tired. If you want to leave before four o'clock, I won't be offended." I assured her I was fine and asked about the pile of paper on the table in the dining area.

"Remember the old map of this property – well, more of a plan really –Nathan dug out of their archives for me? I was trying to work out how it related to the bit I know of the place so far. Do you feel up to helping me work it out?"

As neither of us had seen anything of the property other than the part visible from the track, and the immediate surrounds of the old house, trying to make sense of the drawing was an exercise in futility. Kirsty became frustrated.

"This drawing isn't useful in any way. I don't know why he bothered giving it to me," she wailed.

"I'm not surprised. It's old. I doubt much of the place remains as it was then. Even the fence lines probably are different now.

You might just have to wait until your tractor is mobile again and you are able use it to inspect the property."

With little else to discuss, Kirsty walked me to my car. Her mood still seemed positive, but frustration creeping in wasn't good. "So, now everyone has deserted the place, what are your plans for tomorrow, tomorrow being Friday and almost the end of another week?"

"No firm plans but, as I still can't go back into the house, I'll have to find something to do out here. Before you go, I was thinking… now I have my furniture and everything in my new quarters, how about you and Emily come and stay for the weekend? We could make a sort of housewarming of it. And, I suppose it depends on whether either or both of you are free or working on the weekend."

"As far as I know, I won't be working. I'll talk to Emily to see if it suits her too. It sounds like it should be a good weekend."

My phone played its tune as I was about to turn off the track and onto the road into town; Ben.

"Are you working tonight?"

"At home tonight… and please bring food. Any food would be good tonight."

He chuckled and said, "Okay see you around seven o'clock – or maybe a bit before."

Did I need company tonight? I remained ambivalent about the prospect of an evening with Ben. But, we hadn't spent much time together over the last week, and I did want to know if their work at the old house had turned up anything interesting. Maybe I would feel more enthusiastic after a shower and a few quiet moments alone before he arrived.

Chapter 14

The couple of hours before Ben arrived with dinner were devoted to transcribing the recording of this morning's meeting with Thomas Agnew. It appeared this was my last interview with Thomas. We had reached the end of the story. But had we? As I told myself it was the last of it, a nagging doubt crept in.

What more could there be to know about Regina or her disappearance? My gut sent a prompt reply: what happened after her disappearance was discovered? Who did or said what? What did they find? In general terms, what is the story of the aftermath of her disappearance? Perhaps I would be talking to Thomas again, and sooner than expected.

Another stray thought wandered in as I readied myself to start transcribing. If Thomas managed Regina's affairs before her disappearance, what happened afterwards? If she were declared dead, the terms of her will would kick in. Had she been declared dead? If she wasn't, was Thomas still managing her estate? And, what about the property, how was it being managed now?

Questions were not in short supply this evening, but answers were non-existent. Yep, I would be talking to Thomas again – and soon. As a result of the myriad of questions I conjured up, instead of getting on with the transcription, I slumped back and slid down in my chair. Some of those questions were begging for more thought. Where to start? Which one do I select first?

Something touching my shoulder made my eyes snap open. "Are you all right?" Ben asked. "If you need sleep, for goodness sake, go to bed and be comfortable. I can put your dinner in the fridge and go home. It won't be a problem."

"What time is it," I mumbled.

"Just after seven o'clock… Are you sure you're okay?"

"Apologies; I wasn't aware of being tired. The last thing I remember is sitting here doing some heavy-duty thinking about an investigation."

"Must be a riveting investigation if it sent you to sleep."

"Frustrating more like; too many questions and no answers. But, now you're here, we should eat. What have you brought me tonight?"

"Roast lamb with all the trimmings from the new place in the city heart... and a nice bottle of red to help it go down. I could go and open the wine while you try becoming mobile again. Watch your back as you do. It's likely to be stiff and locked after being in that position for so long."

"I had a mother. I don't need another one," I snarled at his back. On his way to the kitchen, he either didn't hear, or chose to ignore my bitchiness.

After putting our roast dinner in the oven to keep warm, we took our glasses of wine out onto the deck. It was a black night. No stars winked at us as we settled ourselves. The heavy cloud cover which rolled in during my snooze made the night air heavy and still. None of the usual perfumes wafted in tonight, and I noticed the wildlife seemed strangely silent. The crickets which inhabit my rosemary hedge chose not to serenade us. For me, it was altogether too depressing out on the deck. My glass was still half full when I suggested we go back inside.

"Our dinners could dry out and spoil if we leave them in the oven for too long. Perhaps we should go in and get on with the business of eating."

The roast lamb was delicious and done to perfection. Thanks to the food, and perhaps the wine, I felt myself resuming my place in the human race. As soon as we had eaten and cleared the table, we took bowls of fruit salad and mugs of coffee through to the lounge room. We no sooner settled in our chairs than the interrogation commenced.

"What's this investigation you're working on, the one which sent you to sleep earlier?"

"Well, I'm not actually working on an investigation. I was supposed to begin a new job earlier this week, but it didn't happen. The client delayed the start for a couple of days, and said he would contact me as soon as it was right for me to start. On my way home, I realised it's almost a week since my last contact with him. I'll need to talk to him tomorrow, because it's not possible over the weekend. Everything about it is strange so far. If I manage to talk to him tomorrow, and it still doesn't make any sense, I think I'll cancel the job."

"This is not like you. If something about a job doesn't smell right, you usually don't waste time dumping it. Is there something about this one to suggest it needs different treatment?"

"No, I don't suppose so. I suspect the problem is a client who is uncomfortable discussing the work he wants done. Don't get me wrong. There is nothing iffy about the job. He's just not comfortable discussing it… it's not useful when you're trying to work out what it is he wants you to do."

There were no lies in anything I told Ben about the job which seemed to be in a holding pattern at the moment. Talking about it gave the other half of my brain time to think about whether to discuss Regina's story with Ben yet, or if I should wait until I found a few more answers. *A few more answers…* what a joke. I don't have *any* answers. If I share what I know so far, he will have loads of questions – and will expect answers. No, best I do a bit more digging before I discuss any of it with Ben.

To shift the focus from me and my investigation, to Ben and what his mob had been up to, I said, "I noticed your officers are finished with Kirsty's old house. Did they find anything enlightening, or even vaguely interesting?"

"Not a damned thing worth mentioning. I suppose it's no surprise, given it all happened so long ago. Still, I had hoped our more advanced technologies might turn up something. All we can do now is to wait for Emily's team to complete their analyses."

"Disappointing but, as you say, not surprising. Although Kirsty will be pleased to have the old house handed back to her, I suspect the lack of answers will continue to gnaw at her for some time. All I can do is try to keep her outlook on life buoyed up until she is back on an even keel. I still haven't found out what went on in Sydney but, whatever it was, I think it came close to tipping her over the edge."

Mental note to self: coax Kirsty to open up about what went on in Sydney to make her determined to leave the city at any cost. Perhaps the weekend's housewarming might provide the opportunity.

Ben didn't stay late. I think he still believed I was exhausted and needed sleep, so he was gone by around 9.30. I allowed him to maintain such thinking, as I thought it might prompt his early departure and I could go back to my office and have another go at being productive this evening.

As I walked him to his car, a question flew out of my mouth before I even thought about it. "Ben, when they demolished the wall to be able to remove the bones, did they remove the whole wall?"

"No; only the middle section to gain access to the cavity. About half of the wall is still standing, split equally on either side of the bit they removed. It's sound enough not to topple over on anyone who ventures near it. Why do you ask?"

"Just curious; I wondered if they'd found a door or an opening of any sort."

"No openings were found. Although, I suppose there could be something in either parts of the wall which are still standing. Yeah, it's interesting there wasn't a door."

I suspected his last comment would stay with him all the way home... and so it should. The lack of an opening into the cavity struck me as more than 'interesting'. I tapped on the window and gesture for him to roll it down so I could indulge an afterthought. "When are you likely to remove the crime scene tape at Kirsty's place?"

"Depends on when we have Emily's report ... perhaps late tomorrow, or maybe over the weekend. Is it important? Does it matter when it comes down?"

"Not important at all... Kirsty has invited me to spend the weekend. I've other things I could be doing, but I'm keen to support her while she finds her feet again. I'm sure the crime scene tape will come up in conversations."

He stopped his window when it was halfway up again. "Will you still be here tomorrow night?"

"Yes. I won't go out there until Saturday morning."

'Okay; all being well, I'll see you tomorrow night. Now, go to bed and get some sleep. Don't go back into your office."

"Yes, Sir." I flicked him a mock salute as his window rolled all the way up.

The first heavy drops of rain fell as I watched his taillights disappearing down the driveway. I felt the breeze stiffen, and raced inside to close up before the squall hit. As I was on my way through the kitchen to my office (I had no intention of going to bed yet), the power went off.

"Thank you very much," I told the universe. "Now I am going to bed. How much did Ben pay you to do this?" Oh, God, it is time I went to bed. I'm standing in a dark kitchen talking to an empty house.

*****

A gloomy day greeted me this morning. After sleeping later than usual, I became one of a slow-moving tide of cars oozing its way towards the city. This was a definite day for something from the bakery and a newspaper to accompany me to my office. And another coffee was the next priority.

The client I hadn't heard from in days called while I was waiting for my coffee to be ready. Without any apology or pre-amble, he updated me regarding the job he engaged me to carry out.

"As I told you the other day, my wife came home from holidays and went down with flu the next day. She has been quite ill, and yesterday it worsened to the extent she was admitted to hospital. It developed into pneumonia. They expect she will be in hospital for three or four days, so she won't be going anywhere for a while. I'll let you know when the situation changes and you can begin surveillance."

While I was happy to have heard from him, I was no happier about taking the case. The more I had to do with this client, the less I liked him. I found myself feeling sympathy for his wife. If she had managed to find some degree of happiness with someone else, good for her... and I hope they make a go of it. Such biased feelings before I even begin following his wife are not good. I'll leave it until after the weekend but, come Monday, I'll tell him I'm no longer interested in taking his case.

"Right; yesterday's meeting with Thomas Agnew," I announced to the empty office, "transcribe the damned recording before something else gets in the way."

It is not easy to eat custard tarts or drink coffee while trying to type. As a result, an hour later, a mile of recording still remained to transcribe. Once I dealt with the tarts and the coffee, I started making some progress, and all those questions from last evening returned to haunt me. 'The wall' managed to trump everything else.

My gut kept telling me I knew more about the wall than I thought. Resigned to the fact I wasn't making progress with the transcription, I abandoned it and sat back to ponder everything I'd heard about the strange wall in the front room of the old house.

One of the first things the little voice in my head told me was I had neglected to ask Ben if there was any indication of the age of the wall. "Sonny, old girl, you are slipping," I chastised myself aloud.

Should I call him now or wait until tonight? Tonight was the safer option. He would not appreciate being disturbed by something so left-field and inconsequential. And, calling him would open the door to something akin to the Inquisition. He would be around to my office in a flash, and I would spend the morning plying him with cake and coffee while he interrogated me about all I learned from Thomas Agnew. I'm reluctant to share any of it with Ben yet. First, I need to have my head around it so I can sound knowledgeable when I do so.

The morning was slipping away, and I still hadn't told Emily of Kirsty's invitation to spend the weekend at the property. Aware she would either be busy in the lab or writing Ben's report on the bones, I left her a message to call me when she was free.

With everything else attended to, the logical thing to do was to return to transcribing the recording. It wasn't about to happen. My mind refused to focus on the recording. The little voice in my head kept nudging back to *the wall*. I gave in to it. After pushing back from the desk and putting my feet up, I gave my mind free-rein to explore whatever took its fancy. No surprises; without hesitation it returned to the wall in the old house.

Why did it matter when the damned thing was built? It was there and it served a purpose. Was it the wall's intended purpose all along? What did Thomas tell me about the wall? Bugger… if I had finished transcribing the recording, I would be able to look up his exact words. After exercising my powers of recall to their fullest, all I achieved was acceptance I needed to go back and finish the transcription.

Five minutes of typing later, an incoming call caused a further delay. It was Kirsty enquiring as to whether I intended coming out to the property again today. "No, I can't make it today, but I will be there first thing in the morning. Was there any particular reason you might have wanted me to be out there today?"

"No, no reason. I have a few things to do in town and thought I might do them today, unless you were coming out. In which case, I would leave the trip to town until Monday."

"Okay, it looks as though you're safe to come to town today. Is there anything you would like me to bring for the weekend?" She assured me there wasn't, and the call ended moments later.

As Kirsty's call ended, my phone demanded attention again. This time it was Emily. I realised she was calling during her coffee break, so I passed on Kirsty's invitation and kept discussions to a minimum. She thought she might be free tonight, and would join us for dinner if she was.

I checked the time. The temptation was to stop for either another coffee or lunch. It was too late for coffee, but too early for lunch. So, with no other excuse for procrastination available, I returned to pounding the keyboard. It was a late lunch, but the transcription was complete. After a quick trip down to the deli for a chicken and salad roll, I settled in one of the lounge chairs in my interview corner. As I dispatched my lunch, I contemplated the words so recently typed in relation to the wall.

What did I know about the wall? It was started before Raymond Clifford departed the property, supposedly to create his office. Regina was unhappy about its construction. If Thomas' memory is correct, the wall remained unfinished after Clifford left the property. When was the wall finished, and by whom?

If she were unhappy about its presence, it's unlikely Regina completed the wall. If she did, I was sure she would have incorporated a door or some form of access to the space behind it. No, I'm inclined to think she would have demolished it, rather than completing it. Other than Regina, who else would know what was happening on the property at the time? What about the farm manager Regina employed after her husband died?

According to Thomas' account, he was still there after Regina ran Clifford off the place. Was he privy to what might have been happening in the house? Like a whack over the head with something solid, the BIG question managed to slam through the fog to make its presence felt: was the farm manager still around? For a brief moment I wondered whether Thomas would know. Of course he would know if the bloke was still alive ... And he might even know where to find him.

My call to Thomas went unanswered. I didn't leave a message, instead made a mental note to try him again later this afternoon. Monday would be a good time for another meeting with him – if he felt up to it. Long interviews are draining and exhausting for both the interviewer and the interviewee. If I came away from them brain-dead and exhausted, someone Thomas' age probably felt worse.

Emily called again just after three o'clock as I was packing up to go home. "I will be there for dinner tonight. What are we having and what should I bring?"

"As I was about to head home early this afternoon, I thought I might make a stew for tonight. I thought it might be nice after the drizzly, miserable day we've had."

"Sounds good; I'll bring a bottle of red wine to go with it. See you about seven o'clock, if not a bit before."

Now committed to a stew for dinner, I needed to go home via the supermarket. I had tried to convince myself I had sufficient of everything I needed to do some baking to take with me for the weekend. As I now had to visit the supermarket for stew ingredients, I could pick up a bit extra for my baking – just to be sure I had enough of everything.

With the stew ready to go in the oven as soon as I took the batch of muffins out, I felt well and truly ahead of the game this afternoon. With a batch of cupcakes cooling on a rack, I was just about ready for tonight and the weekend. All I had to do before leaving home in the morning was to slap frosting on the cupcakes. Feeling smug, I retreated to my home office to update my McGregor file and the timeline I created to go with it.

My phone chirped just as I plonked my backside down behind my desk. I answered it without checking the caller ID and was startled when Thomas Agnew spoke to me.

"Miss Whittington... Sorry, I forgot. I'll try again. *Sonny*, it's Thomas Agnew. I notice I missed a call from you earlier, but you didn't leave a message."

"Thank you for returning my call. I didn't leave a message because didn't want to bother you. A question occurred to me and, without applying any thought to the matter, I called you. It wasn't urgent, so I didn't leave a message."

"Well, here I am. You are talking to me now. So, what was your question?"

"Okay... At most of our meetings, there has been mention of the farm manager Regina employed after Silas passed away. I don't think I've ever heard the man's name mentioned.

"His name was Peter Griswold, and a more likeable chap would be hard to find."

"Judging by the appearance of the place, nobody has looked after it for quite a while. What happened to Mr Griswold?"

"Nothing happened to him as far as I know. He kept the place in top shape and was an excellent worker. When Regina disappeared, I went to see him and asked him to stay on to keep the place running. After Clifford left, Regina returned managing the affairs of the property to me. So, it was up to me to take the necessary steps … make the necessary arrangements to keep the place going until Regina reappeared. I asked him to stay on and continue running the property as we both knew Regina would expect us to. He agreed, and I increased his wages a bit to cover any extra responsibilities involved."

"But Regina never came back. How long after did he continue to run the property?"

"A lot of years; how long ago was the newspaper article you found written?"

"About ten years ago… So, Regina had been missing for about fifteen years by then."

"It was soon after the article came out. Peter started making noises about retiring. He stayed on for about another twelve months or so before calling it a day. He claimed he was too old, but I think it was more a case of his accepting his adored boss was not coming back which did for him."

"Are you suggesting there was some form of close relationship between Regina and her employee?"

"Good Lord, no. He admired her strength – her resilience. I think he would have walked through fire to maintain the place for her. But, even he couldn't hold on to the belief Regina would reappear one day. So, he retired. I didn't have the heart, or whatever was required, to find someone to replace him. After putting certain arrangements in place to maintain an income from the property, I left it to its own devices."

"Do you know if Peter Griswold is still alive?"

"I haven't heard anything of him for a couple of years but he was up until then."

"Did he remain in Millhaven?"

"Oh yes, he had always lived here. If you have a pencil handy, I can give you the last address I have for him."

After making a note of the address, I asked Thomas if he might be available for a further interview if my investigation unearthed more questions. Not only would he be available, but he hoped I found loads more questions to ask. Our call ended after I promised to keep him updated on anything and everything regarding the McGregor property.

"Right; now for Peter Griswold...," I murmured as I put my phone away. "Is he still alive after all this time?"

Before I had a chance to consider the possibility, my phone played its tune again. This time it was Ben.

"I notice you left your office early today. I hoped you didn't rush home to make something special for me for dinner."

"Gee I wasn't aware I had to check in and out with you. I'll try to remember in future. In the meantime, I can assure you it's not why I left town early."

"Well, it's just as well. I won't be able to make it tonight after all. It's going to be a busy night for my officers tonight."

After making appropriate disappointed-type noises, I said I would catch up with him after the weekend, and ended the call. Sometimes Fate smiles on you. I wasn't devastated by his news. An evening with Emily might be much more productive without Ben, than if he were here.

Chapter 15

After mixing the dumplings and dropping them in on top of the stew to cook, I went back to my office to pursue my latest mission: track down Peter Griswold. With no idea if he were still alive and still living in Millhaven, I prepared for failure.

Sticking with the method which delivered Thomas Agnew to me, I went straight to the old electoral roll. I blinked a couple of times. There was the name *Griswold, Peter Johannes* staring back at me. It was the only entry for the surname, so I felt it safe to assume it belonged to the man who had been Regina McGregor's farm manager. It gave the right address, but,my copy of the electoral roll was old...

Armed with his initials and his address at the time of the election, I searched the white pages for a phone number. Zilch... no listings for Griswold in this area ... And, none with the relevant initials listed anywhere else either. After expressing my disappointment in a few rude words, I sat back to ponder how else I might locate the man in question. "Of course, it has to be Friday evening, doesn't it?" I reminded the universe. My options for pursuing Mr Griswold before Monday at the earliest were zero.

Emily arrived mid-way through my cursing about the way of the world, Fate, and anything else which determined I couldn't do anything about Peter Griswold until next week. "I know I'm early, but I was in a position to escape my office, and desperate to put the week to bed. Shall I open this?" She waved the bottle of red wine she was carrying at me.

"Yes, please. I'm feeling a bit the same about life at the moment."

The drizzle, which persisted for most of the day, had taken time-out. Out on the deck, the air was fresh and a bit cooler. It wafted in tinged with the scent of jasmine and rosemary from the plants in the garden bed along the fence. How long we sat in silence before finding the energy for conversation was an indicator of how our days had been. I roused myself from exploring the far reaches of my mind to break the silence.

"I'm almost not game to ask, but did Ben receive your report on the hidden bones today?"

"Yeah, I dropped it into him when I went out to find something for a late lunch. His phone rang just as I walked into his office, so I dropped it on his desk and left. I've heard nothing from him since. So, he is either still digesting it, or it's okay and there isn't anything to discuss."

"Were there any surprises; anything startling about the bones?"

"Your copy of the report is in my car. I forgot to bring it in. I assumed you didn't want me to give it to you on the weekend in front of Kirsty. I'll fetch it for you when we go in for dinner."

"Do you think you might give me an executive summary of the report while we're out here?"

"Okay… Let's see, where do I start? ... Right, the bones are old but not ancient. I estimate they were in the cavity in the old house for between twenty and thirty years. It might have been for as long as forty years, but I'm inclined to think they are more recent. I did find evidence of peri mortem trauma leading to death. How am I doing so far? How does it fit with what you think you know about the bones?"

"Who said I know anything about them? Until you retrieved them and did your analysis, I didn't know any more about them than anyone else did… and I still don't. So, come on, give me the details please. What about gender?"

"You want the statistical details first? Aren't you even a bit interested in the trauma I mentioned?"

"If you don't stop teasing, I will come around this table and slap you. You know damned well I want to know the 'statistical details' as you call them. Then, afterwards, you may tell me about the trauma you discovered"

"Well, if you insist... But I was enjoying myself there for a moment. Okay, here we go with the details: the body was about 170 centimetres tall, and estimated to be between about 50 and 60 years old at the time of death. The bones showed evidence of a life of hard work, mainly heavy lifting, over a long period of time. There was no evidence of any serious illness or health issues, only the trauma which occurred around the time of death..."

"Yes, thank you, but what about the gender?"

"Oh, didn't I say? You do keep going on about the gender." I pushed my chair back from the table and went to stand up. "Okay, okay; sit down. I'm just teasing. The body was that of a female, and I don't expect it comes as any surprise to you, as I think we both knew it would be."

"Are you saying the body is Regina McGregor's?"

"No. It is not what I said. I have no way of knowing who the person was. Yes, it may be possible to obtain a DNA sample, but I have no other sample for comparison. I might be asked to analyse the DNA. But, with nothing to compare it to, it will become just another piece of information held for future reference."

I gave her a slow hand clap. "Congratulations; a most professional delivery of the details. Now, if you don't mind, I'll reword my earlier question and now I'm asking you and not the forensic scientist. Who do you think those bones might belong to? Come on, honest guesswork required now, not scientific knowledge."

"Who do you think it is? I don't know enough about the person I suspect it is to be able to form any real opinion."

"Okay, I'll say what we're both trying to avoid saying: we have found Regina McGregor."

"It would appear to be the case. And, I wish I could be sure one way or the other. I've seen how it affects people when we can't prove whether a body is a loved one or not. Now I know how they feel. While the bones don't belong to any of my family members, I'm almost desperate to confirm the identity of the

163

woman behind the wall. This has nothing to do with professional pride or the like, and it's not just about Kirsty either. Feeling this way is a whole new experience for me."

"Did your report suggest it might be Regina's remains?"

"No, of course not, it would be unprofessional. Speaking of a certain copper…," Emily glanced at her watch, "isn't he running a bit late tonight?"

"Argh, I forgot to tell you. No, he's not coming tonight. Something looks like blowing up work-wise tonight and he wants to be on hand in case he is needed. So, we don't have to watch what we say." I checked the time too. "Perhaps it's time we rescued the stew…"

"And refill our glasses. I'll slip out to my car for your copy of my report while you dish-up."

Conversation over the rest of the evening was light and of no consequence except for a brief mention of our weekend with Kirsty.

"I might be a bit late heading out to the property in the morning," Emily said. "I need to call in at my office first. Depending on what has come in overnight, I should be at Kirsty's in time for morning coffee." It wasn't a late night. Emily seemed keen to leave and I was more than happy to be alone to glance through Emily's report on the bones.

It was only a slim volume, and didn't tell me much more than I already knew. Within about half an hour of her departure, I was done with the report and slipped it into my file. Of itself, the information in the report didn't solve the riddle of Regina's disappearance. It only added strength to the conviction I held. They had to be Regina's remains. After all, if they weren't hers, whose were they?

My mind spent the best part of the next hour developing speculative scenarios which might have led to Regina's ending up behind the wall. It was not the way to encourage a sound night's sleep and, although I was tired when I crawled into bed, nightmares tormented me all night.

*****

Awake early this morning, I busied myself preparing for my weekend at Kirsty's. I wanted to arrive early, and before Emily, to check on how Kirsty was holding up now she was alone on the property. Depending on how she was, I hoped to elicit more of her story about her departure from Sydney.

Although I was early, it seems other people also were off the mark early this morning. The doors of the tractor shed were open when I arrived and an unfamiliar utility was parked outside it. Kirsty emerged from the shed and came to meet me.

"Good morning, Sonny. It looks as though everyone rose early today. Angus from nextdoor already is here to work on the tractor. He says it will take at least all day and maybe into tomorrow. Can I give you a hand to carry anything?"

She carried the two containers of baking into her digs while I trailed along behind carrying my bag and the esky. She pointed to the esky as I placed it on the floor in the kitchen. "What's in that thing?" she demanded. "I hope you haven't brought food, apart from the baking I mean. This is my weekend. I am your host. I feed you."

"Good to know. But there are some nice steaks in there in case we need them, and I made a batch of cold slaw. Don't get on your high horse about it. You are welcome to fuss about being the host all weekend, if it makes you happy. I have nothing against being pampered. By the way, from the little I've seen of Angus, he is a gorgeous hunk of bloke. What's he doing still living at home? I'm surprised he wasn't snapped up long ago by some enterprising young woman."

"Give me a chance. I haven't had time to extract all his details yet – but I'm working on it. If he joins us for coffee this morning, maybe you could use your investigator's techniques to find out more."

As it would be a couple of hours before Emily arrived, it was an ideal opportunity for us to talk. She didn't have breakfast before Angus arrived so, while she tucked into cereal and toast,

I indulged in another coffee and, at the first opportunity, initiated the conversation I wanted to have.

"Kirsty, at the risk of opening old wounds, I am curious about why you upped and left Sydney when you did. I know you suffered a couple of major upheavals in your life, but your decision was drastic, given the uncertainty regarding Millhaven. It was so unlike your usual way of dealing with crisis. What happened to send you running to Millhaven?"

"It was as though Fate, Karma, or whatever you want to call it, was transpiring against me. After mum died and I was clearing out her house, the stuff I discovered there shook my world to the core. So, I was going through something of an upheaval; a vulnerable time. At the same time, my long-time relationship had lost its lustre. We lived together, worked together, and were held together by a business we owned between us. I suspect, sometime in the future, if I think back on the relationship in those latter days, it might not appear quite so bad. Don't misunderstand me. It wasn't great but, in my then state of mind, I wasn't able to cope with any extra hassles.

For me, the IT business we established remained a sideline. I continued to run the plant breeding program, and a major part of it was using a special program I designed to interrogate and collate our research data. So, software and programming were my main role in our business too. While my partner maintained his unit in the city, we lived in my house in the suburbs. It had a large shed in the backyard, which was where we had our workshop and stored our hardware components and new machines.

Then, more by chance than anything else, I noticed the income from the business had dropped. Cash flow fluctuations are not unusual, but we had been busy over the preceding few months; flat out in fact. The cash flow didn't match the workload. Thinking we might have been undercharging our clients, I checked our rates. They were okay. During the exercise, I thought I detected something else. At first, I didn't know what it was, but I knew something was not quite right.

If we had hardware-type work requests, or new machine purchases, from the city area, we tended to spend a few days – a week if necessary – just dealing with the city work. At those times, my partner stayed in his unit in the city to avoid having to commute every day. To cut a long story shorter, my digging around uncovered a bit of 'extra' work he was doing in the city... And it explained why he was spending so much more time there in those days. He had a lady friend. She had moved into his unit, and they were spending large slabs of time together there whenever he had 'work' to do in the city area."

"Oh dear, I know there is never a good time to make such discoveries, but it could not have been a worse time for you. I assume there was a predictable outcome to the sordid mess?"

"Ah well, my 'journey of discovery' didn't end there. Apart from his bit-on-the-side, I found he had been both skimming from the business, as well as taking on jobs on his own account, which weren't run through the business... although they often involved materials from the business. I threw him out of the house, set things in motion to wind-up the business, and put my house on the market. Selling the house meant there was no workshop area, nowhere to store material and equipment and, from his hardware side of the operation, made life difficult for him. The upside was, it didn't affect my side of the business at all. I continued to take in work, but payments were direct to my account, not the business."

"So, where were you planning to live once your house sold? Did selling trigger your move to Millhaven?"

"Ha hah... no such intelligent thought was behind it. The only plan I had was to move into mum's house if mine sold, and it did sell a little over a week after I listed it. I derived an inordinate amount of pleasure from telling him he had less than two weeks to clear his stuff out of the shed and anything else still in the house. It did not go down well, but he had no choice. At the same time, I told him I already had initiated winding-up of the partnership, and I intended retaining my side of the business."

"How did he react to the news? I understand he would not be happy about losing the shed but, in effect, the business had ceased being run as a partnership anyway."

"Uhmm… it wasn't so simple. The majority of our clients were mine. I mean, I was their point of contact, even if they were buying a new computer. In such cases, the client stayed with me for any future work they required. Although he might prepare the hardware according to the buyer's requirements, I set it up and took care of the programming… and I delivered it to the buyer. If I took my clients with me when we split the business, he would be left with a small client base to build up afterwards."

"I can't believe he agreed to such an arrangement."

"He didn't – not at first anyway. It was a case of solicitors at ten paces arguing it out. Then I called time on it, and headed to court with it. A couple of days before our scheduled court appearance, he folded and agreed to the terms I wanted. So, I still have my client list and can work from Millhaven. I've teamed up with another IT professional to do the legwork of delivering machines around the Sydney area. It's not a partnership or anything. He is just a contractor I employ on an 'as needed' basis."

"If I recall something you told me earlier, your mother's house also sold. It must have been a bit scary finding yourself without a roof over your head. How did you manage the situation?"

"Yeah, everything happened in a rush in the end. While I was clearing mum's house out, I spoke to a real estate agent about selling it. He gave me the spiel about the market being a bit quiet, and there being little interest in anything in the area where mum's house was located. I wasn't in a hurry to sell, and asked him to list it anyway. He agreed to put it on his books, but said he wouldn't advertise it until the market picked up, or someone asked for something in the area."

"It seems the market proved him wrong."

"For a few months, the market was quiet and there was no interest in the house as far as I knew. Then the market picked-up and prices skyrocketed. Out of the blue, the agent called me one day to say he had an interested buyer, and they wanted to inspect the place the following day. When he told me the price he was asking for it, I raced home and spent half the night cleaning and tidying in readiness for the inspection. The buyers already had approved finance. By the end of the day, they had signed a contract … and I had two weeks to move out by the settlement date."

"As I said before: scary to find yourself soon to be out on the street."

"Maybe not as scary as you might think. The solicitor, Nathan Jones, already had contacted me about Silas McGregor's estate, and I felt things were dragging on a bit without much to show for it. While I wasn't so interested in what I might end up with if things went my way, I was curious. Was it possible this was my first tangible evidence of my family – of who I was? So, I think the sale of the house just strengthened my inclination to come to Millhaven to find out more. I had heaps of leave due to me, but I was supposed to give a month's notice. As I didn't want to lose anything owed to me, I took action the next morning after the contract was signed.

I went straight to the personnel department and applied for a month's leave from the following day. Then, on my first day of leave, I resigned, effective from the end of my month-long leave. For whatever the reason, the rules said I had to go back to work for one day after the end of my leave before my resignation could take effect. I wasn't going back to Sydney for one day, so I worked 'from home' here in the unit I was renting in the city. It seemed to satisfy the 'Rules' and I received my full payout from my employer. As soon as the removalists collected my gear and took it to storage, I handed the keys to the real estate agent and was out of Sydney two days before the new owners received the keys to mum's house."

"Now, looking back on everything over your last few months in Sydney, do you have any regrets? Is there anything you would or should have done differently?"

"No... nothing I would change. The crime scene tape came down last thing yesterday afternoon, so I can go back into the house anytime I want to now. Angus is working on the tractor, and it should be ready to use within the next couple of days. I'm feeling excited about exploring the property and starting work on the place. ...And there always will be a spare bed here for my friends."

A vehicle arrived as Kirsty was speaking and, a couple of minutes later, footsteps came up the front stairs. Kirsty rushed to open the door and welcome Emily, who had a bag slung over her shoulder and was carrying a large cardboard carton. She staggered in and dumped the heavy carton on the coffee table in the centre of the lounge area.

"What's in the box?" Kirsty demanded. "I hope you haven't brought any food. This is my weekend for hosting my friends."

"Food...? No, I didn't bring any food. I brought other essential supplies for the weekend."

Kirsty pounced on the box and ripped open the top. "Do you expect us to dispatch all of this in two days?" she asked.

"Of course not..." Emily gave her an innocent smile and shook her head. "We all would end up in hospital drying out if we consumed all of it. What we don't drink over the weekend will be the start of your cellar, and we will continue to visit to help you deal with it." Kirsty, standing there holding a bottle of wine in each hand, looked at a loss as to what to do or say.

"While the two of you work out what to do with the contents of the box, I might busy myself with making morning coffee. Should we invite Angus to join us?" I suggested.

"Oh, yes, I always intended asking him to join us," Kirsty said. "Emily, if you wouldn't mind putting a couple of bottles of white wine in the fridge, while I go and round-up Angus for coffee..."

"Cupcakes or muffins...?" I asked Emily as she made room in the fridge for the wine.

"Dunno... either or both would be good. Why not put four of each out and let people make their own choices?"

It sounded reasonable, so I did. By the time Kirsty returned with Angus in tow, a platter of sweet treats and three mugs of coffee were ready. All I had left to do was to make Angus' coffee. When I joined them at the table, Kirsty was well into cross-examining Angus about the state of her tractor.

"It's in amazing condition, and won't require more than a complete service, but I will replace gaskets and the like as I go along. The only problem I see is the tyres. I'm afraid you are going to be up for a whole set of new tyres. Don't take my word for it though. Let the tyre people have a look and tell you what you need." He gave her the name and contact details of a firm in town which services the rural properties, and which the Walkers use.

Our morning coffee break stretched on much longer than any of us might have envisaged. It was Angus who alerted us to the fact. "God, look at the time. I've wasted half the morning sitting here yapping instead of getting on with the job. Thank you, ladies, but work awaits."

"Join us for lunch, Angus," Kirsty called after him. "I'll let you know when it's ready."

Then, there were just the three of us, and the *girls' weekend* started in earnest. Kirsty led off with her plans to make her new digs more comfortable, and Emily and I had loads of interior decorating ideas to contribute. From there, we went to current fashion and make-up trends, and forthcoming 'entertainment' events in Millhaven. We had no trouble occupying ourselves until it was lunchtime, and Kirsty again went to drag Angus away from his work.

We were clearing the table after lunch when a truck arrived to deliver a side-by-side Quad bike. "What's this all about, Kirsty," I asked.

"It's my new getting-around-the-property mode of transport. I don't have a farm vehicle – other than the tractor when it's finished – and it is not what a tractor is meant for. I bought this little beauty while I was in town yesterday."

A little of the afternoon was devoted to all of us trying out the new machine.

Chapter 16

While we were debating whether to go across to the old house to inspect the damage caused by the police investigation, or to have an early afternoon coffee first, another truck arrived. A large, industrial type mower occupied a good deal of the truck's tray.

"Oh, good; they made it today. I was beginning to think I'd have to wait until Monday for it to arrive." Kirsty said over her shoulder as she strode over to the truck.

Within moments, the ramps were in place and the truck driver's offsider eased the mower down onto the ground. It was all over in a few minutes. Kirsty exchanged a few words with the truck driver while signing the necessary paperwork, and then the truck departed. We watched in silence as it made its way off the property. Sometime during the preceding few minutes, Angus had emerged from the tractor shed. He walked around the new piece of equipment, inspecting it at close range.

"Kirsty, what is this thing all about?" he asked. "Did you buy this thing?" She beamed at him and nodded. "Why? What possessed you to buy it?"

"Well, it's a zero-turn model, the same as used in parks and on playing fields. It allows you to mow right up to trees and buildings. There are acres of knee-high grass here already and, after the recent rains, the situation is about to become worse. I need to be able to mow this area and along the track. This machine will be ideal for those areas. Once the tractor is operational, I'll buy a slasher to keep other areas under control."

"Yes, but you didn't have to buy this mower. You could borrow ours whenever you needed it. As for buying a slasher, let's see what you find when you start mowing before you buy anything more. There is bound to be a slasher, as well as other implements, lying around here somewhere. You can't run a property like this without them. Do you want me to give this the once-over before you use it?"

"It was supposed to be delivered ready to use but, if it makes you happier, feel free to take a look at it. In the meantime, we were just about to have a coffee. Are you free to join us?" As soon as Angus confirmed he would join us as soon as he washed up, we three women traipsed upstairs to make coffee happen.

This afternoon's coffee break was not as protracted as this morning's, probably due to Angus being anxious to return to the tractor shed. After clearing away and stacking everything in the dishwasher, it was time to head to the old house. As we stacked the dishwasher, Emily made a major effort to reassure Kirsty she had no grounds for concern about damage created in the course of the police investigation. While Kirsty tried to appear relaxed about the whole exercise, I sensed a certain degree of tension. The sooner she saw for herself, the sooner she would relax.

Now familiar with the front stairs, the other two bounced up them without a moment's hesitation. They still looked treacherous to me, so I stuck to my earlier approach of placing my feet close to the runner as I climbed up onto the verandah. Kirsty hesitated at the front door. I saw her take a deep breath before positioning herself to open the doors. With Emily and me adding our weight to them, the doors soon stood wide open.

Not surprising I suppose, the moment the three of us stepped across the threshold, our focus was on the wall at the far end of the front room. Somehow, the missing middle section of the wall sent something of a chill through me. It wasn't anything I saw. There wasn't anything untoward to see. I put it down to the thought of what – or who – was the recent occupant of the space behind the wall. In a silent gesture of support, I placed my hand on Kirsty shoulder. If the scene disturbed me, it must be more upsetting for Kirsty.

She gave me a wry smile. "I'll be fine, but I do want a closer look now they've opened up the wall."

I shot Emily and enquiring look. What was behind that wall? Was there anything unpleasant to upset Kirsty? Emily gave a half shake of her head and made a gesture which I interpreted as 'relax'. It was too late to do anything anyway. Kirsty had marched up to the missing section of the wall and now played her torch around the cavity behind it.

"If I didn't know what I saw here a week or so ago, this wall and the space behind it would tell me nothing. There is nothing to see … other than a flimsy wall structure with its centre section removed. There is nothing in there to suggest there was ever anything behind it."

"What did you expect to find?" Emily asked.

"Christ, I don't know. But, I expected there would be some evidence – some tell-tale sign – of what happened here. Maybe, if there were something, it would help me come to terms with it. Not knowing probably is the hardest part."

Both Emily and I sought to ease the situation for Kirsty by telling her it was still early days, and it could be a while before anything from the police investigation was available. My concern was Kirsty now might feel so uncomfortable about what might have happened in this house she wouldn't be able to begin the refurbishment she planned.

Rather than stand around too long peering at an empty space, I suggested Kirsty show us the rest of the ground floor. She seemed reluctant, but we both insisted. She began our tour of inspection and soon warmed to the task and led us down a short hallway to the next set of doors opening off it. To our left was the kitchen and opposite, was what had been the dining room.

Consensus was the whole of the existing kitchen should be ripped out, and the wall between it and the front room removed to create an open plan living area. Kirsty couldn't remember whether the offending wall was one of those Bill Branigan suggested could be removed or not. "I'll find my notes on the subject as soon as we go back to my cottage. While I'm about it, I should have a look at those dining room walls. It would be good to do something there to open it up a bit too."

I heaved a silent sigh of relief. This was what I wanted to hear: Kirsty being enthusiastic and excited about making this the eventual home in which she wanted to live. We didn't explore beyond the kitchen/dining area. Having agreed we had breathed in enough dust and probable mould spores, we abandoned our tour of inspection in favour of fresh air. As we wound our way back towards the cottage, Kirsty detoured to the tractor shed. It already was a bit after five o'clock and I wondered how much longer Angus might stay today. It seems the same question occurred to Kirsty, and she went to find out.

"No, he's not staying for dinner," she reported when she joined us in the kitchen. "What are you two up to?"

"The sun is bound to be over the yardarm somewhere in the world by now, so it's time for a happy hour," Emily announced.

We took our drinks and a selection of nibbles through to the lounge and settled in for what lasted much longer than an hour. There was great conversation and lots of laughter … but not a mention of the hidden bones. I waited until Kirsty went for a shower to check with Emily.

"Has Kirsty mentioned the bones to you at all today?"

She looked surprised and shook her head. "No. I hadn't noticed it until you asked. Had you already shared the key points of my report with her?"

It was my turn to shake my head. "No, I haven't said anything about them. I had no intention to do so unless she mentioned them. She hasn't... and now it concerns me. I thought she might have cornered you for information but, if there's been no mention of them at all, I wonder if we are about to encounter another major problem."

"Now the bones are gone, do you think she might have slipped into some form of denial mode?"

Kirsty's return to the kitchen prevented any further discussion of the bones. It was time to sizzle those steaks I brought, and make salads to go with them. Division of labour kept us all engaged and ensured dinner was ready as soon as the steaks were done. The rest of the evening was a relaxed and pleasant time which stretched on until after midnight.

In spite of the strange bed, I was surprised by how fast asleep arrived, and how deep and restful it was.

*****

Awake at my usual time this morning, I couldn't decide whether to get up and make a start on the day and risk waking the others, or to lie in bed until someone else started moving about. After a few minutes of lying there staring at the ceiling, I couldn't stand it any longer. I was filling the coffee machine when Kirsty, followed by Emily, wandered out to join me. Day two of our weekend on the property had begun. While still seated at the table with our breakfasts, I heard a vehicle arrive and stood up to go and investigate.

"Relax; it will be Angus back to finish off the tractor. Before he left last night, he told me he would be back this morning. He should be finished by lunchtime."

"So, the lovely Angus will be available to have coffee with us again this morning." Emily gave Kirsty a knowing wink as she finished speaking. "You might do well to cultivate your neighbour. Not only is he easy on the eyes, he's also a good catch."

"Oh, no you don't… there will be no match making, thank you. Besides, I think I've developed an allergy to men," Kirsty retorted – but added a wry grin as an afterthought.

Sunday was an altogether lazy day, the highlight of which was a long, l-o-n-g coffee break shared with Angus, who entertained us with stories of farm life. He became almost excited to learn of Kirsty's degree in agricultural science and the plant breeding work she had done. Our extended coffee break meant no one even thought about lunch until after one o'clock. Then there wasn't too much time to fill in until four o'clock when both Emily and I headed home.

Ben called me as I drove into my garage. "Are you home or still out at the McGregor property?"

"…Just arrived home this very minute."

"Okay, I'll pick-up something for dinner and should be at your place a bit before seven o'clock."

"Unless, your tastebuds are suggesting something else, I rather fancy fish and chips tonight."

By the time I unpacked the car and showered, I had about an hour to fill in before Ben arrived. As the copy of the report on the bones Emily gave me would remain Emily's and my secret, I figured Ben would want to tell me what the forensic analysis of the bones produced. Reading my copy of the report before he arrived would allow me to sound more intelligent – and ask more intelligent-sounding questions – during the discussion. Although, knowing Ben as I do, he will require me to almost beg to find out what's in the report before he tells me anything. He liked his ego stroked.

Fish and chips don't wait for anyone so, to avoid tepid fish and soggy chips, we set about eating as soon as he arrived. Tonight, instead of heading for the lounge after dinner, we sat on the back deck. The air tonight was crisp and clear. Rather than waste time, as soon as we were settled on the deck, I initiated the conversation I wanted to have.

"Have you received the forensic report on the bones from the old house?"

"Yeah, Emily dropped it over on Friday."

"And, do we now know anything more than we did before… like was it male or female?"

"It appears to be female and the bones could have been in the cavity behind the wall for up to thirty years. There was nothing else which might help identify the body."

"As it hasn't been there for too long, I thought they might be able to obtain a reliable DNA sample."

They did isolate the DNA from a tooth I think but DNA is useful only if you have another possible sample for comparison. Without any clues as to the identity of the body, it is difficult, if not impossible, to track down a likely match for comparison purposes."

"So, what happens now, with regard to the bones I mean?"

"For the moment, the bones are in the too hard basket. There's been a bit of stuff going on over the last few days, and my whole team has been flat out dealing with it. In fact, given the way things have been, I won't be surprised to be called in again tonight."

"Damn, I hoped you might have some speculation about the identity of the body to share with me. Oh well, I suppose it will have to remain another of life's mysteries... for the present anyway."

No point flogging a dead horse, I reminded myself, and moved the conversation on to what had been happening over the weekend to keep the local detectives so busy. Ben's phone interrupted our conversation just as he began telling me about a series of incidents which occurred in Millhaven since last Thursday night. He wandered inside to take the call, so I knew it was a work call.

"No surprises," he said when he returned. "It appears the current crime spree continues. I have to go. It's not full moon or anything is it? Maybe there is something in the water at the moment causing it."

Too early for bed, and without any clear thought of what I might do, I wandered into my office. Almost as an automatic response, the moment I sat at my desk, I dragged out Kirsty's file. Have I learnt anything more over the weekend to add to the file? Short answer: not much. All I gained was an insight into Kirsty's decision to escape Sydney and relocate to Millhaven. As I stared at the whiteboard on the opposite wall, her story replayed in my head.

I scratched a couple of brief notes on a pad beside me before turning my attention to the rest of the weekend. How pushy and demanding did she have to be to persuade the suppliers to deliver the ATV and the mower on a Saturday? Such places which opened their doors on Saturdays were more interested in selling than delivering.

How much would those two items cost? I did some rough calculations and gulped. "Crikey, she is splashing it about a bit,"

I told the universe. With no faith in my own figures, I checked Google for 'real' prices of the equipment she bought. It still added up to an eye watering amount. When I added it to the likely cost of her new 'cottage', I was stunned. A nervous flutter started in the pit of my stomach.

While it is none of my business, it would be handy to have some idea of the extent of Kirsty's finances. She sold two houses in Sydney and made a killing on the current buoyant real estate market, but what else did she have aside from the profit on those sales? As is the way of it, one rhetorical question gave rise to several others. I needed to speak with Kirsty again – and maybe Thomas Agnew – to find the answers to those questions. And, maybe I needed to talk to Emily too.

Emily almost came to me as an afterthought. It was Ben's comments about the DNA sample they collected from the body in the old house: something to compare it to was required for possible identification. What if the bones were Regina's? Would Kirsty's DNA be a viable option for comparison? While Kirsty was a couple of generations removed from Regina, would her DNA still be close enough for comparison purposes? I sat back to ponder the possibility. It didn't take more than a moment for a negative thought to arrive. If Kirsty's DNA did not show sufficient common markers to be considered a good match, would it be construed as proof the bones were not Regina's?

Although I hadn't found answers to any of my questions, since Ben left, I had fashioned a busy week ahead for myself. First thing tomorrow, I would try to establish whether Peter Griswold was still alive, and to arrange a meeting if he was still in Millhaven. Depending on how my search for Griswold goes, I might have to leave setting up another meeting with Thomas Agnew until Tuesday. Organising a time to speak to Emily when Ben wasn't around might be tricky. It probably needed to be during the day when she wasn't at work. If she wasn't too busy, maybe we could meet for lunch sometime over the next couple of days.

The questions went to bed with me, but didn't keep me awake for long.

*****

In a bid to inject some degree of normalcy into my life again today, I was in my office at my usual time this morning. I spent so little time there over the last few days, it almost felt like being in a foreign country. A check on my messages and emails produced the first disappointment of the day.

I hoped there might be some indication from my new supposed client about when the surveillance work he required might begin. Although I had all but decided to write him off, today would have been his one last chance to have me undertake his work. If I'm honest, I don't want to be tied down with surveillance work this week. I'd be happy not to have any commitments until I finish researching Regina McGregor.

Somehow, I doubted Kirsty would settle to life on her new property unless, and until, she knew all there is to know about Regina and what happened there. While the scant information I'd discovered might help, it does tend to generate further questions. In her current psychological state, Kirsty does not need more questions gnawing at her. Thoughts of Kirsty and Regina reminded me my priority today was to track down Peter Griswold. Having drawn a blank with a phone listing, my only option appeared to be to visit his last known address.

After checking the equipment I might need was in my bag, I headed for my car. About twenty minutes later, I located the address I wanted. In a semi-rural area on the northern extremity of the area considered to be Millhaven, was a small acreage fronted by a simple weatherboard cottage. I guessed the block was about a hectare in size. Visible from the front fence were a number of fruit trees and a large vegetable garden. A few chickens roamed through the orchard.

No one came to the front door. I tried thumping on it once more before accepting no one was at home. Just to be sure, they weren't occupied down the back somewhere and hadn't heard me, I wandered along the side of the cottage and around behind it. Apart from a couple of cows in a paddock at the far end of the block, I discovered nothing else. After scribbling a brief note on my card, I slid it under the front door, and returned to my car.

An old bloke on a horse stopped as he drew level with me. "Are you looking for Peter?" he called out. "He goes into town on Mondays. You'd catch him at home any other day. I often see him when I walk my dogs in the evening. I could give him a message if I see him."

"Thank you. I left a card under his door but, if you do happen to be speaking to him, please tell him I would like to talk to him about Regina McGregor. I don't have his phone number so I can't call him, but my number is on the card I left. I just want to talk to him about a property where he used to work."

"The one where that woman disappeared…?"

"Yeah, there have been a few things happen with the property lately, and I'm putting together some background material for the new owner."

"Are you a journalist?"

His tone suggested it was as well I wasn't, so I hurried to reassure him. "No. I'm just a friend of the new owner, and I thought Mr Griswold might provide information about what the property was like in the past, what it produced, and any other relevant information which might help the new owner re-establish the place. I would have called him first to arrange an appointment, but I couldn't find his phone number."

My heart skipped a beat as I watched him reach into his pocket and drag out his phone. Is he going to call Peter Griswold for me while I am standing here? He did something even better.

"Hang on a minute while check," he muttered. "Yep, I have his number. Do you want to take it down?"

Moments later, Peter Griswold's number was in my contacts list. I thanked him and scrambled into my car. By the time I was making a U-turn to head back into the city, the helpful bloke on the horse already was some distance along the road.

Back in my office, I made a decision about something which nagged me all the way from Griswold's property: should I call him now, or leave it until tonight or tomorrow? If Peter were already in town, and if he didn't have too much else to do, he might agree to talk to me today. It was worth a try. I keyed his number and received an abrupt response. A matter of moments later, I had explained how I had visited his home and left my card, and how a helpful resident from out his way had suggested he might be in town today.

"Why would you be looking for me?"

I gave him the same story about the new owner of the property as I gave the bloke on the horse. "Huh, so what are you suggesting?" With no warmth apparent in his responses so far, I needed to try harder. The problem was how to go about it was a mystery to me. In the end I just gave him my proposal without any embellishment.

"Well, as you are already in town and, if you should happen to have a few minutes spare before you return to you property, we could meet somewhere for a chat."

It worked. He hadn't had lunch yet and was happy to join me for lunch in a small bistro on the north side of the city. While I didn't know of it, he was familiar with the eatery, and I saw it as a comfort zone for him. We agreed to meet at the bistro half an hour later.

Chapter 17

Although not much to look at from the outside, the bistro proved quite pleasant, and its food was excellent. We hadn't arranged whether we would meet out front or inside. No one waited outside, so I went in and scanned the diners. It was well after the lunchtime rush, and only three tables were occupied. Only the occupant of one of them could be Peter Griswold.

One table had a lone occupant, an elderly man. Was this Peter Griswold, or just another elderly bloke who happened to be lunching here today? He saw me and made as if to raise his hand ... then changed his mind. He looked as uncertain as I felt. Flashing my very best smile, I made my way to his table. "Mr Griswold...?" I asked.

He sprang up off his chair and gestured for me to take the chair opposite his. "Please... Please, take a seat. Yes, I am Peter Griswold. Am I right in assuming you are Sonny Whittington whom I arranged to meet here?"

Introductions over, we ordered our meals – but only after I had made it clear lunch was on me. I found it impossible to estimate the age of the man opposite me. In simple terms he was old, but how old? I knew a lifetime spent working outdoors played havoc with one's appearance, but he displayed more damage than I expected. It wasn't just the condition of his wrinkled, leather-like skin burnt to the colour of chocolate. There was something else. Somehow, he looked shrunken within his well-tanned hide. Although he was a big man, who must have looked quite impressive in his younger days, now he looked a withered reflection of his youth.

His snowy white hair was thin and patchy, and his intense blue eyes had a dullness to them. Over the ensuing period I knew him, I did see those eyes light up a couple of times, but mostly they remained lifeless azure orbs. Was all this just part of growing old? Somehow I thought not. To me, his appearance told a story of something more happening in his life; something more sad or sinister than old age alone.

While he was polite and decorous almost in an old-fashioned way, he was guarded and confined himself to one-word answers where possible. I led in with an explanation of how the last couple of weeks had seen a new owner takeover the old McGregor property. My story was embellished with comments about how the new owner was mystified by the way the property had been allowed to fall into disuse, and their concern about rumours associated with the place. In desperation, I told him I was a close friend of the new owner and how I was trying to gather the history of the property for them. I hoped my bland reason for wanting to talk to him would convince him I wasn't in search of sensational 'dirt' about the property and its former owners.

It failed to win him over. He continued to sit tight and unmoving like some stone idol contemplating the tabletop before him. But… he continued to sit there, so I pushed on with initial questions which I thought were 'safe ground': what had the property produced in the past; had there been a long list of previous owners. Answers were brief and to the point, but he was still sitting opposite me, and I hadn't detected any rising hostility…Time to move the questioning closer to 'sensitive territory'.

"The property looks as though it has been neglected for quite some time. Do you know how long the place has been abandoned, or when the last owners left?"

"About twenty-seven years ago, near enough. That be when the last owner left the place is what I mean, but production continued for some years afterwards."

"Did they prefer to live in a more urban environment or the city perhaps, rather than out on the property? The house looks as though it has been uninhabited for at least as long as you suggest. It must have been difficult to keep the place going if they weren't living on it."

I had pushed things too far. At last, Peter Griswold stirred himself. But, it wasn't to answer my questions or talk about the property in any way. He was going home, leaving me alone at the bistro. On his feet and about to depart, he paused for a moment to apologise for running off. He claimed he needed to be elsewhere, but would think about all I had said. He would contact me in a day or two if he felt he had anything worthwhile to tell me. After thanking me for lunch, he was gone, and I was feeling somewhat stunned.

What just happened? Was I losing my touch? I hadn't detected even the slightest twitch, let alone a significant reaction by the man... but something had touched a nerve. While indulging in another coffee, I replayed responses Peter gave to my questions. No, he couldn't be described as 'forthcoming', but he didn't react unfavourably to any of my questions. It seems brevity might be the mark of the man. And, what about his final comment about contacting me *if he felt he had anything to tell me*? To me, it sounded as though he was going home to think about whether he would tell me anything; whether he would talk to me at all.

How well did Thomas Agnew know Peter Griswold? Was Griswold's performance today true to form, or should I read more into it? Were there some sensitivities I was unaware of, and which were likely to survive today? Now I know I need to arrange another chat with Thomas. Back in my office, the clock told me it was not a good time to call him. At this hour of the afternoon, Thomas was bound to be enjoying an afternoon nap. No, it would be much better if I remembered to call him later this afternoon or early this evening.

After my second attempt to call my supposed new client failed to make contact, I settled for sending him a text message and an email asking him to contact me as soon as possible. The remainder of the afternoon I would spend transcribing the recording of my meeting with Peter Griswold. It wouldn't take long to complete. Our meeting scored only a whisker above being a non-event.

A text message from Ben arrived when I was only a few sentences into the transcription: *Can't make it for dinner. The nightingale will sing tonight.*

Cryptic, but its meaning was clear. The reason Ben hadn't made it to dinner on Friday night and was called in to work on Sunday night was to do with Operation Nightingale. He had mentioned the state-wide operation to bust a major drug trafficking network was approaching its final stages after having been ongoing for some time. I interpreted his message to mean tonight would be the drama's final act. And, for me, it was excellent timing.

Emily's phone rang for quite a while before she answered. "Emily, I wondered whether you might be joining me for dinner tonight. It would give me an excuse to leave early to cook something."

"Yes, thanks, but don't go to any trouble. If you are cooking tonight, does it mean Ben won't be dining with us?"

"So it appears, so you are stuck with my cooking instead of something from a takeaway place."

About an hour after a visit to the supermarket, I loaded a casserole into the oven. It was a bit after five o'clock, and perfect timing for it to be ready when Emily arrived. With dinner under control, I took myself into my office to complete the Peter Griswold meeting transcription. It didn't take long and I still was considering what I had learned from the man – if anything – when Emily arrived a little earlier than expected.

"I don't know what you've prepared for dinner, but could we please open this bottle of red I've brought with me, and make a start on it now?"

"It sounds as though your day demands we should, and it suits the kind of day I've had as well."

The silence which hung between us was almost palpable. This was not the silence of conflict, but of comfort shared by friends allowed to be alone with their thoughts while being together. Wildlife surrounded us. They sounded so much louder – so intense – tonight. Even the cricket living in my rosemary hedge seemed to have found a few extra decibels. My favourite songster, a willy wagtail, alternated between raucous screeching and a melodious serenade as he sat on the topmost branch of a shrub next to the deck railing. I heard Emily sigh.

Was it a sigh bred of boredom, exhaustion, or a troubled mind? Although it meant ruining the ambiance, I felt compelled to inquire. "Why the sigh, is everything all right?"

"Eh…? Oh, no, nothing is wrong. I just was relaxing into the moment; losing myself in the world around me."

"Now I am worried. What went wrong today? It might help to talk about it."

"No-o, nothing went wrong, and I am fine. Some days I feel I don't have time to breathe. Today was one of those. It was one of those when I couldn't even manage to fit in a coffee but, at the end of the day, I don't know if I managed to achieve anything. I suppose it comes from spending the whole day on management crap, and no time in the lab. Still, I shouldn't complain. It is what they pay me to do, and pay me well. Now, how about your day, what exciting things happened in your life?"

"If only excitement were even a possibility… I've spent so much time out of my office lately, I spent much of the day catching-up – and thinking. And, my thoughts like to focus on Kirsty's hidden bones."

"Some days I'm of the opinion thinking is overrated. It can lead to more problems than you already have. I suspect your thoughts about the old bones did it for you today."

"What they did was rekindle questions from last night; questions about the identity of the woman whose bones were hidden in the old house for the better part of three decades."

"I think we both have a fair idea whose bones they are. Who else do we know of who has been missing for the same approximate period of time?"

"Yeah… but, I was thinking more of DNA. You managed to isolate DNA from the skeleton, but it is useless without another DNA sample for comparison. What about Kirsty? I realise she is down the family history line a bit from Regina, but might her

DNA still show at least some common markers… if the bones are Regina's?

"The best answer I can give you is: it's possible. And, it also is possible there might be some markers but insufficient to confirm a match. In simple terms, Kirsty will have inherited some of Regina's DNA via her mother, Catherine, but there will be a lot of other traces mixed in with it."

"Okay, I hear you, but it still would be worthwhile obtaining a sample of Kirsty's DNA, wouldn't it?"

"…Without her permission? Shock, horror – as if I would do such a thing as you suggest."

"Aah, I see… and how long will it be before you have the results? Forgive me, if I seem a bit slow on the uptake this evening."

"Well, now you might understand why I'm feeling a bit frustrated. I haven't had any spare time to retreat into my lab to start the process. I plan to go back there on my way home tonight when I will have the place to myself. If we're lucky, I might have something by tomorrow night, but it's more likely to be the next day before the results are through."

"Am I to understand you already have taken a sample for analysis?"

"It might be a bit wide of the truth, but we will stick with your phraseology for now." I demanded more details, but all Emily said was 'I acquired a sample which I believe will be adequate for our needs."

Ben could have been here tonight. Nothing Emily said would have been a problem if he heard it. But, it went without saying, he didn't need to know… and we would make sure it remained so for as long as necessary.

Time was moving on and, with nothing more to say about DNA, we agreed it was time to eat and, not long after, Emily took her leave. She was keen to start work on Kirsty's DNA sample, and I was keen for her to do so. By the time I had cleaned up in the kitchen and showered, it wasn't yet nine o'clock. Although too early for bed on most nights, tonight felt like the perfect opportunity for an early one.

*****

Tuesday developed into almost a non-event from the moment I was in my city office. Only two things stood out over the whole day: two appointments to discuss possible new jobs, and finally making contact with the client whose surveillance work I should be doing now. By the end of the day, I found myself without any definite work prospects for the immediate future.

What didn't happen on Tuesday was contact by Peter Griswold. I reminded myself he had indicated he would be in touch in the next 'day or two'. "No need for concern at least until after tomorrow," I tried reassuring myself and anyone else in the universe within hearing. My gut didn't believe me, and nor did the little voice in my head. They both kept telling me I wouldn't hear from him.

As a result of a day devoid of interest or excitement, I was not much company when Ben and Emily arrived for dinner on Tuesday evening. Emily sensed it first and took me aside to ask if something had happened, and would I prefer to be alone this evening. I assured her being alone would not be a good thing when what I needed was lively conversation and debate. They stayed – and my outlook improved as the evening rolled on and turned itself into a later than usual event.

When I found myself alone again at a bit after eleven o'clock, I was wide awake and with all systems up and running at full speed. Sleep had little to no appeal. I dug out the book I started reading weeks ago and was still bookmarked at page 34. With my feet up in the lounge, I settled down to make serious inroads into it. An hour or so later, I hadn't progressed past page 36. There just was too much competition for my attention. While the book was a page-turner, its storyline competed with my other thoughts.

Why hadn't Peter Griswold contacted me? Would he contact me tomorrow? If not, why not? Why would he want to avoid talking about Westbrook? I had stressed I wanted to talk about the property and its operations over the years which he knew about. And, I had avoided even the least hint I wanted to discuss Regina or her disappearance. Perhaps Peter Griswold had more he could tell me than I realised. What if he did know something about Regina or her disappearance? Was he trying to avoid putting himself in a position where he might inadvertently let slip some long-held secret or clue? Now, there was an interesting thought. And, just the motivation I needed to pursue him further.

Griswold wasn't Tuesday's only disappointment. Emily didn't have anything to say about Kirsty's DNA analysis. While she wouldn't mention it in front of Ben, there were at least a couple of opportunities during the evening when she might have told me the results without Ben overhearing. Again, I reminded myself it was only a possibility results would be available tonight, and they were more likely to be available tomorrow. This waiting around for things to happen and not being able to help hurry them along does not sit well with me.

Frustration made itself at home again and accompanied me to bed. It ensured a restless night followed.

*****

After what felt like little sleep, I overslept by about an hour on Wednesday morning. Then, although awake, I had little inclination to leave my bed and face the day. After all, I had no reason to get up this morning; no appointments and no work to undertake. At any other time, faced with similar circumstance, I would hare off to my beach place for a few days. But, the little voice in my head kept reminding me I did have work to do. I had to get to the bottom of the McGregor story. Kirsty would never settle properly until she knew all there was to know, and it was up to me to dig it up for her.

"Get up and do something," I snarled. "The day is half over and you still are lying in bed sulking." My dressing-down of the sulking me did the trick. An hour or so later I was climbing the stairs to my city office.

In my quest for answers this week, the plan was to call Thomas Agnew to arrange a further interview. I keyed his number. He answered almost on the first ring. We would meet for coffee at his cottage at ten o'clock. His only stipulation was for the meeting not to go too long as he had a lunchtime engagement – a birthday lunch for a fellow resident. To inflict further damage to both our waistlines and our cholesterol levels, I took a box of mixed pastries from the bakery downstairs.

In the scant time after my call and during the drive across town to the retirement village, I tried to develop a list of intelligent questions to put to Thomas. The key word was 'intelligent'. I had a whole raft of 'what if' speculative scenarios to put to him, which I was sure would generate discussion, but I wasn't confident any of them would produce the answers I needed. Then, I arrived at my destination, and there was nothing for it but to wing-it and hope for the best.

Despite my earlier misgivings, the meeting went well. It might have been due to my having nothing prepared and being reduced to asking point blank questions. After the usual initial niceties, I jumped straight into the topic I wanted to pursue.

"I'm sorry, I keep coming back to annoy you, Thomas but, as I start to grasp the story of the property and Regina, I find more I don't understand. As I recall, you said Regina came into some money which you invested for her, and then later you took over managing her affairs. What was to happen to Regina's estate in the event of her death?"

"She made a will, which still exists. Although, I think we know how Regina's story ends: her body has never been found and she has never been declared dead. So, in effect, I continue to manage Regina's estate as I always have done. The sobering aspect is, I am now not just an old man, but an ancient bloke. All is well while my health holds out but, as soon as I start having health problems which herald the beginning of the end for me, I will take steps to protect her estate after I am gone."

"Do you know the terms of her will, and who would benefit in the event of her death under normal circumstances?"

"Yes... She never stopped believing her daughter was alive somewhere and one day she would return. From the time she inherited her grandmother's money, she was determined whatever she had would go towards providing for Catherine."

"Now, with Catherine dead only a few years after running away from home, who benefits from the will? Catherine died intestate. She left no clear instruction regarding what should happen to anything she owned – and I suppose it includes anything she was bequeathed."

"It's not an unfamiliar situation. In fact, it's the same situation as occurred with Silas' estate. It too was to go to Catherine but, once she was deceased, the way was open for Kirsty to claim the estate. In the event Regina is declared dead sometime in the future, Kirsty would have no problem claiming her estate. And, the process would be much simpler than the long, hard slog she was subjected to this time."

"Right... I'm sure you've already tried to explain it to me, but who managed Silas McGregor's estate during the period between when he died and probate was granted in favour of Kirsty?"

"I did. Well, no, that's not quite right. When Silas died, Catherine would have been about seventeen and still a minor. As was the usual practice in such cases, a parent or guardian was granted power to act on behalf of the beneficiary. In the McGregor estate, Regina was empowered to act on behalf of her daughter, Catherine. Almost as soon as that was in place, she came and asked me to manage Silas' estate as well as her own. So, I managed both estates until I retired about five years ago."

"Yet, despite the arrangement, you were unaware probate had been granted to Kirsty and she now owned the property. I remember you saying something about having handed everything into the court when you retired. Would you mind explaining why?"

"You may well ask... I didn't hand the whole estate over to the court. All I handed over was anything to do with the property.

By the time I retired, the place had gone out of production. No one lived there, and no one worked there. What I didn't hand over to the court was the rest of the estate. Subsequent to Silas' death, Peter Griswold maintained the place as a going concern. He was an excellent farm manager, and a number of good years ensured the coffers were healthy. One of the first things I did after taking over was to initiate a regular small wage for Regina as a live-in housekeeper who continued to maintain the home on behalf of Catherine."

"So, cash kept rolling in some years after Silas was no longer around, and I assume you looked after paying all the necessary expenses such as Peter Griswold's wages, rates, and insurance. And, as I understand it, you continued the arrangement for some time after Regina disappeared ... Except for paying her a wage of course. Then, sometime later, Peter Griswold retired, and the place went out of production. Since then, what's happened about recurring expenses, such as the rates for instance?"

"Cash reserves far exceeded those costs over the years. In addition, a few months after Griswold retired, the neighbour, through the bank, tracked me down to ask about the future of the property. Although he never said so, I think he had ideas of leasing the place. I would never have agreed... At least I don't think I would have agreed. In the end, all he asked for was the right to fence off a small area adjoining his farm to use as an agistment paddock for his stock. I saw no problem with such an arrangement and we agreed an annual fee. Once it was settled, I could meet the recurring annual costs from the money paid by the neighbour. The agistment arrangement remains in place today."

"Thomas, at the risk of sounding crass, am I right in suspecting there is quite a bucket of cash now sitting in Silas McGregor's coffers?"

"It is a reasonable question, and your assessment of the situation is correct."

"Might I also be correct in assuming a similar situation also exists with Regina McGregor's estate?"

"Again, your assumption is correct. A great deal of money has accumulated in those accounts over the many years since they were established. And before you ask the next question, yes, if Kirsty has been deemed the legal heir to Silas McGregor's estate, she is indeed a wealthy woman … Or she will be when she claims her inheritance."

"And, in the event of the death or a declaration of death of Regina McGregor, should she be deemed Regina's heir, her fortune would expand by a considerable amount?" Thomas' answer was no more than a nod.

Time was racing towards Thomas' previously arranged lunchtime engagement. I brought the meeting to an end as soon as polite behaviour allowed. After showering him with my heartfelt thanks for his time and honesty, I went back to the solitude of my office to just sit and try to make sense of everything I'd heard this morning.

I was still at it when a call at three o'clock from Ben startled me back to reality. After telling him I would be at home tonight, he confirmed he would bring something for dinner and might arrive a little earlier than usual. As I hadn't heard from Emily by the time I left my office in town, I assumed there would be only two for dinner.

Still somewhat shell-shocked by all I'd learnt today, I was a good match for Ben, whose day appeared to have left him in no better condition. With stilted conversation about nothing of any consequence, and dinner dispatched at an earlier hour than usual, our evening turned into one of the earliest on record when Ben departed soon after eight o'clock.

Lights-out was just after nine o'clock but, before I fell asleep, I spent a long time staring into the darkness as I tried piecing together everything after the death of Silas McGregor and its consequence for Kirsty.

Chapter 18

Everything from my last meeting with Thomas Agnew shared breakfast with me this morning. While no actual figures were mentioned, it was clear Kirsty was not about to run out of cash. Although I didn't know how much Kirsty would inherit from Silas McGregor's estate, Thomas had hinted at a considerable amount.

Kirsty only ever talked about the property as part of his estate, and never mentioned anything about cash. Did she know the full extent of her grandfather's estate? Did she receive the money as part of the grant of probate? It would explain the way she was splashing cash about at present. Somehow, I doubted she knew about anything other than the property.

Apart from her never mentioning it, something else suggested she might be unaware of the cash in his estate. Thomas managed Silas McGregor's estate, and freely admitted he handed everything to do with the property to the court when he retired. It would explain why he wasn't advised when ownership passed to Kirsty. He never mentioned handing over to the court responsibility for the remainder of the estate. His comments suggested quite the contrary: he still managed the property's finances and paid its bills.

Was Regina's estate being handled in a similar fashion to her husband's? The difference was, hers had been kept 'hidden' since its inception; since the bequest from her grandmother. While there were unlikely to be ongoing expenses of any significance to be paid from Regina's account since her disappearance, Thomas held sole authority to act on the account... An account which was unlikely to be known about beyond Thomas and certain bank staff.

As Thomas was unaware of Kirsty, or of her link to the McGregor family until I first met with him, it's likely Kirsty remains unaware her inheritance might be more significant than she realised. If my assumption is correct and Kirsty is unaware of Regina's estate as well as the cash component of her grandfather's estate, then the money she is shelling out at the moment can only be her own, and it caused me concern. I suspect the amount of money she has spent in relation to the property since her arrival – not to mention on legal fees – tallies to a significant figure by now.

Should I be concerned when it is none of my business? I could claim my concern is only as a close friend, but there's more to it I think. A lurking question bobbed up again: is Kirsty's current lavish spending a result of her knowledge of the cash she has inherited?

Although Emily hasn't confirmed it, and it might be premature to speak of Regina in the past tense, both my gut and I are all but convinced the DNA sample Emily is analysing will provide evidence the bones hidden in the old house are those of Regina McGregor. While I hold that conviction, I find it impossible to think of her as anything but deceased. And, it highlights Emily's next potential dilemma.

Kirsty still has a long way to go before she might be considered as having her life together again. Confronting her with the truth about the bones might be more than she can handle. The ideal situation would be to have her settled and fully cognisant of the Silas McGregor part of her family history before introducing another major upheaval. While achieving it might be ideal, I doubt time is on my side. I fear the truth about those bones will be discovered within the next few days, and the subsequent impact of it on Kirsty will be swift and devastating.

How do I lessen the impact? She can't be protected from the truth. The question is, how best to deal with the situation when it arises. My gut kept telling me the key to the story was with Peter Griswold. I don't know what it was – call it sixth sense – but I remained convinced. Although he might not know what happened to Regina, I believed he had information which would help piece the story together.

"So why am I still sitting here?" I demanded of the universe, "When I should be out there prising the truth out of Peter Griswold."

The morning traffic had thinned out to a steady light stream as I made my way into my city office. As I expected, there were no messages or missed calls from Peter Griswold. Okay, so he's going to renege on his promise to talk to me. It was obvious he didn't know me well. If he did, he'd realise I would not go away until I had what I wanted. I snagged my bag off the chair where I dumped it when I came in, and was on my way down to my car again.

My knock received the same response as it did on my previous visit to Griswold's cottage. Thinking he might have been busy somewhere out on his block, I wandered along the side of the house and around to the back. Griswold was nowhere to be seen. After calling out a couple of times, I accepted defeat and returned to my car.

For a few moments I sat there with my frustration level at critical point, and considered my options. Peter Griswold's behaviour suggested he had something – maybe even plenty – he could tell me, but was not about to do so. I needed to devote serious thought to how to crack his defences and have him open up. Sitting in my office for the rest of the day pondering what to do about Griswold didn't appeal.

I remembered a small beach not far from Griswold's place I had visited a couple of times many years ago. In those days, this area was unsettled and the beach, as one of the district's best kept secrets, saw few visitors. Perhaps it might provide the ideal place for me to sit and think. The lovely lady on my car's navigation system soon guided me to my required destination.

Yep, this was the perfect place. The once narrow track through the scrub to the beach now was a well-made road through the bush to a small gavelled carpark. It was obvious the 'locals' now considered this 'their' beach. A stone-pitched wall separated the car park from the sand below, and a row of beach oaks planted along the wall helped hold the bank together. A bottle of water from the centre console went into my tote bag.

Then, minus my shoes and with my tote bag over my shoulder, I made my way down onto the sand. A little way along from the boardwalk leading down onto the beach, a couple of large rocks butted up against the man-made wall. The overhanging oaks shaded the rocks, creating an ideal place to sit and think. I thought the beach deserted, and why not? Today was a weekday and most people would be at work. Not long after settling on my perch atop one of the rocks, I had to reassess the situation. A figure appeared at the northern end of the beach and, accompanied by a dog, was heading my way.

How did he get here? Mine was the only vehicle in the car park. While how the man arrived was of no consequence, his mysterious sudden appearance intrigued me. Thoughts of Peter Griswold were banished to a distant corner of my mind as I focused on the figure advancing along the sand. Even at this distance, there was a familiarity about the man. It didn't look like the bloke I met on the horse the other day. Other than Peter Griswold, I didn't know anyone who lived out there.

He trudged along at a fair pace, and soon I could see the man well enough to recognise him. Peter Griswold was walking his dog on the hard sand close to the water's edge. I sent a silent thank you to the gods. Luck might be on my side today after all. The question now was how to play it from here? Should I march down and accost him? Or, should I remain perched on my rock until he notices me?

The latter wasn't an option. Griswold's eyes appeared glued to his feet as he trudged along the wet sand. If he continued in his present fashion, he wouldn't realise he wasn't alone. I had only one course of action. Leaving my bag on the rocks, I slithered off my perch and strode across the sand towards the man.

His dog was aware of me long before Peter realised I was there. Somehow, the man looked even frailer today. The shock caused by my sudden appearance in front of him might have dire consequences. I didn't want to find myself calling for the paramedics. Although the dog was doing a pretty good job of it already, I called out to alert him to my presence as I crossed the sand towards him.

"Peter… Peter Griswold… It's me, Sonny Whittington." He slowly swung his eyes up to me.

"Why are you here?" There was something about the way he spoke. His voice sounded hollow. Or, maybe, he sounded as though he wasn't quite with it this morning.

"I had no idea anyone would be here today. I had business out this way, and afterwards decided to take a break. This beach is a lovely place to daydream. Do you come here often?" The dog had decided I was okay, and was sat on its haunches beside Peter. He licked my offered hand.

Well, I've won over one half of the cast. Now for the other cast member… Standing there in the sun without a hat was not my idea of fun. Best I moved the meeting to where I wanted it before we both started to sizzle. "I was sitting up there in the shade on those rocks when I recognised you walking your dog. I have bottled water and a couple of muesli bars up there if you'd like to join me for a snack."

He hesitated a few moments before appearing to reach a decision. "I suppose you still want to talk to me about Westbrook?" He spoke barely above a whisper, but I heard every word.

"Yes, I still am interested in what you might feel inclined to tell me about the property and the people who owned it. As I mentioned earlier, knowing something about the place and the people who were there before will help the new owner settle in. And, information on how the place operated will assist in bringing the property back into production. So, yes, I would appreciate anything you might share with me. It doesn't have to be right here and now, but I would like it to be soon."

A brief, weary nod was his only response. Then, he looked over at the rocks for a moment before gesturing for us to head over to them. Maybe my luck was holding today, and he intended talking to me. After settling ourselves comfortably atop the rocks, I offered him a bottle of water and muesli bar. He waved the water away but accepted the bar. While I had rummaged in my bag for the muesli bars, I clicked the record button on my digital recorder and sent silent prayers to the gods. Had I pressed the right button? Was it recording over something vital? Would the recorder pick up everything well enough although it remained hidden in my bag?

On the basis it wouldn't do my cause much good to complain or criticise the man for failing to contact me as promised, I began as though our earlier conversation never happened.

"As you can imagine after being abandoned for so long, the McGregor property is heavily overgrown, and all vestiges of what went before are now lost. The tractor is being overhauled at the moment and, as soon as it has new tyres, the new owner will be able to use it to inspect at least some of the place. But, some information about the farm would be helpful anyway. Such information might include where the fence lines were, soil types across the property, and if and where any cropping occurred. No doubt, the new owner would work most of this out over time, but it would help bring the place back under production sooner if details were available at the outset.

Having been such a major part of the operation of the farm for so long, you would know so much about the place, and your knowledge might prevent a repeat of past unsuccessful initiatives. I'm not asking for anything of a personal or sensitive nature about your association with the property, and I'm sure the new owner also wouldn't expect you to divulge anything of such nature. Please think about what you might be able to contribute to help restore the place. Even just a mud map showing what was where in the past would be useful."

Griswold sat in silence just watching the waves rolling in onto the beach for a few moments. I was beginning to feel my appeal was about to receive outright rejection when I saw him drop his head and study his hands clenched in his lap. A slow turn of his head to face me and a brief nod gave me a moment of hope. I was a ball of nerves as I waited for him to clear his throat and shuffle around on his backside to face me.

"I suppose I could manage something along those lines. I don't know how useful it might be mind you. It's a long while since I've been there... and I don't hold any desire to revisit the place. I come into town most Mondays. Over the weekend, I'll give it some thought and see what I can come up with. If I find there is anything useful I might contribute to help the new owner, I could tell you about it while I'm in town on Monday. How does that suit you?"

It was better than I'd even dared hope for and, regardless of what else might happen on Monday, I would be available whenever it suited him. We agreed on a meeting in my office at about eleven o'clock. While there were still a lot of 'ifs' associated with the arrangement, and in spite of my better judgement, I felt a tingle of excitement. My only problem was, today was Thursday. Monday seemed an age away.

Our business concluded as far as Peter was concerned, he slithered off the rocks, doffed his hat to me, whistled to his dog, and set off back along the beach. His parting comment killed my fleeting moment of excitement.

"Right then, I'll be off. If I manage to come up with anything, I might see you on Monday."

Then, he trudged off across the sand and left me wondering whether I should even bother to pencil him in as an appointment for Monday. For about ten minutes after he disappeared from sight, I remained perched on my rock. What had I achieved this morning, and how confident was I about meeting Peter Griswold on Monday? The jury was out on both those issues. No matter how hard I tried to convince myself my chance meeting with Griswold today had been worthwhile, I'm a pragmatist. I drove back to my office still as unsure as I was while I sat on the rock.

The rest of the week and the weekend were noteworthy for their ordinariness. Nothing worthy of mention happened until I was back in my office on Monday morning.

*****

Monday found me with my enthusiasm level at about zero. My attempts over the weekend to find out more about the McGregor's and their property went nowhere, and left me to start the new week with elevated frustration levels. I almost wished for a herd of new clients demanding I start work for them today. Even the thought Peter Griswold might appear later this morning didn't do anything to lift my spirits. My gut and I both knew there was a fair chance he wouldn't show.

Then, just as I was feeling sorry for myself and sulking about the unfairness of life, a phone call startled me back to reality.

"Miss Whittington, this is Thomas Agnew. I know it's a terrible impertinence to ask, but might you have a few minutes spare to meet with me either today or tomorrow?"

"Thomas, lovely to hear from you... And, of course I have time to meet with you. Did you have any particular time in mind? Would you prefer I visited you at the retirement village, or did you want to come into my office?"

"Well, if it's not too impertinent of me, I have to come into the city later this afternoon and wondered whether you might have some free time, say, after four o'clock at your office."

"I have nothing booked from three o'clock onwards. So, any time after three o'clock works well for me. We could have a coffee – or maybe even something a bit stronger."

Thomas had no way of knowing how cathartic his phone call was. If nothing else, it was a good example of role reversal. All my meetings with Thomas so far have been at my instigation. My question then was: why does he now need to talk to me? Had something happened – gone wrong – with those financial estates he managed? What could possibly go wrong since I last spoke with him? With my mind in negative gear all day, in no time, it came up with several scenarios, none of which were good news.

As it was almost ten o'clock, I allowed myself a mid-morning coffee break, which stretched on way longer than normal as I considered the tone for my meeting with Peter Griswold... if he showed up. When I checked for the umpteenth time, the hands on the clock on the wall seem to be creeping towards eleven o'clock at much slower pace than usual today. I tried reminding myself he hadn't said he would be here at eleven. The key word in our meeting arrangement was 'about'. It might be midday before he arrived ... If he arrived.

Almost convinced Griswold wouldn't show up today, as eleven o'clock rolled by I busied myself with emails. At ten minutes after the hour, a knock on my door made me spring up out of my chair. Griswold, hat in hand and looking as nervous as a kitten, stood in the hallway outside. He accepted my offer of a coffee as he settled himself in one of the lounge chairs in my interview corner.

After again expressing my thanks for coming to talk to me, I nudged our conversation towards what he might tell me and, hopefully, what I wanted to hear. I was surprised when it didn't take too much encouragement for him to launch into his story.

"Yes, well, I don't know how useful any of this is going to be. If the new owner hasn't had a chance yet to look over the place, this might as well be in a foreign language. I'm sure it won't make any sense to them." As he spoke, he scratched around in the bag he had dumped beside his chair. "I took your advice and drew up this here mud map. It sort of shows the arrangements of the paddocks as they were when I was last there. Of course, things could have changed since then ... Before the new owners took over I mean. I don't know what old Agnew had planned for the place after I retired."

With his map unrolled and anchored out flat on the table by our coffee mugs, I inched forward in my chair for a better look at it. "This is brilliant. I'm sure it will be much appreciated. And, I can tell you, your retirement was the end of Westbrook as a productive property ... until now. Your map indicates the owners ran cattle and some areas were fenced off for them. But, it appears some areas were under crops. What did they grow?"

"It depended on the seasonal conditions – and the markets." While I knew what he meant, I indicated I didn't understand. I must have looked convincing because it triggered an explanation. "Sometimes they were put under pasture crops. Other times, if the weather and market indications were favourable, we might plant peanuts or other vegetable crops. And, of course, you had to ensure the crop you wanted to plant suited the soil type in the area you were to plant. Soil types vary across the property and not all of them are suitable for growing anything other than grass."

"I'm sure the new owner has no idea about such variations. Your information will be invaluable in getting the place up and running again."

"From what I've heard from you so far, I'm guessing the new owner is a city slicker with no knowledge of agriculture. They are going to struggle. They have a colossal job ahead of them if the current situation with the property is as bad as you make out. With no experience behind them, they will struggle to make a go of it at all, let alone bring it back to the standard it maintained in the past."

"Again, I only can tell you how much the new owner would benefit from any of your expertise you might be inclined to pass on."

"Well, by the sounds of things, they still haven't been able to explore the place, so they are nowhere near ready to be worrying about what to plant where. I'll have a think about whether there is anything I might be able to help them with in the future. In the meantime, you know where to find me if the situation changes, and you need to talk to me again."

For a moment after Peter left my office, I felt guilty about not having enlightened him about the new owner... but only for a moment. I needed to keep Griswold onside and talking to me for a bit longer. Telling him Westbrook's new owner was a woman – a *single* woman – who has a degree in Ag Science might prove counterproductive. He struck me as 'old school' and would throw up his hands in disgust at the thought of a woman running Westbrook ... regardless of the fact Regina ran it after her husband's death.

Shoving such thoughts aside for the moment, I turned my attention to the mud map he left with me. It was obvious he put considerable thought and effort into producing it. While I knew nothing of the intricacies involved in running a property such as Westbrook, I felt Kirsty would appreciate the map when I gave it to her … just as soon as I had it copied for my files. The map was too big to copy on my machine. Although I could copy it in a number of pieces and stick them together later, I preferred it was copied in one piece. A copy place near the Post Office could do it in a flash on their big machine.

A check on the time told me, if I went now, I could have the map copied and be back in my office before my meeting with Thomas Agnew later this afternoon.

Chapter 19

An apologetic Thomas Agnew arrived at 3.45PM. "I do apologise for my early arrival. I know my appointment was for four o'clock, but my previous appointment finished earlier than anticipated. They usually run so far behind time, but today I had to wait only seven or eight minutes. I took a chance you might be free a bit earlier too."

"And, as you can see, I am. So, come in and take a seat." I gestured to the lounge chairs in my interview corner. "You've saved me from the dreaded filing I was going to do to fill in time until you arrived. Can I offer you a coffee before we start?" My offer was accepted with enthusiasm.

On my way across to the coffee machine, I realised I had left Peter Griswold's mud map of Westbrook spread out on the coffee table where I studied it after having it copied. When I glanced back, Thomas was subjecting it to intense scrutiny. As the machine was completing the second mug of coffee, I called out.

"Thomas, would you mind rolling up the map on the table please so I can put the coffees down without slopping them all over it?"

He sprang into action and, without a word, the map was rolled up and pushed to one side. But, his eyes lingered on it. As I placed his coffee in front of him, he looked up at me. Sadness was in his eyes. He indicated the map with a jerk of his head and said, "Peter Griswold's handiwork I presume?"

"Yes. I asked him to put together something which might help the new owner gain an understanding of how the place operated in the past. He dropped the map in this morning. The map appears to concern you. Is there something I should know about it?"

"No. No, not at all. I was surprised Peter produced it for you. He is the best person – the only person – able to provide such information, but I'm surprised he bothered to do so. I found he went a little strange when he retired. He became surly and a bit of a recluse."

"I understood he retired of his own volition. He can't blame you for his decision can he?"

"Perhaps not, but I don't think it was so simple not to his way of thinking anyway. For some reason, I think he held me responsible for Regina's disappearance, and the fact she was never found. Although he never said anything to me, there were hints; inferences I hadn't cared enough or done enough. He remained civil but distant during the last few weeks before his retirement. I don't think we've spoken more than half a dozen words since then. I don't have a problem with him. Whatever the problem is, it is all Peter's."

"He was prickly when we first met, and I made a point of chasing him when he reneged on our arrangement. I admit I wasn't confident he would produce the promised map, or if I would see him today. He appeared convinced the new owner wouldn't have a clue about running the place and would need all the help they could get. I don't think his concern was for the owner so much as for the property. He sees an opportunity for the property to become productive, and he doesn't want to see it fail and be abandoned again."

"What does he know about the new owner?"

"Not a lot; he hasn't sought details and I haven't provided any. For a start, I don't think he would approve of the owner, and would see all his misgivings confirmed. I'll be happy to share the information with him, but it will be when and if he asks for it."

"Probably a good move on your part, but don't hold your breath waiting for him to become interested."

"Okay, but this is your appointment. So, what did you want to talk to me about?"

"Well, I realise it is a tad impertinent of me, but I wondered if it might be possible for me to meet the new owner of Westbrook. I will understand if, for whatever reason, it is not possible. All I hoped to do was to explain the cash component of Silas McGregor's estate, about which only I appear to have knowledge."

"While it seems a fair enough request to me, I will need to run it past the person concerned before I can say more. I doubt there will be a problem. It also means I will have to come clean about the research I have been doing, and I had hoped to be a bit further advanced with it before sharing the information. Leave it with me. I'll see what I can do and will let you know the outcome. Is there any particular time, day or date which wouldn't suit you if I am to set up a meeting?"

"Set it up for whenever you can if you can and I will make sure I am available. Just bear in mind, I am old and can give no guarantees about how much longer I will be around." Although he ended with a wry smile, I had received the implied message not to leave it too long.

After assuring him I would try to set something up as soon as possible, he thanked me and left. Apart from his sound reason for wanting to meet with Kirsty, I owed him for all the time and information he had given me. I resolved to give Kirsty a call this evening to discuss going out to the property to talk to her tomorrow.

With nothing more to keep me at my city office, I gave myself an early mark and headed home. As I crawled along with end-of-day city traffic, I realised I hadn't heard from Ben or Emily today. Perhaps I would be dining alone this evening. Such a situation at any other time would be a welcome change, but not tonight. Eating alone didn't bother me, but I did want to know the results of the DNA tests Emily had carried out. While I could call and ask about the results, held greater appeal.

Soon after I arrived home, Ben called to say he was working late and wouldn't join me for dinner. No surprises there, I had assumed he wasn't coming. His call was followed a few minutes later by one from Emily; could she pick up something and join me for dinner. It looks as though everything is falling into place for me this evening after all.

Before I did anything else, and before Emily arrived, I needed to talk to Kirsty. When my call went unanswered, I went for a shower and intended trying Kirsty again later. She returned my call as I emerged from the bathroom.

"Sorry I missed your call earlier. I was being reminded why I hated Sydney's traffic as my taxi fought its way to my hotel."

"You're in Sydney? Why are you there?"

"I think I told you I agreed to work on contract for my previous employer. They have a new research project starting soon and I will be working on it. Today was a briefing session for everyone involved. While I didn't need to participate, I decided it would be best to do so. And my tax accountant had the final tax return ready for the business I ran with my ex-partner. As I was going to be in Sydney, I could deal with the tax return while I was here, and visit my Sydney-based solicitor to sign some registration document for the new business I set up after our break-up of the partnership."

"So, how long do you plan to be in Sydney?"

"No longer than required... I'm booked on the late plane home tomorrow night. Is there a problem you called to tell me about?"

"Everything is fine here as far as I know. I hadn't spoken to you for a few days and wanted to catch up again. As I'm having a quiet time at the moment, I thought I might take a drive out to the property to see how thing were progressing – and have a coffee with you."

"Sounds great... Although you won't notice much has happened since you were there last. How about you come out in time for coffee on Wednesday morning?"

A few minutes after talking to Kirsty, Emily arrived with great looking steaks to barbeque and a selection of salads to accompany them. While the barbeque on the deck heated up, Emily and I sat in silence with a glass of wine and soaked up the ambiance of the evening. The fragrance of jasmine and rosemary drifted in on the cool, light breeze, while the vibrant sunset colours enhanced the solitude offered by my deck. It was heady stuff, and hard to abandon in favour of cooking steaks. By the time we returned to a functional state, the barbeque was well and truly ready to do its job.

It was an unspoken agreement we would eat out on the deck. While I carefully timed cooking the steaks, Emily fetched the salads and other necessary equipment from the kitchen. Little conversation interrupted our eating until the food was dispatched. "Demanding kind of day…?" I asked Emily. She looked weary.

"Yes… no, not really… just never-ending more of the same; more of man's inhumanity to man."

"Finding those hidden bones didn't help I don't suppose. They just gave you one more case to deal with."

"God, no, they are the only exciting thing to happen over the last couple of weeks. There has been a continual stream of material coming into the lab – and just when my key staff member was off through illness for the week. I already was owed a few days off, and then I worked all weekend. Once my staff bloke returns later this week, I think I'll take those few days off. If you see Ben in the meantime, tell him not to find any new cases for us to work on until at least the end of next week. So, what about your day… anything interesting happen?"

"Interesting is one word to describe it, but I'm inclined to say today has been just as confusing as it was interesting."

I told her of my meetings with Peter Griswold and the map of the property he produced, and of Thomas Agnew's visit this afternoon. Then I moved our conversation around to the question I wanted to ask since she arrived.

"Earlier this evening, I discovered Kirsty will be in Sydney until tomorrow night. I'll have coffee with her at the property on Wednesday morning. As Thomas Agnew wants to meet her, it means I have to tell her about the research I've been doing on her behalf; preferably before she meets Thomas Agnew. Anyway,

Wednesday is looking like my 'tell all day'. Although, it might depend on her frame of mind after her trip of Sydney. But, it brings me to my big question once again: what did analysis of Kirsty's DNA show? As you haven't mentioned it, I suspect it's not good news."

"It depends on your point of view, and whether you consider no news to be good news. The results were inconclusive. The sample I had to analyse was a bit 'iffy' to begin with, and the results it produced were not much better than rubbish. I'm thinking I should see if she will agree to a proper sample. And, I suspect it won't be too much longer before Ben starts demanding one. I too might be visiting Kirsty at home before the end of the week."

"Try to avoid Wednesday if you can. I would like to break the news of my research to her while we are alone. Thanks to her recent frame of mind, I don't know how she will react. Although she sounded all right over the phone this evening, she still has another day in Sydney, and it has the potential to be traumatic. Wednesday might not prove the 'right' time to talk to her."

"Yeah, Wednesday might not be a good time. I was aiming for Thursday or Friday, depending on when I am able to start my few days off. My thinking is, if she agrees to provide a sample, I'll go in at night to set up the analysis. I wouldn't be doing anything questionable, but I do want to keep it quiet until I have the results."

The answer to my question about Kirsty's DNA wasn't helpful. I knew I would feel more confident telling Kirsty about the work I had done if I could offer something solid about the bones. Now it looks as though such discussion will have to wait for another day. Conversation for the remainder of the evening was light and general until Emily left at a bit after nine o'clock.

As it was too early for bed, and in the hope some new line of enquiry might emerge, I spent the next hour or so poring over the information I had amassed so far on the McGregor family. It appears my muse had clocked off early for the day. Not even a hint of inspiration was forthcoming.

Disgusted and cranky, I called it a night and went to bed. After lying awake in the dark for quite some time trying to think of some new angle to research tomorrow, I accepted there was unlikely to be anything more I could achieve before meeting with Kirsty on Wednesday.

*****

Thanks to the appearance throughout the day of a number of potential new clients, Tuesday morning did not drag on as I had expected – and, I signed up one new client. It would take her until the end of the week to round up the necessary background information I required to start work on her case. We agreed I would start work on her case after she delivered the information, probably early next week.

The highlight of the day occurred just as I was considering what I might like for lunch. An unexpected visit by Peter Griswold shoved all thoughts of lunch aside. He looked awkward and apologised at least twice for arriving without an appointment. After my profuse reassurance his presence was most welcome, he opened up about his unscheduled trip to town.

"I got to thinking about the map of Westbrook I gave you and realised I might have done the wrong thing." My heart sank. I hoped he wasn't going to demand its return, but he continued before I could comment.

"When I thought about it, I wasn't sure what information would be most useful. I mean, I wasn't sure a map of the property from which era would be the most useful to the new owner. I'm probably not making much sense. Please bear with me while I explain. The map I gave you shows how the property operated in earlier times. In more recent times, some of the information was different – different from how I showed it on the map. I'm concerned what's on the map might not be helpful today. Perhaps, if you might clarify the situation for me, I'll be able to work out what to do for the best."

"Well, I think the new owner would welcome any information you can provide. Maybe, if I understood the differences between the two eras you are talking about, I might be in a position to give you a better answer."

"It's complicated." I gestured for him to tell me about it. "Okay, the map I gave you shows the way the property operated during the time of Silas McGregor, and then later when Regina ran the place. Lots of changes happened in more recent times when Regina had little say in what went on. You have to understand when I say 'recent times', I mean twenty years ago, not last year."

No further information required. Instinct told me he referred to the period after Raymond Clifford took control of the place. While I was interested in the changes Clifford instigated during his time, I also wanted to know more about Clifford the man. It might be worth the cost of lunch to find out what Griswold might have to say about Mr Clifford.

"Peter, are you in a hurry to return to your farm?"

"No-o, not in a hurry … Why do you ask?"

"Just before you arrived, I was thinking about what I might have for lunch. How would you like to join me for lunch somewhere? There's a nice little bistro a bit further along the street from here. We could grab a bite to eat there if you have time."

His token resistance was short lived. We soon were seated in the bistro and waiting for our meals to arrive. While we waited, I asked a few questions about his farm: how long he'd had it and what he produced there? I waited until our meals were delivered and there was less chance of interruption before I asked about Raymond Clifford. At first, Griswold hedged around the topic, but I managed to pin him down.

"Peter, it's obvious you are reluctant to talk about the bloke Clifford, but you would have had a lot to do with him during his time on Westbrook. From the little you have said, I gather he took over running the property from Regina. Was there some reason Regina handed over the reins although she appeared capable of running the place?"

"How it came about is something I was not privy to, but I don't think it was a simple case of *handing over the reins*, as you put it. I suspect it was more a case of pressure being brought to bear. More like the reins being yanked away from her, rather than handed over."

"What can you tell me about Raymond Clifford? Was he a good farm manager? And, how did he come to be there in the first place?"

"Argh, anything I could tell you would be no better than gossip. The one thing I can tell you is, Clifford was no farmer. He had no idea about running a farming property like Westbrook. I don't think he'd ever been on a farm before he arrived. But, as I said before, I wasn't privy to anything that went on in the household."

"Okay, it's obvious you didn't think much of the bloke. Why? Or, perhaps the question should be: why don't you want to tell me about it?"

"I was brought up to say nothing, rather than to speak ill of people. I cannot say anything good about Raymond Clifford, why he came to Westbrook in the first place, or about his ultimate intention. I will tell you he was wrong'un through and through. There wasn't a decent bone in his body. And, a lot of the changes he insisted we made on Westbrook were rubbish. No, not just rubbish, they were just plain the wrong thing to do.

He had fences pulled down so cattle could roam on good cultivated paddocks, and then he tried to grow crops on areas where the soil was so poor it barely grew decent grass. I tried talking him out of some of the stuff he wanted to do. He threatened me with the sack. While it held a certain appeal, I owed it to Mrs McGregor and her daughter, Catherine, to stay on and protect their interests as best I could. It was no easy chore, and I didn't have much success."

"Working under his direction must've been almost unbearable for you. Did Regina have much say in what went on, or did she try to intervene in any way?"

"It's difficult to say. I wasn't to know what went on behind closed doors, but I don't think she had any say. He might have threatened me with the sack, but I often wondered what he held over her. It disgusted me to see her so cowered down while he was around. It's not how she was. She was a strong, knowledgeable lady … a real lady. Clifford, on the other hand, came out of some gutter somewhere. There was nothing refined or decent about him."

Our conversation stalled while bistro staff cleared our table and brought us coffee. In spite of my best efforts afterwards, I was unable to reignite our discussion of Raymond Clifford. With little reason to drag lunch on longer, I moved to wrap up Peter's visit.

"I suppose I haven't been much help to you in deciding whether the map you have produced – or another map you might produce – is the best option for the new owner. If I'm honest, I'm inclined to suggest the map you gave me yesterday will suffice. What I can't do, is guarantee the new owner won't want to ask questions, or seek further information."

"Yeah, a similar thought had occurred to me. The best outcome I suppose would be achieved if I sat down with the new owner to discuss the property in detail." By the time he finished speaking, Peter was on his feet and ready to leave. "Let's play it by ear," he suggested. "Give them the map, and we'll see what happens afterwards."

Oh, you can bet your boots I'll give Kirsty your map I thought as I watched him make his way out of the bistro. Had I read too much into his final comments? Was he suggesting he might be amenable to a meeting with Kirsty? The first and perhaps the major hurdle, before such a meeting can take place, is for Peter Griswold to accept the fact the new owner of Westbrook is a woman. Although, he seemed okay about Regina running the place all those years ago. Maybe another woman in charge won't faze him too much.

The short walk back to my office provided me with an opportunity to consider a strategy to facilitate a meeting between

Kirsty and Peter Griswold ... and preferably at Westbrook. If all else failed as far as Peter was concerned, perhaps the fact Kirsty is Regina McGregor's granddaughter might sweeten the deal. A key factor in engineering any such meeting might be the new case I am to start work on next week. Some urgency might attach to whatever strategy I devise.

My afternoon went past in a blur. Before I knew it, I was on my way home to have Ben join me for dinner. Tonight, I would have preferred to be alone. But, maybe his company will help take my mind off a possible Kirsty/Griswold meeting. I did need something to take my mind off it, if I was to have anything resembling a decent night's sleep.

Chapter 20

On the early drive into my city office, and later all the way out to Westbrook, I struggled with how to lead into the conversation I needed to have with Kirsty. I arrived at the property no wiser than when I left home this morning. "Just wing it," I told myself without conviction as I pulled up out front of the old house.

Kirsty came out onto the verandah of the old place and bounced down the stairs to meet me. "I was just doing a bit of exploring. I haven't been in there since the last time we were all here, and I decided it was time I started devoting some thought to the old place. How to rearrange the upper floor is going to be challenging. My comfortable 'temporary quarters' seem to have taken some of the urgency out of the refurbishment."

"I'm not surprised. With so much to do on the property, the house is bound to be way down the list. What do you see as your priority tasks? To my way of thinking, clearing the ground so the place can become productive again might top the list." By the time I finished speaking, we were climbing the stairs of her quarters.

"Yeah, I suppose it tops my list too. Apart from a bit of mowing around this immediate area, nothing much has happened yet. But, the mowing did help me discover all the implements for the tractor. So I've no excuse for not doing anything. Angus Walker from nextdoor has made helpful suggestions about how to make a start… and where to start. I suppose the whole thing was a bit overwhelming, so I shoved it in the too hard basket and left it there. With all the Sydney stuff out of the way, I might be able to think and operate better."

This was going to be too easy, I told myself. Everything was going so well. It was setting everything up for the conversation I wanted. As soon as we sat down with our coffee and wedges of the cake I brought with me, I dived straight in before the conversation's thread was lost.

"It's interesting to hear you are struggling to commence what must be a huge job ahead. With the place so overgrown, it's impossible to see if there is anything out there, or how the place was laid out, or anything else about the property. But, I do have something in the car which might help with some of the unknown factors. I'll fetch it after we finish our coffees. Between now and then, I have something to tell you... Well, it's more like I need to come clean about something."

"Okay, I'm intrigued. You have my undivided attention. So, come on; spit it out. What's your big revelation then?"

"Right well, I suppose it all started with your story of discovering who you were and your inheritance from grandparents whom you knew nothing about before you learned you were adopted. Then, for me, finding the bones just elevated the mystery to the point where I felt there were too many unanswered questions. With so many other things happening in your life, I knew you didn't have the headspace even to think beyond one day at a time. Also, I knew, even after you managed to bring everything else under control, you would not be able to settle properly until you knew the whole story.

Those unanswered questions were critical pieces of the story. At least, from the way I saw the situation, knowing the whole story was important to your being able to move on with your life here. So, while you were dealing with everything else, I set about finding the answers we needed."

"You are right about the almost overwhelming amount of stuff I don't know. Sometimes in the dark of night, when sleep is being elusive, all sorts of questions come to haunt me. The only way I've been able to cope – with everything, not just those questions – was to ignore them and keep them corralled in a dark corner of my mind. I'm almost not game to ask what you managed to dig up. And, am I able to cope with whatever it is? But, as I am curious, perhaps you should tell me your story and then we will work out how I'm going to deal with it."

"Before I begin, there is something I need to know. Are you aware if there is any more to Silas McGregor's estate than this property?"

"No, there is nothing more as far as I know. I was going to make an appointment to see Nathan last week but, when the Sydney trip came up, I put it off until after I was back."

"Was there something in particular you needed to discuss with him? I'm sorry. I sound as though I'm trying to pry into your private life. I'm not. I just wondered whether there was something more to do with the estate to sort out."

"Relax. It was nothing complicated. Nathan called as a follow-up to confirm everything had gone according to plan and I had taken over the property as expected. I assured him everything was okay. When I thought about it later, I wondered if there was anything more I should know. I've never received a copy of Silas' will, and I thought it would be nice to have a copy, and to know the precise wording of the document. As my first port of call, I was going to ask Nathan if he had a copy. Have I set you mind at ease about why I was going to talk to Nathan?"

"I can't say you have, but we will come back to it later."

"Right… it's your story, so let's hear it. Please begin."

Where to begin? After a moment's hesitation, I decided to start my 'confession' from the point of having tracked down Thomas Agnew as someone who might be knowledgeable about the McGregor's.

"He is a retired solicitor, and was Nathan Jones' boss from when Nathan started at his current legal practice. Thomas had been Regina McGregor's legal representative and, after the death of Silas McGregor when Regina began managing his estate on behalf of her daughter, Catherine, she handed over running the estate to Thomas. When he retired about five years ago, in the hope one day Catherine, Regina, or someone, would come forward to claim it, he handed over to the court everything relating to the property. Thanks to Nathan's efforts, the property now has a new and rightful owner."

"So…? This is all old news. When do we start on the new stuff you're going to tell me?"

"Argh… I'm not doing this well, and I know why. The next part is a bit more confronting and difficult to tell. In fact, I'm going to give you an 'executive summary' for now. The detailed version will come later.

Suffice to say Thomas knew Regina for a lot of years, both as a client and a friend. He speaks highly of her … but not of Silas. Amongst everything else we talked about, he mentioned Peter Griswold. Also now retired for some time, Griswold was the farm manager here for a long time. I figured his knowledge of the place might be of interest to you, and maybe helpful in re-establishing the place."

"Anything I can learn about how the place used to be would be wonderful."

"He has produced a rough, hand-drawn map of the property showing fence lines and the likes, and has added notations where he thought explanation might be necessary. His map is in my car and I will fetch it for you in a moment. As well as what Thomas Agnew knows about the place, Peter Griswold is bound to know other stuff as well. So, between the pair of them, it's possible to generate a picture of not only how the property operated, but what life was like here before Regina disappeared."

"You have spoken with both men? Are you going to share what you have gathered from your meetings with them, or are you going to keep me guessing?"

"I could share their stories, but I thought you might like to hear them from the blokes themselves, rather than second hand through me. They both have expressed an interest in meeting you."

"But, if you have heard their stories, why do I need to meet them? Tell me, and I will be happy with however much you managed to gather."

"It would be better if you talked to them directly. Then you could ask question and seek clarification, if needed. I can't give you the same background information as they can."

"How do you know what they can tell me – or how much they can tell me – if they haven't told it to you already? I'm not keen… I don't think I'm up to having such discussions. And, look at the place. If they see the property looking like this, they will think I'm a total loser who won't do any good here."

This was not going as I hoped it would, and I suspected it was not going to be easy to turn things around. Once again, I checked my own motives for withholding the information I had gathered. Some of it was explosive stuff. Maybe coming to talk to her today was too soon. Her frame of mind is not yet sound enough to handle some of the details. Should I just deliver an overview which omits some of the rougher information?

No; today was not the right time for even an overview. But, having started down this track, I had to go some way along it. "Well, Kirsty, what you do is up to you. I'm not here to push you into doing something you'd prefer not to. But, I will go out to my car now to fetch Peter Griswold's map. Again, what you do with it afterwards is up to you."

My car was parked too close to the quarters for me to waste much time walking to it, retrieving the map, and walking back to Kirsty. Nevertheless, I didn't rush. I was working on the assumption giving her a little time to think things over might change her mind. It didn't, and I was less than happy about it. Smile and keep it friendly, I reminded myself as I returned to Kirsty. Being cranky about her attitude wasn't going to help.

"Come and help me roll this out on the dining room table," I said as I walked into the lounge room where Kirsty remained seated where I left her. "We'll need weights of some sort to hold the corners down. Can you find something we can use please?" She grabbed another couple of mugs, and then scratched around in a cupboard to come up with a tin of tomatoes and one of chick peas.

"Here, this lot should hold it flat enough. So, let's have a look at what we have here." I rolled the map out and held it flat while Kirsty plonked the four 'weights' on its corners.

"There you go, Kirsty. This is how the place used to look all those years ago."

My not mentioning how long ago or in which 'era' the place looked as it did on the map was a deliberate ploy. Given her lack of knowledge of how life here was back then, my trying to explain the time period the map represented would confuse the situation.

"Goodness, he put a lot of work into this. It will take me a while to absorb it all." After bending over the table to scan the map from side to side, she eased herself upright again and stretched her back. "Some of his comments are fascinating. I'll need to apply some thought to them before I do too much about the place."

I allowed myself a moment of triumph. Was this the start of a breakthrough? I hoped so, as I wanted her to meet with both Thomas and Peter to hear their stories firsthand. Rather than continue to advocate for meetings with those two men, I felt it wise to change the topic for a while and, hopefully, return to it later.

"Earlier, you mentioned Angus Walker. Has he been here again since he serviced the tractor?"

"Uhmm… yeah, Angus has come over a couple of times. He wanted to follow-up and make sure everything went okay with having the new tyres fitted. Oh, and then he came over again after I cleared the long grass from around the implements lying out there in the open beyond the outbuildings. He was concerned some of them might be dangerous to use if they had built up heavy rust over however long they were idle."

"What was his assessment of the equipment?"

"He was a bit concerned about the condition of the slasher but, after he did a bit of work on it, it is now passed fit for use. A couple of other implements were a bit dodgy too, but there was nothing serious. The disc harrows needed new discs, and a few of the tines on the rakes needed replacing. He sent me off with a shopping list for all the required replacement bits and pieces.

All the new stuff has been fitted now and everything is ready to start working-up ground… soon."

"Why 'soon'…? What is stopping you, now everything has been assessed as in sound working order?"

"Honestly…? I wish I knew. I just don't seem able to make myself hop on the tractor and do some work on the place. Every time I think about making a start, the thought of it is too overwhelming … and I find something 'important' I need to do first."

"Is it why you were wandering around in the old house instead of clearing paddocks?"

Kirsty shrugged and then nodded. "Yeah, perhaps you're right. It is what I've been doing. It not as though I don't know what I have to do, or how to do it. It's about not being able to get started."

"Perhaps Peter's mud map will inspire or motivate you. I'm afraid there is little I can contribute to help you jump into farming mode. Instead, how about you show me around the old house? I've never ventured much beyond the front room. On the few occasions I was in the house, a strange wall and the things it hid seemed to keep us anchored in the front room." Although I had no particular interest in a tour of the house, I felt it sensible to shift the focus to the house for a while, and away from work required in the paddocks.

A call on Kirsty's phone rescued me from a long, boring wander through the building. It was filthy, with the crud of decades of neglect on every surface … and so was I by the time my tour ended sooner than expected. While Kirsty dealt with her phone call, I retreated to the verandah – and fresh air.

It was a few minutes later before Kirsty joined me there. Those few minutes gave me time to survey as much of the property as was visible from my elevated vantage point. I developed a new appreciation of what faced Kirsty in making the place a going concern again. Although I knew she was capable of the work required, because of the extent of the task ahead, she would need help.

Another big question elbowed its way into my train of thought: can she manage to employ someone to help? With no knowledge of her financial situation, it was difficult to know. And, it occurred to me how careful Thomas Agnew was in avoiding giving me any clues as to the amount of cash he still managed in the estates of Silas and Regina McGregor. I accepted it was appropriate for him to treat such information as confidential, but it didn't stop me wanting to know how much Kirsty stood to inherit.

Two issues were clear: she needed help on the property, and she needed to talk to Thomas Agnew. It was imperative I make the latter of the two happen as, to my mind, it would facilitate the solution to the first issue. It was then, Kirsty wandered out to join me.

"Sorry about the call, but I had to take it. It was from my Sydney-based accountant. She has submitted the final tax return to the Tax Office, and wanted to tell me I would receive a small refund."

"Now there's a surprise… a refund from the Tax Office. It's not every day you receive one of those."

"Don't get too excited. She said it was 'small', so I don't doubt it won't be much. Anyway, I won't know how much until I read the email she sent me. Now, as we both look as though we've spent the morning down in the mines, I suggest we wash off the grime and then have lunch."

"Regardless of how small your refund is, I guess every bit helps at the moment. You've already had massive expenditure, and there are heaps more expenses to come." I couldn't help myself. This felt like a good opportunity to bring up the matter of money and again try to persuade Kirsty to meet with Thomas Agnew.

"Yeah, there's been a bit of outlay involved so far, but it shouldn't be too bad for a while now. If, for the moment, we ignore what refurbishing the old house might cost, the next major expenses will come when I need to restock the property.

So, there shouldn't be any further major expenses for a while yet … not until after I find the paddocks I need for the stock."

"What about fuel for the tractor? You will chew up a fair bit of diesel clearing this place. I'm surprised there isn't a bulk tank for diesel somewhere close to the sheds. Have you come across one anywhere? You will need to have one filled before you start work. And you will need to hold quantities of petrol on the place, not only for your car, but also the mower and the ATV. It looks to me as though you still have some preparatory work to do before you can start the real task ahead of you. The price of fuel these days means you will have a further couple of large expenses to meet."

"You're right. I hadn't thought about installing a couple of fuel tanks, but I do need them before I start any clearing operations. One of the joys of life on the land: there is never a shortage of things on which to spend money. The trick is being able to recoup it from what you produce."

"Maybe, if you knew someone with a herd of goats, you could bring them in on agistment. They would help clear some of the brambles and stuff, and you could charge an agistment fee. Feel free to tell me it's none of my business but how are your finances holding up?"

"I admit they have taken a bit of a caning in the last couple of weeks or so, but I'm okay. And, yes, I am aware I need to get stuck in so I can start generating an income stream. It's not as grim as you might imagine though. I'm still paid by my former employer for the work on the plant breeding project, and a bit of work still trickles in since we split the computer business."

"Good… so you will be able to continue to eat. But, I doubt those income streams are sufficient to fund the work required on this place."

"No, but I'm not stony broke yet, and I think I'll be okay until the place starts paying its way… if I'm careful. Look, I know you are worried about me, and I do appreciate your concern. But, I will work it out somehow … I have to."

"Right, it's time I stopped dancing around this issue, and told it as it is. Please note before we go any further, I do not have details to give you other than what I am about to say. You need to meet with and talk to Thomas Agnew. *You will learn something to your advantage* – as they used to say in the good old days. So, stop mucking about and tell me when would be a good time for him to come to see you."

"Well, no. I don't...."

"I'm not interested in what you don't want so, if it was what you were about to say, don't bother. If you don't agree, and give me a day and time which suits you, I will bring him out here anyway whenever it suits him to come. And, while we are on the subject of people who are willing to help you, if you don't change your attitude, I will arrive out here one day with Peter Griswold in tow as well. Now, is there anything in any of what I've said you don't understand? If there is, we should clarify it now, as I will do as I said, if you don't stop playing silly buggers and apply some intelligence to the situation."

Kirsty stiffened and I knew a tirade would follow. Before she could utter a word, I set my jaw and gave her a hard, unwavering stare. It was one she encountered quite a few times in our youth. After a moment, I watched her back down. Maybe victory would be mine after all.

"You haven't changed one damned bit over the years, have you? Okay, I'll meet this geriatric solicitor of yours. Make it tomorrow and let's have it over and done with."

"Wonderful… I'll call him to see if he is available tomorrow."

"While you are about it, I will do something about making us lunch." As I picked up my phone and headed for the door, she called after me, "And you had better give the Griswold bloke a call to see if he is available too … Might as well deal with the lot while we are about it."

Victory is mine! "Happy to oblige… I'll help with lunch as soon as I make the calls."

By the time I returned from calling Thomas and Peter, lunch was ready and waiting for me. Thomas had jumped at the opportunity to meet with Kirsty. A previous commitment on Friday meant tomorrow, Thursday, was best for him. Unlike Thomas, now the chance to meet with Westbrook's new owner presented itself, Peter dithered about taking up the offer. Nothing had changed, except he was nervous about meeting a stranger. I thought I also detected a reluctance to visit Westbrook.

It seemed as though he favoured meeting the new owner in town, or somewhere other than on the property. I stressed how more effective a meeting would be on the site they were to discuss, but he took some convincing. My offer to Peter was the same as the one to Thomas: I would collect him and drive him out to Westbrook. Then, I would stay out of the way while the meeting happened, so I wasn't hanging around to overhear or interfere. When the meeting concluded, I would drive him home again.

Thomas had accepted my offer of transport, but wanted me to be a part of his discussions. Peter rejected the same offer. He would drive himself out, and thought he would be more comfortable talking to the owner without me present. Tomorrow was not a good day for him to visit Westbrook but, if it suited the owner, Friday would be good. If Kirsty dithered about it, I would work damned hard to make sure Friday did suit.

Over lunch, I outlined the plans in place for the visits by Thomas and Peter. Kirsty didn't quibble about either of the arrangements, but insisted she wanted me present on both occasions. Although I cited Peter's request for me not to be present, my argument against Kirsty's request fell on deaf ears. So, while I told Kirsty I would be there, I was determined to make my own arrangements on the day, to suit the day.

The only real problem with everything arranged and agreed to so far was the timing of Peter Griswold's visit. He only stipulated his preferred day, but not the time. I resolved to call him later to find out – on the basis the owner might like to know when to expect him.

Chapter 21

Thursday morning saw me at my city office early. I wanted to deal with routine admin tasks and collect all the material from my research into the McGregors before I collected Thomas. Kirsty expected us at ten o'clock, so there was little time to spare before I drove across town to pick-up Thomas and head out to the property. On my way down to my car, I remembered something for morning tea would be nice, and detoured to the bakery for a box of cupcakes.

Thomas was out the door and striding towards the car the moment I pulled up out front of his cottage. I suspected he stood at his front window all morning waiting for me to arrive. He carried a small satchel, which appeared heavy for its size. I opened a rear door and he dumped the case on the back seat... and gave it a reassuring pat before closing the door and scrambling into the passenger's seat.

"Is everything okay and ready for your meeting this morning?" I asked. He didn't reply until he finished struggling to clip up his seat belt.

"Yes... at least, I think so. I've been waiting for this day ever since you first told me about the new owner, and now I'm so nervous... I've presented in court so many times over my lifetime and never turned a hair while about it. Today, I'm not even sure where to start, or what to say, or how much to share. Do you have any clues you might give me... like where to focus, or if there is any particular area of interest I should make a priority?"

"Well, as I'm not privy to the nature of the information you wish to pass on, it is a bit hard for me to advise you. I'm sure everything will fall into place once we are there. Just relax and be yourself and you'll be fine." All fine words coming from someone who struggled with a similar situation yesterday, but true nevertheless.

On our arrival, Kirsty surprised me. If I didn't know her so well, I might not have picked up on it, but I detected a hint of nervousness about her. She is one of the most confident people I know, and meeting new people never fazes her. To save Thomas a long walk, I pulled up almost at the bottom of the steps to her quarters.

As Thomas eased himself out of the car, Kirsty rushed out onto the landing and called out, "Come in, come in... I have coffee on the go, and I hope the box you're carrying contains something to go with it."

"Oh, there is. I decided we had to have something to go with our coffee. Kirsty, this is Thomas Agnew, a man who has been giving freely of his time to me over the last couple of weeks. And Thomas, meet Kirsty Shelby McGregor. There my official duties are over. Now where is the coffee you promised us?"

Coffee and cake was a great icebreaker. Any signs of nervousness on the part of either of the key players disappeared. Thomas looked as though he was in his element talking to Kirsty. His eyes sparkled and, as he worked up to the main subject he came to discuss, his speech became increasingly lively. For her part, Kirsty appeared to hang on his every word. I sat back and let it roll on without my input. One thing was obvious, unless something untoward happened to upset things, Kirsty and Thomas were fast on the way to becoming best friends.

While watching their interaction was fascinating, it was fast becoming a case of three's-a-crowd... and one of us was playing no part in proceedings other than occupying a third chair. There was nothing new for me in anything said so far. Thomas was recounting his memories of Regina, and Kirsty had a never-ending supply of questions to keep him recounting tales from years now long gone. I needed to stretch my legs.

At the first break in conversation, I made a move. "Would you excuse me for a few minutes please? I've remembered a couple of phone calls I promised to make today. I'll just be outside if any major revelations are about to occur." Of course I had no 'promised calls' to make, but they provided a plausible white lie to use as an excuse.

Once outside, I was at a loss as to what to do with myself. The ideal would be something interesting and exciting to keep me entertained for at least an hour, but I was wishful thinking. I settled for wandering around along the front of the row out outbuildings. Now the grass had been tamed, the various farm implements were obvious on a patch of ground past the last shed in the row. With nothing better to do, I wandered along to look at them. While I could work out what some of them might be for, others could be from a distant planet for all I knew.

As I walked past the last shed on my way to inspect the implements, I noticed the shed's doors stood slightly open. Having inspected every one of the implements in the laydown area, a quick look inside the nearest shed had a certain appeal. It didn't require much effort to have its doors almost fully open. The light streaming in through the open doors revealed an Aladdin's cave from another era. This was the possible blacksmith's shop Kirsty had mentioned previously.

After poking about in there for a while, I decided to work my way back along the row of outbuildings. To my disappointment, all the others were locked, including the tractor's shed. It was while standing outside the tractor's shed debating what else to do, I heard Kirsty calling me. My heart skipped a beat at the urgency in her voice. I rushed back around to her quarters and found her standing on the landing at the front door. 'Standing' might not be the best descriptor. It seemed more like she was bouncing up and down on the spot.

"Where have you been?" she demanded as I set foot on the bottom step. "You've missed the most exciting news."

No further encouragement required, I bounded up the stairs and followed her into the lounge room, where Thomas sat looking pleased with himself. Kirsty was almost tripping over her tongue as she tried telling me all she had learned from Thomas.

"I can't believe it, Sonny. Thomas has been looking after the rest of my inheritance for all these years. It's almost impossible to believe the amounts of money he is talking about, but he has shown me statements and other documents. Everything he said is true, and it's all beyond comprehension." I saw her check the time. She bounced up out of her chair.

"God, look at the time. We should have eaten by now. Come through and talk to me while I make lunch. Sonny, you know where everything is by now. Would you mind setting the table please? I'm sorry. It's only cold chicken and salad today," she apologised to Thomas and me.

Gallant as always, Thomas replied, "It sounds just about perfect, thank you, Kirsty."

"Oh, and there's cold white wine to wash it down. I wish I had champagne instead. It's what the occasion demands," she added.

"White wine will be perfect," Thomas assured her.

"Not for me thanks, I'm driving," I told them.

Lunch was a wonderful vibrant event which stretched on longer than demanded by chicken and salad. Over the course of it, I discovered Kirsty was having trouble absorbing all Thomas had told her. Not surprising, I suppose coming out of the blue as it did.

"I will be spending quite a bit of time with Thomas in the future," Kirsty announced, as we made our way back to the lounge room after clearing the table. "By the time I fall asleep tonight, I will have a list of questions a mile long which I should have asked while he was here this morning. I suspect he already has answered them but the information hasn't sunk in."

Aware Thomas needed to take some medication at a set time every afternoon, I kept a close eye on the time. About ten minutes after we were settled in the lounge room again, my best intentions were scuttled. "It sounds as though a visitor is about to arrive," I told Kirsty. "Were you expecting anyone? Thomas and I should be going soon anyway, so we will leave you in peace to deal with whoever it is."

"Don't rush off… I wasn't expecting anyone, so it won't take me long to get rid of them."

As Kirsty spoke, I heard a car door slam, followed by a familiar voice calling Kirsty's name. Emily Ibbotson had arrived. She looked uncomfortable and was most apologetic when she saw us.

"I'm sorry. I should have called before I came. If I'd know you had people with you, I would have left it for another time."

"What are you on about?" Kirsty demanded. "There are no people here, only Sonny and Thomas. So, come on in and join us. We were just sitting yapping. Uhmm… this is just a friend's visit isn't it, or are you here for a specific reason?"

This seemed an appropriate time for me to suggest Thomas and I might leave. Both Kirsty and Emily howled me down. After the initial hoo-hah was done, it was Emily's cue to explain her visit.

"My intention was to call this morning to ask if I could come out here sometime today. It was supposed to be the first of my few days off, but I had to go into work first thing, and I wasn't sure when I could get away. Then, when the opportunity presented to leave, I just bolted for it and drove out here. And, yes, I'm afraid there is a reason for my uninvited visit. Kirsty, as you know, I analysed the DNA of the bones found in the old house, which is all well and good as far as it goes. The problem is, DNA in such situations is useless unless you have something to compare it to… and, in this instance, we don't."

"I can see the difficulty, Emily," Thomas said. "Goodness knows how long those bones were there, or why they were there. You don't have much to go on when it comes to finding out whose bones they were."

"Yeah, you've just about summed it up. And any day now, I'm sure the police are going to start looking into every possible way of finding even the tiniest clue to the identity of the bones. When they do, they will descend on this place again, and I'm sure they will want a DNA sample from you, Kirsty, to eliminate any possible match."

"Why me...? I didn't hide the bones there. I don't know whose they are."

"No. Nobody was suggesting it. They would want to compare your DNA to the bones' sample to see if there are any similarities. Then, the first thing they would do is to call me in to take a sample from you. And, I wouldn't look good for not having taken one at the time the bones were retrieved. I thought, if I took a sample now and had it analysed before they came looking for it, I could save you having the police tramping all over the place again."

"But, until I moved here a few weeks ago, I had never been to this property. I doubt there could be any connection to me." Although Kirsty appeared confused by Emily's request, she agreed to give Emily a sample. "How do you think this might be useful to the police?" she asked.

"We won't know the answer to your question until we have the results. It's possible it won't be useful at all. Nevertheless, something to keep in mind, and I'm sure the police will think of it in time, is your relationship to the McGregors who owned this place. While you are a couple of generations removed from your grandparents, and your DNA also will contain traces of both your parents, there might be enough markers present to either indicate a connection to the bones, or to eliminate you altogether." I admired Emily's attempts to simplify the explanation as much as possible, but Kirsty remained confused.

"But, I don't know anything about my father. So, you won't be out to get a sample from him to be able to work out which part of my DNA comes from him, and which part belongs to my mother."

"This is true, but DNA comparisons are complicated and not quite as straightforward as you might think. Given Regina McGregor's mysterious disappearance all those years ago, you are your grandmother's closest living relative. Your DNA is the only chance we have to prove whether those bones might belong to your grandmother or someone else. You see, even your mother's DNA, if she were alive today, would be a mixture of both her mother's and father's DNA.

When we take it to the next generation, which is you, traces of your grandmother's DNA become further diluted by whatever came across from your father and your grandfather. So, even if those bones do belong to your grandmother, the analysis of your DNA won't produce a 'eureka' moment. It will require an extensive comparative process to identify any connection."

"Wow, the stuff you do is complicated. Right, how do we take this sample you require? Let's do it. The sooner we get it over and done with, the sooner we might have some answers." I breathed a quiet sigh of relief. Kirsty was now fully committed, and some of the questions dogging all of us might be closer to answers.

Collecting a sample took a matter of moments. As Emily labelled it before placing it in her bag, she said, "Thanks guys for your patience, and apologies once again for my intrusion. I'll leave you to it now and head back into town to begin the analysis of the sample."

"We should be going too, Kirsty, as Thomas has something he needs to be home for about now." Thomas didn't argue, so I assumed he was ready to leave. It didn't go to plan.

"Thomas could come back into town with me," Emily offered. "I'm not in any hurry and would be happy to drop him at home."

"Thank you. It would suit me just fine to go back with you," Thomas replied. "And, it will give me a chance to find out more about this DNA sampling process. If you're ready to go, I'll walk you to your car. If I go with you, it will allow Sonny and Kirsty some time to wander down memory lane again without my hanging around to interfere."

My protests fell on deaf ears, and within moments, Kirsty and I were seeing them off. As we walked back inside, Kirsty seemed deep in thought.

"What do you suppose that was all about?" she asked.

"What... I didn't see anything."

"Thomas had a brief but serious conversation with Emily as she was loading her bag into the car. There was just something about the way he looked when he spoke to her."

"Sorry, I can't help you. I didn't notice anything. But, my guess would be it was the beginning of Thomas' quest for more knowledge about DNA. He might be getting on a bit, but he still possesses a lively and enquiring mind." Kirsty nodded but I could see my answer didn't settle the question for her.

About half an hour later, I too was on my way back into town. I toyed with the idea of going into my city office for an hour or so, but decided to go home instead. As I drove into my garage, Ben called to say he was working late tonight. I wasn't disappointed. Some time alone to digest all I had been witness to this morning suited me fine. In the end I had to settle for about three hours alone.

Emily called about ten minutes after I spoke to Ben. "Could you stand some company for dinner tonight?"

"You're always welcome ... see you later. How do you feel about quiche and salad for dinner?"

"…Sounds good. If we're having quiche, I take it Ben won't be joining us tonight?"

"No, he just called to say he was working late."

"Good…" With that, she ended the call and I was left wondering what was so good about Ben's absence tonight.

After calling Thomas out of courtesy to check he arrived home okay, I plonked myself down in my office and sat back to replay my memories of this morning's meeting between Thomas Agnew and Kirsty McGregor.

Regardless of what Kirsty's existing financial state was, she is about to inherit a great deal of cash – buckets of the stuff. She will be an extremely rich woman ... and more than able to afford to employ someone to help her re-establish Westbrook.

My time alone ended with Emily's arrival at seven o'clock. Neither of us felt like wine, so we took long glasses of iced tea out onto the deck. Emily appeared a bit uptight when she arrived. Not long after we sat down outside, I discovered why.

"This is a bit unprofessional of me, but I think you need to know. An interesting thing happened as Thomas and I were about to leave Kirsty's place. He spoke to me as I was loading my bag into the car:

If Kirsty's grandfather's DNA will help in the identification of those bones, perhaps you should take a sample from me. I won't say more until after you have the results, and I am in a position to know whether more needs to be said or not.

"I might be reading too much into it, but it sounded as though... What did you do about it?"

"At first, I didn't know what to say. I just nodded, and we drove off. When I stopped at his cottage, he asked again if I would take a sample. So, I did. As a result of today's excursion to the property, I now have two samples being processed."

"How long before you have the results. And, if it's much longer than 24 hours, I don't know if I'll survive the wait."

After she said she might have the results by sometime tomorrow night, we both lapsed into silence. The implications of Thomas' action were almost too much to comprehend. Sounds of a cat fight on a neighbouring property interrupted our period of silent contemplation and sent me inside to make a salad to have with the quiche which was ready to come out of the oven.

Later, when sleep was proving elusive, I spent a long time considering the possible implications of Thomas' request.

*****

"Why did I ever agree to go out to Westbrook again today?" I asked the universe as I waited for my first coffee of the day. Sleep deprived and the prospect of a difficult meeting between Peter Griswold and Kirsty did not bode well for a great morning. Still, I promised Kirsty to be there for her meeting with Griswold. So, after a slow start to the day, I was at Westbrook a little ahead of the appointed hour, and spent the brief time prior to Peter's arrival reassuring Kirsty meeting him was well worth her while.

Although his initial reaction to my presence was not good, Peter accepted it was what Kirsty wanted. From then on, everything went well. Kirsty had his map anchored out on the dining room table, and we congregated around it. Once he started explaining his map, I saw Peter relax and rise to the task at hand. His only reservation which lingered a while longer was about the new owner's being a woman. But, any concerns he had in this regard disappeared.

Kirsty and Peter were in a world of their own as they discussed crops, soil types, and breeds of cattle. And, I think I saw evidence Kirsty's knowledge of agriculture had won him over. The meeting proved well worthwhile, especially from my point of view as, for most of the time, I was ignored. My role became one of providing coffee and other sustenance, and at all other time remaining invisible. Discussions progressed well until Kirsty asked a key question.

"So, the fence lines you have drawn on the map are where I will find them now? It will be good to know where they are when I start clearing paddocks."

Peter hesitated before answering. "I've shown them as they were almost from the time Silas took over the property."

"Did some of them change at some point?"

"In more recent times, different thinking saw some changes made."

"Okay, so what were the reasons for the changes? Was it due to new seeds more suited to other areas of the place becoming available, or was it down to changes in weather conditions affecting water supplies to some areas?"

"No. I was unaware of the reasons for the changes. As the farm worker, my job was to carry out instructions, not to question them."

It was obvious Peter was avoiding mentioning Raymond Clifford and the role he had in the changes. I decided to stir things up a little. After all, Kirsty was entitled to know the whole story … and where she might find fence lines today.

"So, Peter, do those changes you referred to mean, once Kirsty starts clearing land, she might encounter fences where she least expects them?" He snarled a single word confirmation.

"Were those changes instigated by the bloke Clifford who was here for a while?" Although aware my comments might bring the meeting to a sudden and unpleasant end, I felt it my duty to try eliciting the whole story for Kirsty.

"Yeah, something along those lines, but they were not successful changes. He didn't understand the property. Anyway, after he left sudden like, I put some of them back the way they always were."

Okay, message received loud and clear: there would be no discussion of Raymond Clifford. It didn't matter, because Kirsty had moved on to asking about crop varieties and their respective yields. I suffered another half hour of being a spectator before I decided they wouldn't miss me.

"All of this is beyond my knowledge of farming. I think I might leave the two of you to continue without me."

"There isn't much more to tell," Peter said. "The best thing would be for me to come out again when you are ready to start work on the paddocks."

"Right… Yes, I think it might be the way to go forward. What about next week, what days are you free to come out?"

Their final arrangement was for Kirsty to call Peter the night before she thought she was ready to attack clearing the first small area of the property. A few minutes later, Peter was gone and I was on my way home as well.

Within minutes of arriving home, both Ben and Emily called to say they wouldn't be joining me tonight. Ben said he would be working. Emily was a bit more expansive and said she expected to be working most of the night. It sounds as though crime was alive and well in Millhaven tonight. The solitude it granted me was most welcome. So much had happened over the last couple of days, some time alone to ponder it was a gift.

Chapter 22

While time alone last evening was appreciated, it was disappointing not to have the DNA sample results from the those Emily took. If, as I suspect, she spent a large slab of the night 'on the job', somehow I would curb my curiosity and not call her today. I had hoped to wrap up my research into the McGregor family and Regina's disappearance by this weekend. My new client promised to deliver on Monday the necessary information for me to start work for her. Once I start the new job, it will be difficult to do more on the McGregor story. It's frustrating, as I believe I'm close to unravelling the story … and the mystery.

To tidy up my files before Monday, I spent a large slab of the weekend reading everything in them and adding my notes from the recent meetings between Kirsty and Thomas Agnew and Peter Griswold. Relief came on Sunday evening, when Emily announced she would join me for dinner. I asked her to come a little earlier if possible so we could talk before Ben arrived. In the end, it didn't matter. Ben sent a message to say he was working again this evening. Then, as so often happens, everything fell in a heap.

A six o'clock call from Emily cancelled our dinner arrangements. I knew she would be working on the same as whatever was occupying Ben, but I was not happy. I was desperate to know the results of those DNA samples, but Fate was determined to make me wait. My one option for the evening was surfing TV channels for something worth watching. It was pointless to try reading my book. My mind would be elsewhere.

As I sat down to reheated leftovers for dinner Kirsty called. "I asked Peter Griswold to come out on Monday, but he said he couldn't come until Tuesday. It's good he can't come until

Tuesday. It gives me a chance to clear some of the headlands and other flat areas before we start to look at the paddocks. I know I've taken up a lot of your time already, but could you come out on Tuesday morning too?"

"At this stage, Tuesday remains a mystery to me. I expect to be busy with a new client tomorrow. What happens then will determine what my Tuesday might be like. If I'm free, I could take a drive out to the property, but I don't know why you want me there. You and Peter will be off looking at paddocks, or whatever you plan on doing, and I would be superfluous to requirements."

Kirsty was determined, and pleaded her case. The call ended when, for the sake of peace, I agreed to drive out on Tuesday morning. Kirsty dealt with, I turned my attention to interrogating the TV channels. I was sound asleep in front of some foreign ice hockey game when my phone woke me. It had just gone nine o'clock, and it was Emily.

"I thought you might still be up. Could you stand some company?"

"Of course; come around. It sounds like you finished early for a change."

About ten minutes later, Emily parked out front. She looked worn out when she dragged herself through the door.

"Good evening... and have you eaten this evening," I asked.

"No time for food or anything else today; almost no time to breathe."

"Right, let's get some food into you before anything else. I can do hot or cold. What appeals to you?"

"Until you mentioned food, I didn't think I was hungry. Now my taste buds are screaming out for scrambled eggs on toast. If you have eggs, I'll make it."

"Not likely; in my kitchen, I do the cooking. Sit down and talk to me while I cook. What would you like to drink? There is white wine opened in the fridge, or I could make you a coffee."

"Ooh, coffee please... It feels like a month since I last tasted coffee."

Soon we were seated at the table. While Emily tucked into her scrambled eggs and sipped coffee, I munched on buttered toast. Conversation was non-existent. Reluctant to initiate anything until she finished eating, I allowed the silence to stretch on. At last her plate was scraped clean. She took it through and added it to the dishwasher.

While still in the kitchen, she announced, "That's better. Now I feel ready for a glass of wine. Will you join me?"

How could I say no? We took our glasses through to the lounge. The next few minutes were taken up with Emily's commentary on the case she'd been called out to at around midday. Then it was my turn to drive the conversation.

"I don't suppose you need me to remind you I'm dying to know the results of those DNA samples you took last Thursday. I'm assuming you have some clear results. Are there any surprises ... such as whose bones they might be?"

"Sorry, sorry... It's why I wanted to talk to you. Yes, I knew you were waiting for the results, and so was Thomas. I had a word to him this morning about his results."

"Well, are you going to tell me about them now?"

"Uhmm... No." Stunned, I couldn't respond. She rushed on to explain. "You won't find out until tomorrow. I'm taking Thomas out to Kirsty's in time for morning coffee tomorrow. It would be good – better than good – if you could be there too. I'll be giving Kirsty the results of her sample then."

There was no way I wouldn't be there, but therein was the problem. I expected my new client to deliver critical information tomorrow so I could start work on her case. Most people attend to such matters in the morning... when I would be out at Westbrook. I resolved to call her first thing, and hoped she wouldn't leave home before I called. Decision made, I could give Emily her answer.

"Yes, I can be there. I assume you're planning morning coffee will be about ten o'clock, and Kirsty already is aware she is to have visitors tomorrow morning."

"Let's just say she knows I will be coming to see her in time for coffee. She is under the impression I'm coming to talk to her about her DNA sample."

"…And she would be correct?"

"Okay, yes, she would be correct. But, she doesn't know about the rest of her guests who also will join us for coffee."

My efforts to prise more information out of her failed. She wasn't about to hand out any clues about the results or the need for such covert arrangements. Conversation lapsed into inconsequential generalities until Emily left a bit after eleven o'clock. While grateful to fall into bed, I knew sleep would not accompany me. Curiosity is not a good bed mate and, on this occasion, it proved the worst possible one.

*****

An early start saw me avoid the worst of the morning's traffic on my way into the city. As soon as I was in my office, I called my new client, and hoped it wasn't too early for her. She sounded groggy when she answered. I cursed myself for having woken her and rushed to apologise.

"No, you didn't wake me. It's the medication they give me at night. I've been awake for a while, but I don't think I'm functioning yet."

"Who is giving you medication, and why?"

"I intended calling you today to let you know I wouldn't be seeing you until later this week. I'm in hospital, and have been since Friday night. They say, if all goes well, I might be discharged on Wednesday. So, the earliest I might meet with you is Thursday."

"When we next meet is not an issue. But, tell me why you are in hospital … if it is nothing too personal to tell me."

"Oh, it's not personal. Someone knocked me off my bike on Friday night. I know it was deliberate, but the police believe otherwise. It looks as though you might have a bit extra to investigate once I escape from here."

"Okay, I'm happy to wait for all the details until we meet. In the meantime, can you give me just a basic outline of why you think your accident was deliberate?"

242

"Because the bloke on the motorbike who rammed me while I was out for my regular evening ride had hazed me for quite a while before he made his big move. I think he waited until I was in the right spot before sending me into the brick wall. Of course, the motorbike was nowhere in sight when they found me unconscious and I was carted off to hospital."

"Hmm… I will be interested to hear all the details. Don't worry about our meeting. It can happen whenever you are up to it."

"Sorry, Sonny; the doctor is here. I have to go. Talk to you again soon."

As it was too early to head out to Westbrook, I made another coffee and sat back to think about what my new client had shared with me. It was obvious there was no doubt in her mind her 'accident' was deliberate. The longer I thought about it, the more I was inclined to agree. My new case – whenever it starts – shows promise of being v-e-r-y interesting.

In the remaining time I had available before heading to Westbrook, I thought about Emily's visit last night. Her reluctance to discuss the results of the DNA tests was intriguing, as was her request for my presence at the gathering at Westbrook this morning. Should I read more into it? I'm sure I should, but I have no idea what to make of any of it.

My timing proved spot-on. I followed Emily's car up the track to the old house and parked beside her. The three of us, Thomas carrying a cake box from the bakers, Emily toting an attaché case, and me with only my bag over my shoulder, marched in single file up the stairs and into Kirsty's cottage. I noted how nervous Kirsty appeared.

"How do you want to play this?" she asked Emily. "Do you want to sit in the lounge or at the table? And, do you want to have coffee first, or go straight to business?"

"As it is everyone's normal coffee time, perhaps we should have coffee before anything else."

Good on you, Emily, I thought. There's nothing like stretching it out to heighten curiosity and add to the intrigue.

Somehow, I managed not to voice my thoughts while agreeing coffee first might be good.

The cake was wonderful, the coffee was good, and conversation was pleasant, but I was fidgeting on my chair and wishing morning tea was over. At last, after longer than I wanted, the time had come. As soon as Kirsty noted everyone appeared to have finished their coffee, she whipped the mugs and plates off the table, and I removed the cake.

Back at the table, Kirsty demanded, "Right, now the coffee routine is over, can those of us still in the dark about this morning's meeting please be enlightened as to why we are gathered here. As it was at your request, Emily, perhaps you should explain."

Emily cleared her throat and squirmed on her chair before sliding forward to perch on the front edge of it. "Yes, of course… I'm just not sure how to begin. So, I'll jump straight in. You will remember I took a sample for DNA analysis from Kirsty the last time I was here. The object of the exercise was to obtain a result for comparison with the DNA of the bones hidden in the old house. As the police haven't made progress with identifying the bones, as a routine procedure, I expected them to want to know whether there was any similarity between Kirsty's DNA and that of the bones. I decided to jump in first and have the information ready before they asked for it."

"Okay, I understood the reasons for it at the time," Kirsty reminded Emily. "So what did you discover?"

"Quite a few markers are common to both samples. Whether they would be enough to prove a link between both samples – both people – might be open to argument by professionals in a court of law… No, don't interrupt, Kirsty, not yet anyway… The story doesn't end there. At the time, another party came forward to provide a separate sample for analysis, and the results for this too are available."

"Why would someone else want their DNA tested – at coincidentally the same time as mine? Anyway, why is it significant?" Kirsty was becoming impatient, and it wasn't making Emily's job any easier.

"Bear with me, Kirsty, and all will be revealed."

"Yeah, yeah, all right... so what about this other mysterious sample, is it important?"

"The DNA results of the other, or third, sample produced no surprises as far as the old bones were concerned. But what they did show was even more exciting. Out of curiosity, I compared those DNA results with yours Kirsty. Again, quite a few markers were common to both samples."

"So... it proves the donor of the third samples is related to the old bones – is that what you're telling us?" Kirsty asked.

"No, Kirsty. It proved there is no relationship between the bones (the first sample) and the donor of the third sample." I saw Kirsty shake her head to indicate she didn't understand. "The third sample's DNA is a close match to yours."

"To mine...? But... that's not possible. I mean, it's not possible unless you've uncovered some family I didn't know I had."

"Well, in essence, it's what has happened. After finding a close match between you and the old bones, and then another close match between you and the third sample, it is impossible to escape the truth: both of those donors have close familial connections to you. Or, to put it another way, you are related to both those other donors.

To put it in simple terms, a part of the little bit of your sample which doesn't match either of those other samples probably comes from your father."

"Emily, I think you're telling me, if I ignore the involvement of my father's possible DNA, the other two donors are close relatives. How close?

"It is probable the other two donors are your grandparents."

A long silence ensued as I watched Kirsty grapple with the information. Then, still shaking her head in disbelief, she sat upright and challenged Emily.

"You expect me to believe those hidden bones belong to one of my grandparents...? Well, come on, explain it. Which one was it?"

"Based on the DNA analysis, those bones found hidden in the old house belonged to your grandmother...."

"My grandmother...? Regina McGregor...? No... No, is it possible?" Kirsty wailed.

"I'm sorry, but yes, it is what I'm telling you. I don't expect you to be able to absorb the enormity of this right now, but I wanted to tell you before I give the information to the police."

"Thank you. You're right. I'm struggling to understand what it all means. Hang on a minute... What about the other donor? ...The third donor who, if your information is correct, must be my grandfather. If he came forward to volunteer a sample, he must still be alive."

Before Emily could reply, a chair scraped a little way back from the table, and a throat was cleared.

"Ahem... yes, I am still alive, at least for a bit longer I hope – now I've found my granddaughter."

"You...? Thomas Agnew...! How is it possible you are my grandfather? I don't mean to be rude, and finding my grandfather is a lovely thought, but something must have happened to the samples. It can't be right."

"Nothing went wrong with the samples. I'm afraid the results don't lie. None of us here expects you to take all this on board today, or for some time yet. But, Kirsty, I'm staking my professional reputation on it," Emily said.

"It will take longer than today for me to grasp it. Look, while I try to digest all I've heard this morning, how about we take a break for lunch?" Kirsty suggested.

"Good idea. Kirsty, you take yourself of for a walk somewhere while I make it. I assume what I saw earlier in the fridge is intended for lunch. Go ... take a bottle of water with you if you need it... but just go; get out of here." I helped lift her up off her chair as I spoke. Then I grabbed a bottle of water out of the fridge before propelling her out the front door and down the stairs. "Now walk... go on... go. I'll call you when lunch is ready."

No one had shown any interest in lunch, and I hadn't noticed anyone check the time, but it was well past a normal lunch hour. Waiting a bit longer before eating was unlikely to cause starvation. I suggested everyone might like to freshen up before lunch and maybe have a drink or a coffee... or anything else which might delay my having to call Kirsty to join us.

Maybe a bit shell-shocked after this morning's revelations, lunch was prepared on autopilot. What a Trojan Thomas is. He sat through the whole event without blinking or flinching right up until he spoke at the end. But, is he coping, or is this the courtroom Thomas Agnew we're seeing today? Only one way to find out...

"How are you holding up, Thomas? All this comes as a shock to us but, for you, it's more personal. I can't begin to imagine the emotional turmoil you must be going through right now."

"Unlike the rest of you, I've had twenty-four hours to come to terms with it. I still have a long way to go. Behind all this is a long story. But, it is one I want to share with Kirsty first. No doubt she will share it with you later, Sonny, and then might be a good time to share with her the story you've put together of her background."

Emily had remained silent since Kirsty left for her walk. At last I realised there might be something needing attention happening there. "Emily, is everything all right? You haven't said a word since Kirsty left. Are you okay?"

"Argh, yes, I'm okay... or, I will be when I see how Kirsty is handling the situation. I did try to lead her to the big reveal as gently as I could, but I accept the news is a monumental thing to accept. Not only was her grandmother murdered (I think we must accept that) but Kirsty has discovered she had a grandfather alive and well for all these years. And he is not the grandfather she thought she had. Tough stuff to take on board when it comes at you without warning."

"True... and I will do all I can to help her with whatever emotional upheaval it might cause. But, first things first, lunch is ready and I'm going to call her back to eat with us... and see how she is holding up."

It didn't require a loud yell. Kirsty already was on her way back to the cottage. "I was just coming to call you."

"Saved you the trouble; I'm starving, so let's eat shall we?"

I waited on the landing for her so I could have a word before we joined the others. My concern about whether she was up to having lunch with all of us, or if she might prefer more time alone, was brushed aside.

"Stop fussing, Sonny. This is a great day for me; a monumental day. I have a grandfather. I have a living family member, and he will have lots to tell me about my family and this property... And, especially about how he came to be my grandfather. Yes, it is a lot to take on board. But, all it has done is made me want to know every last detail of every aspect of who I am and about those from whom I've come. If anything, Sonny, I'm feeling hyped-up and elated... and starving!"

Lunch was a lively affair with conversation flowing constantly, and with each excited input often being spoken over someone else's. When we were done eating, Emily and I cleared the table before returning to join the other two who remained at the table. We hadn't long sat down again when a vehicle arrived. Kirsty went to investigate and met the new visitor on the landing.

"Peter, this is a surprise. Come on in and join us. It must be just about time for coffee. Before we go in though, as I wasn't expecting you until tomorrow, has something happened. Is there a reason for your visit today, or is it of a social nature? "

"Nothing serious has happened. I just thought I'd come to make sure everything was ready for the work we were going to tackle tomorrow."

"We are right to go tomorrow. But, come in now and have a coffee with us. I think you might know at least some of us already." Kirsty and Peter Griswold came to join us in the dining room.

Kirsty realised, the only person present whom Peter hadn't met before was Emily. Introductions over, Peter apologised for intruding on our get together of friends. We all spoke at once as we tried to assure him he wasn't intruding. Kirsty won the battle.

"It was a surprise get-together, Peter, but it has produced the most amazing news. Sit yourself down. While Sonny and Emily make the coffees, I'll tell you the most astonishing thing I've heard today." He did as instructed, as Emily and I shuffled around delivering coffees and wedges of cake.

Although I knew Peter's habit was to come into town on Mondays, I thought it odd he came all the way out to Westbrook. In fact, I was almost sure his regular Monday trips to town had something to do with his health: to visit his doctor or something else health related. Today, he looked more washed out than on any previous occasion. I felt a twinge of concern developing.

As soon as everyone had engaged with the coffee and cake, Kirsty launched into a recap of all she learned this morning. When she delivered her bombshell about her new grandfather, Peter dropped his fork in shock. His gaze swung to Thomas and, for a few moments, he looked stunned.

"You... You and Regina...?" he blurted out. "Did Silas know?"

Thomas chuckled. I noticed a pink tinge slide from under his collar and settle on his cheeks. "We were both still alive long after Silas had departed this mortal coil so, no, I don't believe he knew."

"But, it means Catherine was your daughter and not Silas'."
A beaming Thomas nodded in reply.

For a few moments, Peter appeared to struggle with the concept of Thomas being Catherine's father. Then his eyes lit up and he was babbling on about how wonderful it was to have the family back on Westbrook and looking to restore it to its former glory. We all joined in sharing his excitement. But, the interlude was short lived.

Without warning, Peter slumped over and fell off his chair. It was fortunate he didn't hit his head on anything on the way down. Thomas and Emily helped him up and laid him out on the sofa in the lounge room. Moments later, he was sitting up and apologising for giving us a scare. He rummaged in his pocket and produced a bottle of pills and an inhaler gadget.

After a couple of pills and a few puffs on the inhaler, his colour returned and he claimed to be 'right as rain again'. Our next cause for concern came when he insisted on driving himself home. He assured us his turn was because he hadn't eaten at the right time or taken his medication when he was supposed to but, now he had dealt with it, he was fine to drive home.

In spite of howls of protest from all of us, he insisted he would be back in the morning to inspect the property with Kirsty. His only demand was for us all to be here again in the morning. He assured us it was important and we must make every effort to be at Westbrook by nine o'clock at the latest.

Then, he was gone and we three visitors were making a move to follow him, until Kirsty intervened.

"Thomas, unless you must rush off, would you mind staying behind for a while? I will run you home later, if it's okay with you."

None of us needed to belong to Mensa to work out Kirsty wanted private time with her grandfather, and Thomas was keen to oblige. Moments later, Emily and I were on our way into town. I was pleased traffic was light. My mind focused on other things rather than driving.

Emily must have had plenty to occupy her mind as well. She opted to eat at home, and Ben said he was working to catch up on paperwork, so I was to eat alone… and it suited me fine tonight.

Chapter 23

As instructed, we reconvened at Westbrook at about nine o'clock. Peter insisted his and Kirsty's inspection of the property could wait. He had something to share with us. The call came for coffee – and yesterday's leftover cake – while we heard what he had to say. Before he could start, another arrived to join our ranks, and was not much pleased to find us all there. Ben, in his official capacity as Millhaven's top cop, had arrived.

"Apologies for interrupting, but I wonder if I might have a word with Miss McGregor?"

"Of course; what can I do for you?"

"Well, I was hoping for a private word, if you don't… Emily what are you doing here?"

Emily wandered out from the bathroom as Ben spoke. I'm not sure who looked most surprised, but Emily recovered first. She gave Ben a wide smile and said, "I was invited. I didn't know you also received an invitation. Anyway, you're too late for cake and coffee."

"No, I wasn't invited. I came to ask Miss McGregor to provide us with a DNA sample the next time she was in town. We just want to eliminate any possibility of contamination with the bones found in the old house. But, as you are here now, and if you have your kit with you, would you mind taking a sample?" He looked stunned when we all roared laughing.

As soon as she could speak, Emily said, "Aah, right … Ben, now it's my turn to apologise. You're a bit late. It's already been done… and there has been an interesting development."

"Am I allowed to know what the 'interesting development' might be, or is it for a restricted audience only?" Okay, perhaps with some justification, Ben was not a happy chap.

Between Emily and Kirsty, they managed to deliver what amounted to an executive summary of everything we learned yesterday. Their story told, they sat back and waited for Ben's reaction. It was a while coming. It seemed as though it was taking him more than a moment or two to absorb all he had been told. But, at last, his face told me he had grasped it. Thomas pushed a chair out to Ben and suggested Ben sit down and join us. I bounced up and went to make him a coffee. The last slim sliver of cake and a coffee were soon on the table in front of him. And, it appeared it helped him find his voice again.

"So... correct me if I'm wrong ... it sounded like you told me those bones we removed from the old house probably are those of the missing woman, Regina McGregor, who we know was Miss McGregor's grandmother. Am I right?" His question met with enthusiastic nodding from the rest of us around the table. He continued, "And, am I also correct in believing I now have a murder investigation to undertake – as opposed to a search for a missing woman?"

A loud chorus of *Yes* was our reply. Ben shook his head in disbelief before doing what police officers do: asking his next question. "I don't suppose you've made my job easier by identifying the murderer as well, have you?" His question met with silence. "No, I thought not. This means we have to clean the slate of everything my team has done so far and start again. I'm assuming you all want to know *who did it* as much as we do. So, do any of you have any thoughts, ideas, evidence, or anything at all after all this time, which might help solve the mystery of who murdered Regina McGregor, and might help to put the culprit behind bars?"

"While we all want to know, and I *need* to know, I doubt anyone here can help you," Kirsty told Ben.

"I do have a question though," Thomas began. "Did you ever track down the bloke who claimed to be Regina's son, Raymond Clifford?"

"No. We found no record of a Raymond Clifford anywhere. There was no birth recorded to Regina Shelby prior to her marriage, and we found no death for Raymond Clifford; no driver's licence or registration as an elector. Nothing; not only in this state but anywhere in this country… perhaps a little more information about the man might have helped."

"Well, when he first arrived on the scene, in a way for Regina, it confirmed a suspicion which lingered in the back of her mind. A part of her believed her son didn't die, and the family had taken him and handed him over for adoption. If it were the case, she accepted it would explain his name being something quite unfamiliar to her." The whole time he spoke, Thomas hadn't lifted his eyes from his hands clenched on the table.

"Thomas, you said *when he first arrived*," Kirsty began and then paused for a moment before completing her question. "Are you suggesting Regina later discarded her acceptance of Clifford as her son?"

"Yes… It took her a while, but in time, she came to doubt his claim to be her son. On one of her visits to town, she came to see me and asked me to undertake some research for her. She gave me the name of the person and asked me to see if I could locate her. At the time, she didn't give me a reason, but I was happy to do what I could. Later, she explained the person she had asked me to find had been the cook's assistant in the Shelby household. When she was due to give birth, the young lass was promoted to the position of nursery maid. Before the baby arrived, the girl had about a week's training in what her new job would entail." Thomas still hadn't lifted his eyes from his hands on the table.

"So, what happened, did you find this woman?" Ben demanded.

"Although she no longer worked for the Shelbys and had moved to live in the next township, I did find her and passed on her current address to Regina. Although I didn't know at the time, the following weekend Regina went to visit the woman. After visiting the woman, Regina threw Clifford off the property."

"It's obvious she discovered something contrary to what Clifford had been telling her about his connection to Regina. Did she tell you about it?" Ben asked.

"On her next trip to town, Regina called in to see me and told me of her meeting with the ex-nursery maid. At the time of the birth, the housekeeper acted as midwife. It was a difficult birth and the baby's health was not good. The housekeeper stayed with the baby to care for it and give him every chance of surviving, while the nursery maid stayed in the background to bring and fetch as demanded by the housekeeper. In the early hours of the next morning, the baby died. It seems the family considered it the best possible outcome."

"I doubt that is what happened," Ben announced. The angry tone of his voice made me flinch, and I felt concerned Thomas was being subjected to such treatment, but Ben continued. "Had the child died, there would be records of its birth and subsequent death. None exists. It sounds like a great story, but it has no credence. Perhaps you should rethink it and try again – employing the truth this time."

I felt my anger towards Ben rising to dangerous levels. I knew he had a job to do, but was this the place or the time to be doing it? And, why was he treating Thomas like some criminal bought in for interrogation? Thomas was giving him information to help with the investigation. He didn't need to be treated in such a way. Regardless, this is no way to treat an old man. As I was about to voice my objection, Thomas continued the story.

"You found no record of birth or death for the child because it was never registered. As the child's birth had not been registered, and it died so soon afterwards, Regina's father saw no need to register its death. He ordered the child be buried on the property. With Regina forced to remain at home throughout her pregnancy, no one other than the household staff knew she was pregnant. If they wanted to keep their jobs, they would forget she had been pregnant, had given birth to a son who died soon after, and that his body was buried in an unmarked grave on the property."

"This supposedly ex-nursery maid, who had kept silent for so many years, was now prepared to come clean? You expect me to believe this rather fanciful story? It's obvious you had a soft spot for Regina McGregor, so what's to be gained by lying about her now? How does any of this cock-and-bull story you've come up with help her now, or even help protect her reputation in some way?"

Yep, Ben had better not come to my place for dinner tonight. He would be much safer if he stayed home. But, another question had occurred to Ben.

"From what I've heard, it appears Mr Clifford had been on the property for some time before Mrs McGregor went on this so-called fact-finding mission to talk to the ex-nursery maid. Why did she have a change of heart about the man which caused her to doubt he might be her son?"

"Clifford abused her. In spite of her best efforts, I saw the bruises – at least some of them. And, only several months before she went on her 'fact-finding mission' as you call it, she presented in my office with a broken arm. Oh, yes, she spun me a line about how she fallen down the stairs. I saw the other bruises which accompanied the broken arm. There had been no fall down stairs. It was Clifford's handiwork." This time, Thomas had raised his eyes from his hands on the table, and they were filled with venom. He was angry, and I suspected Ben was about to receive full blast of Thomas' court room persona.

"So you say, Mr Agnew, but I think it's time you accompanied me to the station. It's time we had a formal interview and a signed statement."

I sprang up from the table knocking my chair over as I did so. "How dare you? Who the hell do you think you are? You might be the top cop in this precinct, but your behaviour is deplorable, and your superiors should be made aware of it. You disgust me." Ben looked suitably stunned by my outburst. I wasn't sure I was finished, but Thomas interceded.

"Thank you, Sonny, but it's not necessary. I can fight my own battles. Even though I'm a bit long in the tooth these days, I'm quite capable of dealing with bullies. And, I would enjoy tearing this bloke to pieces in front of a judge and jury. He has a job to do and, if he believes his job requires he charge me with the murder of somebody – or whatever – he should get on with it."

"While I believe Miss Whittington's assessment of the officer is an accurate one. I see no reason why he should be allowed to continue this farce any longer. Please sit down again, Miss Whittington." Peter Griswold had stood to deliver his speech and, although urging me to sit again, he showed no inclination to do so himself. After clearing his throat, and appearing to take a moment to organise his thoughts, Peter continued.

"Inspector, there's no point in giving Thomas Agnew a hard time. He doesn't know anything more than he's told you so far. He doesn't know anything about what happened to Regina McGregor or why you can't find Raymond Clifford… *But I do.* I intended taking what I know to the grave with me, and I almost have. Those of you who were here yesterday would realise the turn I took is indicative of what lies ahead for me. It's fortunate I won't have to put up with it for too long."

"Peter, what are you saying?" Kirsty asked. "Are you saying you are ill, so ill you won't be around much longer?"

"For some time now, I've come into town every Monday for treatment. It's been working, but it's only been holding the inevitable at bay. The word I received yesterday morning, in effect, told me the treatment no longer worked and I should put my affairs in order as soon as possible. So, in view of yesterday's bad news and all we've endured this morning, perhaps part of 'putting my affairs in order' might be to share what I know about the day Regina McGregor disappeared."

"The exact date of Regina McGregor's disappearance has never been identified. Are you now saying you know the exact day on which she disappeared?" Ben asked.

"No, I'm saying I know the exact night on which she disappeared. If you bear with me, I'll share with you the events of the night in question and what happened afterwards." We all murmured encouragement for Peter to continue his story, and he obliged.

"One of the cows was about to calve. She always had trouble and needed assistance. I came out to Westbrook at about ten o'clock and went straight to her in the home paddock. I sat with her there in the dark until soon after midnight when I heard a scream from inside the house. Of course I knew Clifford had knocked Regina around when he was here, but he was gone, and had been for some while. So, I assumed Regina must've had an accident – or a nightmare. As I was only the farmhand, I wasn't sure what to do, but I didn't think it appropriate for me to go rushing into the house. Instead, I sneaked up to the house and peered in the windows.

At first I didn't see anything. Then the horror of that night became obvious. I saw Clifford coming from the direction of the kitchen. He was carrying Regina. I could tell she was dead. There was blood down the side of her face and a large bloody patch on the front of her frock. He carried her into the front room and over to the ridiculous wall he had started to build across one end of the room. The wall had never been completed. Most of it had been clad, but an area remained open as if a door were to be fitted.

Clifford stepped through the opening in the wall and stood just inside. I had to stifle a scream as I watched him toss Regina's body onto the floor behind the wall. Then I heard the cow bellowing. I didn't want Clifford to find me peering through the window. I rushed back to the cow and waited with her until she delivered the calf. While I sat with her, I heard hammering in the house.

As soon as I knew the cow and calf were okay, I snuck back to the house and risked another peep through the window. There no longer was a hole in the wall. It had been sheeted over and Clifford was standing back admiring his handiwork. But, with the job finished, he picked up a couple of tools and started walking towards the front door. I dived back into the bushes and watched him walk across to the tool shed. He didn't put things away properly; just threw them in on the bench. Then, after closing the door of the tool shed, he stood outside it for a few moments scanning the area around him. I suppose, once he was confident nobody was around, he walked back along the line of outbuildings to the tractor shed.

The tractor shed was always kept closed when the tractor was inside, as it was on the night in question. He threw the doors open wide to let in the pale moonlight to assist the weak light from the torch he carried. Clifford had no reason to go into the tractor shed. He never went in there. I feared he had a plan to sabotage the tractor, or use it to damage something around the property. He was whistling as he made his way through the shed and didn't hear me sneak up to see what he was doing.

It was payday. Regina had been to town during the day and brought my pay home with her. After she arrived home, as she always did, she put my pay envelope in the drawer under the bench along the back wall of the tractor shed. I watched Clifford go straight to that drawer and take out my pay packet. He extracted the money and fanned through it as if to see how much was there.

I guess by then, I had lost all sense of reason. Not only had he killed a woman who I admired and who was my employer, he was now stuffing my money into his pocket. I picked up an old tyre iron which had rested against the shed wall since it was last used years ago. I yelled at him *this is for Regina* as I struck him across the head with it. He crumpled to the ground. Although I knew he was dead, I couldn't help myself. My anger was still at full flood. I gave him two or three more wallops with the tyre iron.

Then, common sense kicked in. I now had a body to do something about. As it happened, Regina had decided to concrete the floor in the dairy. The foundations had been dug, and the formwork and reinforcing mesh were in place ready for the concrete to be poured first thing next morning. I dug a hole – a grave – roughly in the middle of the floor, and dropped Clifford's body into it. The whole floor area had been dug up and raked and levelled, so it didn't take much to put it back to the way it looked beforehand.

There was nothing more for me to do except to go home, change my clothes, clean myself up, and be back at work in time to meet the concrete truck when it arrived. As scheduled, the dairy received its new concrete floor. After the job was done, I turned my attention to the tractor shed, and spent quite some time cleaning up the mess I'd made in there. Then I took the spare key and locked the front door of the house. I didn't want anyone finding Regina. It was an undignified end for such a gracious lady. I wanted to spare her any further indignity.

About then, I discovered a car parked in close behind the house. The keys were still in the ignition. I had to get rid of it. So, I drove it to Ralston, left it in the long-term carpark at the airport there, and caught a plane back to Millhaven. My truck remained out here on the property, so I grabbed a lift with a farmer from further along the road from here. He was on his way home from town and was happy to drop me at Westbrook's gate. I walked to the home yard, collected my truck and went home."

"What happened next? It appears you went on working here in spite of everything you witnessed and were a party to." Ben's tone had moderated to almost a polite level.

"How did you cope with coming to work every day knowing those two bodies were here?" Emily asked.

"Although it took me a while to recover from that night, the bodies never bothered me. The old house was Regina's mausoleum; a monument to the woman she had been. As for Raymond Clifford, I doubt I gave him much thought after I disposed of him. But, on occasions as I passed the dairy, I would allow myself a smug feeling. He might have killed a woman I admired, but I had made sure he paid for what he did.

Afterwards, I just kept working as normal until my next pay day rolled around. Of course, there was no pay put in the drawer in the tractor shed as was the practice over many years. But, at about six o'clock the next day, Thomas arrived with my pay. I saw him arrive and start towards the house. I intercepted him before he reached the front stairs and told him I didn't think

Regina was at home. I suggested she must have been away somewhere because I hadn't seen her around in about a week.

Thomas said he was concerned when she hadn't called to collect my pay, and was worried she might be sick or injured. I spun him a yarn about Regina's finding out something about where Catherine might be and had gone to investigate. We agreed, if it were the case, she would be back in a few days and everything should keep going as normal. When the second pay day arrived and Regina again failed to collect my pay from Thomas, he chose to deliver it again. On that occasion, we discussed the future. Thomas was concerned for Regina, but we both knew what she had wanted. She had made it clear to me the place had to be kept in top condition for when Catherine returned."

"Peter is right," Thomas agreed. "Regina never gave up hope Catherine would return one day. Some time after the girl ran away from home, Regina confessed to me she believed her husband, Silas was responsible for the girl's departure. She always felt he showed too much interest in Catherine – more than normal for a parent. Then, in the few months before she ran away, Regina thought she detected a change. Silas was showing more than interest, and she suspected he was abusing Catherine or working up to doing so... sexual abuse is what I'm talking about. I think the knowledge Catherine was safe from Silas helped her cope when Catherine absconded."

"Right, this is all quite interesting," Ben began, "But would someone mind telling me who this Catherine is I'm hearing about?"

"My Mother..." Kirsty barked. "Regina McGregor's daughter...."

"Oh, I see. So, although Catherine hadn't returned home, after Regina disappeared, Catherine was in line to inherit everything." We exchanged glances, but it was Thomas who stepped in to enlighten Ben.

"No, the situation was quite different. Silas left everything to Catherine when he died, and nothing – not a penny even – to

Regina. Catherine was only about sixteen or seventeen when Silas died and not yet of legal age to claim her inheritance. Regina sought and was granted the court's permission to manage Silas' estate on behalf of her daughter. I had been Regina's legal representative for some years by then. She approached me to take over managing Silas' estate as well as her own. I have been doing so ever since."

"So, between you, Thomas and Peter, you kept the place going much as if nothing had happened.... But for how long? It's obvious, from the look of the place, no one has been running it for quite a few years." I knew I was stating the obvious but curiosity was at fault.

Thomas chuckled. "About ten years ago, Peter came to me and said he was too old and tired to keep working. He wanted to retire. On the basis it would be better for his tax, I persuaded him to stay on for a couple of months until after the end of the financial year. It gave me time to put in a place an agreement which would bring in an annual sum of money sufficient to pay the rates and insurance on the property. And, my friends, it is what remains in place today. Now there is a new owner, I'm not sure about the legality of the contract – not since probate was granted."

Peter chose to expand Thomas' response. "It was when I first noticed my health wasn't all it should be. I put it down to old age, but I soon realised it was something else. After a whole barrage of tests, they confirmed I had a serious health problem and needed to start treatment if I were to have any hope of beating it. I chose to go with the treatment, even though it meant retiring. After a couple of years, I was declared free of the problem, but I was warned it might return. It did, about eighteen months ago. So, more treatment from then until now but, as of yesterday, I am at the virtual end of the road. Well, I suppose, Mr Policeman, if you are going to charge me and lock me up, you had better get on with it. There isn't too much time to waste."

"No one is going to charge you, not yet anyway. Everything I've heard here today needs to be investigated. And. I'm sorry, Miss McGregor, but we are going to have to remove your dairy's concrete floor. There is a whole mountain of work to do before we can think of charging anyone. For a start, we will need to investigate the car you abandoned at Ralston to determine the owner's name. Of course, it might be another alias, but we would have to investigate who it was. Investigating those things will take a while. Given the recent crime spate in Millhaven and its surrounds, it will be weeks before such investigations rise to the top of the pile. So, Mr Griswold, I suggest you go home and relax." I sent Ben a mental apology for my earlier outburst and dark thoughts about him. This was more like the Ben I knew.

"There is one thing I don't understand," Emily confessed. "If Regina's husband's death left her penniless, how did she survive all those years until her death?"

It was Peter's turn to chuckle. "You had to know Regina to understand. Silas gave her nothing while she was alive, so she was used to making ends meet as best she could. She raised pigs and chickens and grew vegetables. Anything surplus to her own needs she sold."

"And it was how she intended to cope after her husband's death," Thomas added, "but, I wouldn't hear of it. She was running the place as the property manager. It was appropriate she be paid as such. In spite of her initial refusal to accept payment, I managed to win her over. She was paid a regular wage, albeit well below what she should have been paid for the work she did."

"Well, all I can say is thank you all for your patience and perseverance. It has been an interesting morning to say the least. Sometime over the next day or two, a team of my men will descend on the place to dig up the concrete floor. In the meantime, I have to try tracking down Catherine McGregor," Ben said as he stood and made ready to leave.

"I shouldn't bother if I were you," Kirsty said between giggles. "She ran away at about age fifteen, had me at seventeen

and was dead by nineteen. If we hadn't proved she was dead –
and I was her daughter – how do you think I could inherit this
place?"

Then it was time to follow Ben's example and leave Kirsty
and Peter to make a start on the inspection of the property they
planned for today. Emily, Thomas and I walked out together.
Twenty minutes after dropping Thomas at the retirement village,
I was home and pouring myself a scotch to have with crackers
and cheese to keep me going until later.

Fate smiled on me again, when both Ben and Emily called to
say they wouldn't be joining me for dinner tonight.

Chapter 24

Wednesday found me back in my city office striving for normalcy. It was fortunate nothing too demanding required my attention. As I worked my way through admin and other overdue tasks, about half my mind was on the job. The other part, and perhaps the larger part, continued to deal with the events of the previous couple of days. It still felt as though I had inhabited some alternate universe for those days.

Somehow, I managed to make it through the day and felt good about it by the time I was on my way home. After persevering today, tomorrow I would have a clean slate, and I would be ready for my new client – if she were out of hospital and able to come to see me. No one joined me for dinner thanks to texts I'd sent telling them I was working. It wasn't a lie. I wanted to reacquaint myself with my new client and her case, and to do some pre-emptive research to be better placed should she arrive at my office tomorrow.

The highlight of Thursday was a meeting with my new client, Janine. We revisited all she told me on her previous visit, which amounted to the sum total of information in my case file so far. Then, I chose to focus on the recent accident which put her in hospital for a few days. She remained adamant it wasn't an accident, and was convinced being rammed by the bloke on the motorbike was deliberate.

"After hazing me for some distance through the park, he chose the best place to execute his plan. His only problem was, the plan didn't come off quite as he expected. The little bridge across the stormwater drain in a more deserted area of the park has waist-high stone pitched walls along both sides. I was halfway across the bridge when he chose to ram my rear wheel. Except for some quirk of fate, the incident should have sent me over the wall and down about three metres into the concrete lined stormwater drain below. Instead of flying over the wall as intended, I struck the wall and bounced back onto the side of the bridge decking."

As the case she wanted me to investigate was about her husband, I felt it appropriate to ask where he was when her 'accident' occurred.

"It happened on Friday night. He left on Friday morning to fly to Tasmania for a week of trout fishing with a couple of his mate who live there. He wasn't home when it happened so, if the joggers hadn't found me when they did, I could have been lying injured on the bridge for goodness knows how long."

While, to a sceptic like me, it all appeared just a touch to convenient for him to be so far away when it happened, it did provide me with a wonderful starting point for my investigation. As soon as Janine left my office, I checked her husband did indeed fly to Tasmania on Friday morning, and whether he had a return flight booked.

By lunchtime, I knew his story, as Janine recounted it, did not hold up. Neither had he flown to Tasmania on Friday morning, nor did he have a return flight booked for any time in the next fortnight. Aah, yes… I sensed a quite interesting investigation ahead. And, I saw a client shedding quite a few tears before the case was closed. In spite of everything, she seemed fond of the man she married. It's possible her feelings might change in the near future.

Again tonight, no one joined me for dinner. While I was happy to share the evening with only my own company, I did wonder whether I'd insulted everybody during proceedings earlier in the week.

*****

Friday started out in the worst sluggish way. Although intrigued by the case I was about to embark on, I struggled to gain traction. After another coffee, I began to remember how this investigation stuff is supposed to happen. By lunchtime, I was in the thick of research and feeling confident I had remembered how to do my job. I risked a quick trip away from my desk to find something to eat and a newspaper to read while I chewed.

As four o'clock slipped past, I had explored a mountain of information without having much to show for it. It seemed like a good time to take an early mark and go home. I told myself I could continue my research at home over the weekend, so I wasn't avoiding the job I had to do. As I picked up my bag, my phone demanded attention. I felt my stomach tighten when I saw it was Kirsty calling.

"No, nothing is wrong," she assured me. I wondered whether you were working tonight, or if we might have dinner somewhere."

"Dinner sounds great. Do you want me to bring anything out with me?"

"Eh... No; I wasn't talking about having dinner at Westbrook. I'm in town and thought we might eat at a restaurant."

It didn't take long to agree a time and place – and it left me with about an hour to fill in beforehand. "I could spend the time going through everything I dug up today... or I could finish reading the paper," I told my empty office. The newspaper won out, and kept me occupied until about 5.30PM when I needed to freshen up before heading to the restaurant.

Although it was early, quite a few patrons already took advantage of the establishment's wine bar, which served as an antechamber to the restaurant. I wove my way through those congregating in front of the bar and made my way to a table at the back where Kirsty waited.

As I pulled out my chair, I said, "I'm surprised you're wasting time in town. Has Peter given you time off from clearing the property to wine and dine with me?"

She laughed. "I've been in town most of the afternoon. There were a few things I needed to do, including buying groceries, before I collected Thomas at three o'clock. Then we spent just over an hour at the bank before I took him home again. Nothing is ever simple or easy to achieve in banks, and today was no exception. All we had to do was a hand-over to me those accounts Thomas has been managing for both Regina's and Silas' estates. Once it was done, I took Thomas home, and we indulged in coffee and chat until it was time for me to leave. I asked him to join us, but he preferred to watch some favourite show on TV instead."

"So, apart from your expedition to the bank this afternoon, what else has happened at Westbrook since I left there on Tuesday?"

"A team of blokes from the police arrived mid-morning yesterday and started removing the concrete floor of the dairy. After a couple of hours or so, they discovered they needed some heavy equipment to lift the slabs of concrete out of the building and the machine hadn't arrived as planned. So, they left early, and came back this morning to finish the job. They found the bones just as Peter described and remove them for analysis. I insisted they shift the concrete slabs out of the way and not leave them lying around out front of the dairy. Once they shifted them to where I indicated, they packed up and left.

The only other happening was a visit from Angus Walker. It was his day off today and, when he saw the police vehicles and blokes messing about around the sheds, he came over to see if I was okay. It seems Angus, like me, didn't know anything about the bit of Westbrook his father, Neil Walker, has leased for years for agistment purposes. I only found out about it after you all went home on Tuesday, and Thomas and I had a chance to chat about things.

Neil gave Angus the third degree about me after he had been over here working on the tractor. It seems Neil became nervous after I arrived on the scene, and he had been trying to track down Thomas to establish the situation regarding his agistment block now there was a new owner in residence."

"Has the situation regarding the block been resolved?"

"Yeah, Thomas and I discussed the arrangement and agreed it should continue for at least another twelve months. It would provide an income stream, albeit quite small, until the property is productive again. It's likely the arrangement can stay in place for longer than a year, but it's the length of time we've agreed for now."

"It was decent of Angus to come over and make sure you're all right. Like his father, he seems a decent sort of bloke. Now you've mentioned bringing the property into production again, there is something I've wanted to talk to you about. Perhaps you should give some thought to employing a farmhand, at least to help with the initial clearing and cultivation work. Once the place is up and running again, you'll be able to decide whether you still need someone or not. If everything is now sorted out with the bank, there should be enough cash available to be able to employ someone without causing concern."

"Funny you should mention employing someone... Angus told me he was taking all the leave he is due to give himself some time to think about what he wants to do in the future. For some time now, he entertained the idea of setting himself up as a mobile diesel fitter, who is happy to travel around the farms attending to tractors and any other diesel equipment in situ. I don't think his father is too impressed with the idea, but Angus seems keen to give it a go.

Anyway, when we were discussing his future, I suggested, if he became bored during his holidays, I'd be happy to pay him to give me a hand on Westbrook. We had a bit of an argument about it being paid work, but I insisted, and I won. He starts work with me on Monday. We seem to get on well, so I think it's the right move."

While there was no question about it being the right move, I thought I detected something more than just a neighbourly interest developing when she spoke of Angus. She could do a lot worse, and having him in her life would relieve some of my concern for her. Then, with all the main topics dealt with, conversation wandered off down memory lane again, with lots of 'whatever happened to' questions raised about mutual friends from the past.

Cognisant of her long drive back to Westbrook, I made sure our night didn't run too late. On my way home, I realised I felt as though a weight had lifted from my shoulders. Although I wasn't aware of it at the time, I had been concerned about Kirsty's wellbeing now she was at Westbrook on her own and isolated from any support. It appears Angus had already taken it upon himself to keep a watchful eye on his neighbour. I would sleep well tonight, and over the weekend, I would document all the research I had done into Kirsty's background and her family. My plan being, at an appropriate time next week, to present her with a bound copy of all I had discovered.

*****

The weekend saw another return to normal. Ben joined me for dinner on Saturday night, but I didn't hear from Emily. Everything appeared back to normal as far as Ben and I were concerned. No apologies were sought or given for events which occurred earlier in the week. As expected, conversation moved to Peter Griswold's story, with particular emphasis on the demise of Raymond Clifford, and his body in the dairy.

Ben confirmed Kirsty's version of the removal of the concrete floor in the dairy and the discovery of what was assumed to be Clifford's body in the exact place Peter had indicated. Emily now had another bundle of bones to play with, and Ben admitted to pressuring her to produce results as soon as possible. No further explanation for Emily's absence tonight was necessary. I pictured her working into the wee hours of the morning to meet Ben's demands.

While it was a companionable night, apart from discussing Clifford, conversation was sparse and of no consequence. The only other notable point of interest came when Ben admitted solving the mystery of Regina McGregor's disappearance hadn't done his career any harm. His boss had called and made veiled reference to a possible promotion in the near future. Ben wouldn't be drawn on the subject, claiming it was only speculation at this stage.

In bed later, when sleep was being elusive, my thoughts returned to Ben's possible promotion. I didn't need to be a genius to realise, if such a promotion occurred, it was probable he would leave Millhaven to take up a new posting elsewhere. Now, how did I feel about the possibility of his leaving Millhaven? Of course, it might not happen I told myself, as I tried to put aside any further thought on the subject.

The weekend seemed to evaporate into the ether. I felt as though I'd turned around twice and it was Sunday night already. Both Emily and Ben were coming to dinner tonight, and I'd asked Emily to come a little earlier if possible so I could quiz her about the body in the dairy.

"Ah, yes. The bones retrieved from Kirsty's dairy... All I can tell you is their DNA shows they are no possible match to Regina McGregor. So, the former nursery maid's story about the death of Regina's son is confirmed. I don't know how Kirsty will cope with the dairy building after what was removed from it... And, she now needs to pour a new floor."

"It won't be a problem. She was thinking about a larger, more modern dairy before all this happened. Now, as soon as she and Angus Walker agree a suitable site for the new building, construction will begin. The old dairy is to be pulled down and where it now stands will become somewhere to store the ATV and the ride-on mower."

"Ooh, should I read something into Angus' being involved?"

"Maybe it's a case of watch this space to see what develops."

Both Ben and Emily left early tonight, allowing me plenty of time to sit and think. Tomorrow was the start of a new week and time I returned to 'work' mode after the last couple of weeks spent more away from my office than in it. I'm looking forward to it. My new case has all the indications of an investigation jam-packed with intrigue, and horror; just the stuff to get my bloodhound juices flowing again.

Tonight, sleep will come easily.

The End

Other Books by the Author

About the Author

Neive Denis is the creator of the series featuring the Private Investigator, Sonoma (Sonny) Whittington. Neive Denis is the pen name of a writer who was lured from her usual genre to focus on the mystery and excitement that are a part of Sonoma Whittington's world. Neive came into being specifically for this series and had intended remaining faithful to only stories from Sonny's case files. Her focus now has broadened and also includes another new series as well.

The Sonoma Whittington series tells of the intrigue and scrapes – some on occasion life threatening – that are part of the life of Sonoma Whittington, an Australian Private Investigator based in a Central Queensland coastal city. However, Sonny doesn't confine her escapades to Australia, and that provides Neive with an opportunity to weave some of her other areas of interest into Sonny's hair-raising adventures.

See more about Neive Denis and her work at

www.eaglemountbooks.com.au/neivedenis

or contact her at

admin@eaglemountbooks.com.au

Dear Reader

Thank you for reading my book.

If you enjoyed it, please consider leaving a review on your favourite bookseller's website.

Thank you

Neive